ROMAN COLLAR CRIME

VIOLATED!

THE TRANSGRESSIONS OF A SMALL-TOWN PRIEST

CHARLES A UTTER

This is a book of fiction based on actual historical events surrounding the life of Father Joseph Brennan (not his real name) and the people whose lives he touched. Peoples names and the names of some of the places have been changed and are used in a fictitious manner. The author has taken significant literary license in describing events that actually occurred. The way these events unfolded is the product of the authors imagination or are used in a fictitious manner.

ISBN-13: 9781984195432

ISBN-10: 1984195433

Library of Congress Control Number: 2017919026

CreateSpace Independent Publishing Platform, North Charleston, SC

Contents

This book is dedicated to my mentor, George Ryan, and my friend Dick Ryan, his son. Of all those whose lives collided with Father Joseph Brennan, the Ryan family experience was the most deplorable. George had his flaws, but was the best basketball coach I have ever known. He taught me well and lifted my self-confidence at a time when there was very little confidence to work with. Dick worked with me on the research for what I have always termed, THE BOOK, and was with me when we confronted the Bishop of the Bismarck Diocese with the crimes committed by Brennan. His life struggle can be traced directly to Brennan's evil influence on his family at a time when he was the most impressionable.

Authors Preface

I met Father Joe Brennan when I was eight years old. I feared him from the start. Manifesting love was not one of his strong points. As a teenager I had frequent confrontations with him. I always reveled in the rumors about his depredations. My sister and her husband poured their souls into the effort to remove him from the priesthood.

Many graduates of Our Lady of Perpetual Help School, greatly resent my writing this book, and are skeptical of my motives. They wonder about the need to dredge up old scandals. While I fully respect their concerns, I believe that exposure of what we used to call MORTAL SINS, is the only way to save our church.

I am saddened by the "negligence and fraud" perpetrated by the church, to which I remain loyal, by its mindlessly clueless leadership. In choosing to protect the church as its first priority, it is devastating the mental health of the victims of its priests. Not even Francis of Assisi , a revered saint of the church who 800 years ago recognized the age-old problem, could affect the obvious need to openly condemn the perpetrators.

A man, stained with sin, despises and tramples on the Lamb of God, when, as the Apostle says, not discerning the sacred Bread, which is Christ, from other food, he eats unworthily by being guilty of unworthy actions; for the Lord has said by His Prophet: *"Cursed is the man who does the work of God with negligence or fraud."* And on account of those priests who will not lay these things seriously to heart, we are condemned, when Our Lord says: *"I will curse your blessings."'*

St. Francis of Assisi

It is my hope that, in exposing the depredations of an extraordinarily destructive clergyman, the pressure on the church to reform will someday culminate in a victory for its founder, Jesus, who asked us to "Love one another as I have loved you"

Introduction

Having lived through the life changing events described in this book, I can only thank God that the Roman Catholic church was finally forced to right the egregious evil of priests unable to commit themselves to celibacy as preached to them in seminaries all over the world. Despite that, I confess to moments Of despair upon reading the story of the unmitigated horrors brought upon so many good people by a person who sullied the whole meaning of priesthood. The power of the priest in the days when a mere man was considered to be a representative of God himself created a 20 year horror story lived out by many of those under his charge. His sexual degradation of innocent women, as well as his egotistical need to be in power, led to tragedy in the lives of many.

His perversions were enabled by his brilliant financial success using parish funds in the stock market and later in real estate. At the same time, he cleverly used his ability to blackmail those powerful clergy in the diocese who had their own sinful reasons to ignore the needs of the people in his parish. His creation of a sports empire in small town America was the pride of his Bishop, most of his parishioners, and many others who saw only the outside of this broken man. I am so proud of the author of this book and the small group of good priests, nuns and parish people who were able to withstand public degradations in the church bulletin. The weekly prayer and support group they formed did, in the end, see grace prevail over evil. I say this with apologies to those people whose lives were ruined.

Vaudeth Oberlander
Sister of the author

Prologue

"Father why?" Nevada moaned when Father Joe Brennan shouted in ecstasy as his final thrust pierced her tender heart. Nineteen-year-old Nevada Black was unable to understand what was happening when her pastor, superintendent, and confessor suddenly grabbed her and started caressing her breasts. The confusion she felt paralyzed her and precluded even modest resistance. When he pulled off his pants revealing his erect penis she became faint and almost lost consciousness. She could only close her eyes and passively submit. When it was over she lay on the couch and sobbed uncontrollably. This was her first sexual experience.

Brennan watched her sob for a few minutes and then began berating her for her naiveté and weakness. "Do you not understand that you should never be alone with a man without expecting that he might try something? Did you not listen to my warnings about human nature in religion class? You came into my office expecting what? But do not fret too much, I can hear your confession and I have the power to forgive sins. Please, get dressed and say a prayer."

"In nomine Patris et Filii et Spiritus Sancti......" "Go my child and sin nor more." With that he ushered her out of his office. As she left, he cautioned her to never tell anyone. I can ruin your father's business, and no one would believe you anyway."

It was June of 1954 barely a year since Brennan took over Our Lady of Perpetual Help Parish.

Chapter 1

A Gifted Administrator

PARISH TROUBLES BY A FEW WILL NOT QUIT.... If the things said about me were so true don't you think that the bishop.... would have removed me.... instead of asking me to stay?

Sunday Bulletin March 14,1971

With 1:30 left in the championship game, they were ahead by five points. The Perpetual Help crowd was going crazy, finally smelling victory and their first state championship. As the sports reporter for The Dickinson Press, Frank Nash was supposed to be objective, but he was perched on the end of his chair, his hands gripping the table in front of him, eyes glued to Hope's point guard as he scored the third of three quick buckets, pulling his team ahead by one. Frank's heart sank when on its next possession Ricky Bryan, Perpetual Help's star forward blew a layup and was forced to foul in a final effort to get the ball back. Angry with himself, Bryan instinctively reacted by fouling Hope's best free throw shooter who had gotten the rebound. As he stood at the free throw line, the arena went dead silent with anticipation as they contemplated a Hope victory over the Perpetual Help team that had knocked them out of the tournament in each of the last two years. Hope was in a one and one situation. Make two free throws and the game was over. Frank dropped his eyes to the floor. He could not bear to watch. Suddenly the Perpetual Help crowd exploded and as Frank looked up he saw that the free throw had been missed, and Ricky Bryan was sprinting down court with no defender in sight. A teammate got the rebound, and the pass was perfect. Bryan's slam dunk at the buzzer gave Perpetual Help their first state title after nine tournament appearances.

Pandemonium erupted as the Perpetual Help fans rushed onto the floor. Frank, despite himself, was overjoyed as he joined in the celebration. But, he was shocked when, out of nowhere, he found himself in a bear hug from the usually stoic Father Joe Brennan, the architect of Perpetual Help's nine year run of great state tournament teams.

"Write a great story Frank, these boys deserve it," he implored.

"Congratulations, you made it happen, awesome, fantastic job. We need to get together. You are the architect of all this. Sports fans will want to know how you put this all together"

Joe nodded in agreement as he turned to players and parents eager to offer their congratulations. Frank walked off wondering if he had just been played by the padre or if he really was a truly unusual and amazing priest.

Chapter 2

Mixed Messages

To make accusations is one thing and to prove them is another. You know that people can work and talk about things so long that they begin to believe them as truth even though they have never proved them.

Sunday Bulletin March 14, 1971

It was a two-and-a-half-hour drive home from Minot to Frank's home in Dickinson. He had plenty of time to think about his upcoming interview with Brennan. He was excited about the potential that this story could be the break in his career that had been so long delayed. He thought back on the days when he had been aggressively recruited by Brennan, and his father had refused to send him to Perpetual Help.

He always said, "We have chores to do. I need Frank's help. He is no help to me 60 miles from home."

His high school teams had been regular victims of Perpetual Help. He felt a degree of irony that Brennan could be his ticket out of small town journalism to the big time on one of the coasts.

He arrived home to a half-hearted greeting from Sandy, his wife of ten years, who was becoming increasingly disenchanted with their marriage. Low pay combined with a perpetual sense of optimism had made Frank less than responsible with his money. He tried to keep Sandy happy by taking her on trips that they really could not afford and lavishing her with expensive gifts at Christmas and on her birthday. When his buddies went on their annual fishing trips to Canada and hunting trips to Colorado, Frank never hesitated to join them. The trips and the gifts were often paid for with credit cards. He was confident that his big break was just around the corner and the credit cards would get paid off. Sandy dearly loved him but was gradually losing faith that he would become anything other than a low paid small-town sports writer.

Joe ignored Sandy's tepid greeting and gave her a big hug,

"I think I've finally gotten the break I have been waiting for, "he proclaimed. "Father Brennan at Perpetual Help is going to give me an interview. With his track record, it has to be a hit." Everyone loves a story about the small-town boy who makes it big."

*****

Frank drove to New London the day prior to his meeting with Brennan. The late March weather had returned temporarily to winter. The northwest wind was bone chillingly cold, and he suspected that the Golden West Bar would begin to fill up in the late afternoon. He wanted to get a feel for how the locals felt about their rock star priest and there was no better place to find out than the Golden West. He had been in the bar often as he covered Perpetual Help ball games. Invariably the fans would retire there to rehash the games, along with the referees who had worked the game. After a few drinks the conversations became increasingly lively. Frank knew that he would get candid opinions at the Golden West.

It seemed like nearly every farmer in Hettinger County that could, had showed up. Frank smiled when he thought of the standing joke he had heard so often,

"What else is there to do? It's too wet to plow and too windy to haul rocks"

He was greeted by a stale beer smell, and smoke drifting from every corner. Many farmers were sitting together talking and shots of Calvert Whisky lined the bar. It looked like everybody in the place had a pony bottle of Grain Belt in their hands. Father and Son were lined up at the bar, standing back to back, talking with others about the weather, and arguing over the local gossip.

"Mr. Nash, welcome," Joe the bar owner, yelled above the din as he walked through the door.

The New London folks were a friendly group and were especially proud of their first state championship. They knew Frank because of his regular coverage of the games. They greatly appreciated his laudatory reporting. Joe's loud greeting alerted the growing crowd to Frank's presence and they responded with back slapping and handshakes. It was a typical New London welcome in these heady days following their greatest victory.

"Hey bartender, give this man a drink." Frank looked around to see who his new friend was and found himself face to face with Cleo Sieger. Sieger was Perpetual Help's biggest fan and had formerly been its head basketball coach.

"What brings you to New London?"

Before he could answer, three more of the patrons were asking the bartender to, "set one up for Nash!"

Frank yelled back, "no, no, I've got to drive home, but thanks."

"What," they responded, "are you too good for us?"

"Bartender, give him his drink."

Frank wondered how in the world he was going to be able to stay sober enough to focus on his mission, but reluctantly accepted the drinks, which he asked to be delivered to a nearby table where he sat down to visit with Sieger.

The excitement quickly died down and the crowd returned to what they did best at this time of the day, which was to hand over their emotional pressures to Dr. Buzz. After a few drinks, all their inhibitions were gone and the b.s. began to flow. There would be hell to pay when they got home as 'Ma" was already mad because they were gone most of the day to get "parts". No one cared.

"I'm here to interview Father Brennan," he finally answered Sieger.

"What do you think of him?"

"Well, he can be a bit overbearing from the pulpit. He talks about money damn near every Sunday, but he has put this town on the map. We are very fortunate to have him." Cleo's brother, Floyd happened to be standing nearby and overheard the conversation and chimed in,

"There are some rumors about Brennan that are going around and there is no place where they are more rampant than in this bar. When these guys get a few drinks under their belt, their tongues start wagging. Don't believe a word they say. None of it is true. Brennan is a saint. He has done more for Perpetual Help and New London North Dakota than any man, ever. The Protestants and those Catholics who won't send their kids to Perpetual Help, love to spread the rumors, but there is nothing to them."

This was information of which Frank was not previously aware, and he thought it to be a bit strange that Floyd would begin a conversation that way. He filed the information in the back of his mind and decided that it might be interesting to explore later.

Turning back to Cleo, Frank said,

"You were saying that Brennan has put this town on the map. I couldn't agree more. How has he accomplished so much at a small Catholic School?"

"He is just driven to excellence," responded Sieger. I was the head basketball coach when he first came to town and my dad had written the first $100 check to start Perpetual Help School. My sister is a nun, and the whole family has been committed to helping Perpetual Help be the best school it can be. We've contributed some of its best athletes too. I used to coach without pay just so we could have a sports program. I know the game pretty well. But we never had a winning season. He came to me in July the year he arrived in town and said that he appreciated all I had done, but he had a friend by the name of Ted Holbrook, who he thought he could get to come to New London to coach the basketball team. He had been a star ballplayer at St. John's University in Minnesota and Brennan thought he had the potential to be a great high school coach. I was happy to step down even though I loved the game. I was working at my brother's hardware store and farming as well. One less job was a relief. Brennan was right about Holbrook too. He went on to become head basketball coach at his alma mater. He put the Perpetual Help program on a winning path. We went to the regional tournament a couple of times for the first time in school history."

"Wasn't that about the same time that Don Earnhardt was hired to coach the football team?" asked Frank,

"Yes, that was the following year. You know as well as anyone how that worked out. I doubt that there has been a more successful football program in the country than ours. We had a 25-game winning streak when he left here. Undefeated seasons have been the standard every year since. Earnhardt went on to Minot Ryan and had the same success. His two Division II titles at North Dakota State put the school on the map. He's now an assistant at the New England Patriots and I have no doubt that he will be an NFL head coach someday."

Frank knew the story well.

~ 7 ~

He said, "I'm not sure if you remember, but Brennan recruited me to play football at Perpetual Help. My dad played for the Dodgers in the 50's and I was fortunate enough to get his athletic genes. We lived on a ranch near Marmath, so I wasn't around football as a kid, but I played baseball for the local farm team. I was the best hitter on the team by the time I was 14 years old. Somehow, Brennan found out about me and started coming to our games. I was big for my age and he told me I would be an excellent football player. But, my dad didn't like him very well. He thought he was pushy and he talked down the other schools in the conference. He was insulted when Brennan suggested that I would be wasting my time at Bowman High, and he literally threw him out of the house the night he tried to recruit me. He was right though about my potential. I would have played for Earnhardt at North Dakota State if I hadn't blown out my knee my senior year in high school. It was frustrating to lose to Perpetual Help every year. We only got close once. That was in my senior year. In fact, it was the night I injured my knee."

"The coach who took over for Holbrook, wasn't that Dan Thomas?"

"Yes," replied Sieger, "and he did a great job in the short time he was here. We went to our first state tournament in 1962 and might have won it if Mott hadn't had the team of the century. They beat us five times including the state championship game."

"I remember that year," Frank said, "we weren't too impressed. You had a bunch of recruits. Not one kid from New London started for that team, we thought it was unfair."

"Well," Sieger said, "there is no doubt that Brennan has a knack for recruiting students to Perpetual Help. The fact that some of them are athletes is really a coincidence though. Catholic families want their kids to play here. More important, they know that they will get the best education available anywhere. Brennan and the Notre Dame nuns have built a great educational institution. We love Brennan as much for the quality of education at Perpetual help as for the athletics."

"I was surprised that Thomas left after that one good year, remarked Frank, "if I was a coach in a program like Perpetual Help's I would milk it if I could. I guess he did pretty well anyway getting the job at Dawson County Community College. He's done a great job there."

"If you talk to enough people," Sieger responded, "you'll hear some outrageous rumors about Thomas's departure. I recommend you stay as far away from them as you can. Most of the people in this town love what this man has done for Perpetual Help School. They don't take kindly to those who spread these rumors. They think they are out to destroy the school. Some of them are. There are plenty of non-Catholics in town who would love to take Perpetual Help down. They hate getting their butts beat every year in basketball. A few years back we beat Public by 25 points and none of our starters played in the game. Even I was embarrassed by that one. Grower and Sieger Hardware suffers a bit because they have to cater to everyone in town not just the Catholics. Sometimes the competition between the schools hurts."

By now the din in the bar was so loud that Frank and Cleo were shouting to hear each other. The bar was jammed with patrons, some playing pool, others cards, but they were there to drink. Small towns in North Dakota were famous for the number of alcoholics they produced and New London was no exception.

The conversation with Sieger broke up as Cleo excused himself to join a game of pinochle with his cronies. Frank moved on to talk with others in the bar. He found almost universal admiration for Brennan. However, someone in the crowd called him "Big Dad," and sounded a bit cynical about all the adulation of Brennan. Frank wondered where that came from and made a mental note to explore it later, but for now the alcohol was starting to get to him. Virtually everyone he stopped to talk to offered him a drink and he felt it was impolite to turn them down. He decided he had better get home while he could still drive.

As he walked out of the bar a blast of wind caused him to stagger a little. The North Dakota spring had returned to winter with a vengeance. He shivered as he pulled the too light coat he was wearing tightly around himself. As he hurried to his car he heard someone yell his name. He turned to look and was confronted by Larry Kronk, whom he didn't know, but who seemed a bit agitated by all the adulation he had heard inside the bar.

"Big Dad is not the person you just heard about, Kronk yelled as they left the bar."

"What do you mean," Frank responded, "you sound like one of those people Cleo Sieger just warned me about."

"Cleo is a Big Dad toady, as long as they keep winning football and basketball games you won't hear any criticism from him. His kid is one of the best football players who ever played here. He's not going to say anything

~ 9 ~

that might jeopardize his kid's future. If you are doing a story about Big Dad and you don't talk to the women in the community who have been abused by him, you will have missed the real story. He ruined Dan Thomas's marriage; one of the nicest guys who ever coached at Perpetual Help, and he messed up my sister so badly that she has literally abandoned us as her family."

The biting cold was getting to Frank and he couldn't go back into the bar for fear of having more drinks imposed on him, so he asked Larry if he could talk to him later.

"No, I don't have a lot of credibility around here. Talk to Therese Koch. She knows all the dirt."

Frank shivered as he got into his car and was relieved to get out of what now was a gale force wind, but as he was about to start his car, the effect of the booze hit him harder than ever. He saw no way that he could drive home in his condition. He was familiar with the Gardner Hotel down the street because this wasn't the first time had had too much to drink while covering Perpetual Help sports. It was an old and dingy place, but nonetheless, he decided to stay the night.

Chapter 3

New London

The parish and the school are being done untold harm by these trouble makers in the parish. They will get a few to go along with them because in 18 years here I have stepped on a lot of toes, especially at school in the matters of discipline.

Sunday Bulletin March 14, 1971

New London North Dakota was a typical Southwestern North Dakota farming community. The windswept, treeless prairie, that surrounded it had some of the most fertile farm ground outside the Red River Valley. The winds were constant. In the spring, the east winds would often bring three-day rains everyone prayed for, and that got the crops started, but in the summer temperatures could rise well into triple digits and were sometimes accompanied by high winds. When you stepped outdoors it felt like you were walking into an oven. Too much hot wind would destroy the crops. In the winter, the periodic Canadian Clippers, brought high winds out of the Northwest that would trigger massive blizzards, closing many of the roads and isolating farm families for days at a time. Once the blizzards calmed, the steady winds caused the snow to drift over plowed roads closing them repeatedly. At a minimum, the winds would blast through the best of winter wear. Winters were just plain miserable.

The hardy residents endured the weather with a toughness and pride that bespoke their German and Norwegian heritage and appreciated what was good about prairie living. Springtime brought beautiful prairie sunsets, the fragrance of newly cut hay, crystal clear air with its refreshingly clean smell, and the quiet mornings when all you would hear were the Meadowlarks performing the most melodious of bird symphonies.

More than anything, though, they appreciated what they always referred to as, the smell of money. Springs work was followed by the flourishing of the freshly planted grain that grew ever taller over the following weeks till it flowed in the wind like waves in an ocean squall. If they "got a crop," the banks got paid, and they could support their families and continue to raise their children to be good Christians; or Catholics, as the case may be. To jigger the odds in their favor, the Catholics said novenas, worked in an occasional weekday Mass, and plied God's favor with extra contributions in the Sunday offertory. These were simple but good people.

Virtually all the businesses in town were on Main Street, the most prosperous of which were the four bars. The people were mostly second and third generation German Catholics and Norwegian Lutherans. They were a conservative and fun-loving lot. They generally got along well, even though some of the Protestants thought that Catholics were not really Christian. The economy depended almost exclusively on how good the crops were from year to year, and that was determined more by the weather than anything else. Farming methods didn't vary much from farm to farm in those days, so the weather was all that really mattered. When the crops were good and commodity prices high, both the farmers and the businesses they patronized, prospered. There were two hardware stores, three grocery stores, a couple of implement dealerships, two car dealers, a drug store and the four bars. There were also the typical service businesses that supported all the rest. The people were fortunate to have a Doctor, Chiropractor, and Dentist who served the communities health care needs. The hospital was 25 miles away. Getting there was easy since the roads were good.

One feature though distinguished New London from all the other small towns around it. It was the biggest farm to market transportation hub in the world. It had an impressive skyline made up of a row of elevators that jutted out of the prairie not unlike the skyscrapers in the far away big cities. The Wheat, Barley, and Oats that were raised on the surrounding farms filled the elevators to the brim every fall, and often overflowed into huge piles of grain precariously exposed to the elements until the Milwaukie and St. Paul Railroad could transport it to the big city markets in Minneapolis and Chicago. Occasionally, heavy fall rains ruined a big part of the overflow grain. Such was the life of the farmer. The rewards could be great, but the risks could overwhelm them.

The people of New London were not atypical of those you would find anywhere in SW North Dakota. They got along reasonably well despite the occasional bar fights and the constant gossip. Everyone knew everyone else's business, and when things got stressful for one family or another, everyone knew about it. Not a few of the bar fights resulted from the gossip, but mostly they resulted from too much alcohol. Fights between good friends out for a good time were common. All it took was a playful shove and an insult often said in jest, and the battle was on. When they sobered up, they forgot about the fight and remained friends.

There was one strong undercurrent in New London though that always bode ill for community relationships. Both the Catholics and the Lutherans felt strongly about their religious beliefs. Problems typically lay just below the surface. When Father Joe Brennan became pastor of Our Lady of Perpetual Help Catholic Church, he brought with him a personality and an agenda that were hardwired to bring all the self-righteous prejudices and doctrinal conflicts to the surface. The sleepy town of New London was not the better for it. Part of that agenda was to elevate Our Lady of Perpetual Help School's athletic program.

Chapter 4

Suspicions Raised

I could not even begin to count up the lies going on about me. I cannot fight lies as fast as some people make them up. Lies have become a tool to get me out of here by character assassination.

Sunday Bulletin March 14, 1971

Frank awakened with a start, shouting. "What the hell was that?" He quickly realized he had been dreaming, but the image of some dark, ghostly, presence hovering over his first child, who hadn't been born yet, with an incredibly evil grin on his face, was enough to ruin the start of one of the most eagerly anticipated days of Franks career.

Speaking to himself aloud, he said, "I need to get that one out of my mind. This is too important a day to let a silly dream ruin it."

He realized that he had been shivering in a bed with too few blankets and a room that was inadequately heated. He hated staying at the Gardner and, even more, the thought of having to bathe in a dilapidated old bath tub. He couldn't believe that the Gardner hadn't installed showers in the guest rooms yet.

The one good thing about the Gardner was the restaurant in the lobby. Babe Miller ran it and did all the cooking. Her bacon and eggs were second to none, but the caramel roles were notorious. Babe was known far and wide for them.

She greeted Frank as he entered the restaurant. "Fancy meeting you here. What brings you to New London? The basketball season is over."

Frank explained about his upcoming meeting with Father Brennan and mentioned how impressed he was with how he had built the Perpetual Help sports program. Babe looked at him with amusement and said,

"It sounds like you think Brennan is some kind of hero. Trust me, you don't even want to know the real Joe Brennan."

"Tell me about that," Frank responded.

"Naah, I ain't getting into that. I've got a business to run, and there is nothing but trouble in talking about Brennan. Talk to Therese Koch, she has the goods on him."

"You're the second person to mention Therese Koch. Something must be brewing; do you want to tell me a little more?"

"Like I said, Mr. Nash, that topic is off limits in the restaurant. Therese is a very nice person. You'll enjoy visiting with her."

"Well then, I better get going. The padre has a full schedule and wants to get this meeting out of the way as early today as possible. Thanks for the best caramel roll in town. It was worth the hard bed and cold room."

Babe's scrumptious breakfast had partially alleviated Frank's hangover a and he felt ready for his interview with Brennan. He arrived at the appointed time and was shocked to see the run-down state of the rectory. It had not been painted for too long and the white paint was flaking off the siding. The roof was in disrepair and Frank wondered if it might leak. It was long and narrow with too few windows and looked almost like an abandoned farm house.

He had expected to see the plush accommodations that were so common amongst the clergy even in small towns. His first impression added to the positive image he carried with him while witnessing Perpetual Help's successes. Not only was Brennan apparently highly capable, but seemingly very humble as well. It caused him to reflect on the prior evenings encounter with Larry Kronk.

I wonder if Kronk might just be looking for revenge because of some conflict he had with Brennan., he thought.

He knocked on the door and was shocked to find Brennan dressed in a white tank top t-shirt, with his suspenders hanging at his side. His hair was disheveled, and he looked like he had just gotten out of bed.

"Is it eight o'clock already?" he said, as he closed the door to a crack, embarrassed that he had been caught off guard.

"Just a minute while I make myself more presentable."

While he was waiting, Frank heard the muffled sound of the back-door closing. It sounded like someone was exiting in a hurry.

Strange, he thought to himself.

After just a few seconds Brennan yelled, "Why don't you just come in and wait in my office, I will be only a few minutes."

Frank, pushed the door open tentatively, not wanting to invade Brennan's privacy. Not seeing anyone, he stepped into Brennan's office. He was impressed by its simplicity. The desk was old and beat up just like the sides of the house. Papers were piled in a disorderly fashion all over the desk. There was only a small space in which to work. Drawers were left open, and the whole place was a mess. The rest of the home opened up from the office. In contrast to the office, the rest of the place was well kept and orderly. He had an excellent house keeper. However, the early morning sun was insufficient to penetrate the dark shadows that resulted from so few windows. It made for a very dreary place. Frank wondered if it didn't depress Brennan at times.

There was one exception to the overall simplicity of Brennan's surroundings. Behind his desk was a massive plush brown leather chair and ottoman.

Must be Brennan's one exception to the simple life, Frank thought. *He probably feels like he deserves it.*

"Good to see you Frank," Brennan said as he strode into the office. "Please accept my apology for so rudely asking you to wait at my doorstep. I had a long night and got very little sleep. Running a school like Perpetual Help can be very tiring at times."

"You have done such a wonderful job here," said Frank, "people need uplifting stories, I am hopeful that Hollywood will view it as compelling as I do. That would be a public relations coup of the first order for Perpetual Help School."

"Well Frank, I am happy to answer your questions. I hadn't thought of our story in the same terms as you." He lied. "But what you say has appeal. I'm ready whenever you are."

~ 16 ~

"I've known a lot of priests over the years, but I've never met anyone like you. How did you get so interested in sports?

"Frank, I played some high school ball, but I'm not really that interested in sports. I don't even follow any college or professional teams. My job is to protect the Church and spread the faith. Catholics believe the best way to do this is through our schools. Building a reputation for excellence is my primary goal. We strive for excellence in every aspect. Sports are only one of them, but, frankly, the most important. Good athletic teams create immense pride in the school and the general community at large. They help to attract students from a wide area and keep the school workable. We can support a good student population while growing the number of those we nurture in the true faith. We have mandatory daily Mass and religion classes. The Church is always under great scrutiny and the object of a lot of unfair discrimination. We can't afford to be anything less than excellent. The Bishop appointed me to Our Lady of Perpetual Help because I have a successful record of accomplishment. I've improved every parish I've been assigned to. Appointments to parishes with schools are reserved for the most successful pastors."

"I remember how hard you tried to recruit me," Frank said.

"Yeah," Brennan responded with a wry grin and a twinkle in his eye, "your dad wouldn't give me the time of day. No matter how hard I tried, he would have nothing to do with sending you off to boarding school. I tried to impress him with our great coaches and excellent education, but he wanted you at home. He said you were too valuable at home and he needed you on the ranch. I was disappointed, but not discouraged. I made several attempts to get you. You might remember that I even went behind his back and talked to you directly, but that really made him mad. The rest is history. Instead of playing for Perpetual Help you became one of our biggest nightmares. Coach Earnhardt always game planned around how to stop you. He used to give me a tough time about not getting you to come here."

"I venture to guess that, year in and year out, Perpetual Help has the best coaches in the entire state. Where do you find them?

"I have relationships at the athletic departments at most of the area colleges and I attend every state tournament. When I see a successful football program, I make it a point to attend a few of their games. I travel a lot. I look for a coach that is obsessed with winning and keeps great discipline on his teams. Some come highly recommended right out of college. I am more interested in psychology than sports per se. In athletics, the best psychologists make the best coaches. Then, of course, if they have a good-looking wife they are a candidate to coach at Perpetual Help."

After a short pause, he added, "Just kidding about that."

"Yeah, pretty women aren't much good to a celibate priest I suppose," responded Frank.

"That would depend on the priest," Brennan said under his breath.

"*Hmm*, thought Nash as he smiled, "*that was interesting. I wonder....*"

"I've heard people, jealous people; say that Perpetual Help is nothing more than a sports factory, what is your response to that?"

"Well Frank, let's look at the record. You will find that we excel at everything that we do. Our students finish at the top in music, drama, speech, debate, science fair, spelling bee, you name it. We will stand for nothing less than excellence, and the Notre Dame nuns are the best teachers in the business. Send your kids to Perpetual Help, and they will be well prepared for college and beyond.

Our athletic teams are just the most fun aspect of education at Perpetual Help and, not surprisingly, the best recruiting tool. We also send more young men and women to the convent and seminary than any Catholic School in the state. This is our primary mission. When a young person makes this commitment, they are well rewarded by both myself and the Diocese. I reward them with some great trips after they graduate and make sure that their education is taken care of where there is a need for help."

"Tell me about the trips, I bet the kids really enjoy them."

"Usually, we go to Disney Land. My brother runs a string of motels there, so we always have affordable accommodations. The parents of the girls worry about their children being alone for the first time, but I assure them that they will be well taken care of. Being with their pastor and confessor is very reassuring. Typically, we go by car, so expenses are manageable. I am fortunate to have extra funds. The families are not burdened."

"That's interesting; you pay for the trips out of your own pocket? I thought Catholic priests took vows of poverty."

"That's a misconception many have, but vows of poverty are limited to the monks. I've acquired some resources through smart investing that are helpful in running my operation."

"This is off the record Joe, but when a parish accumulates funds over and above the cost of operation, the bishop always claims those funds for the dioceses. I've chosen to invest that money personally and use it to grow our programs without having to ask for permission. The bishop would not be happy if he knew how much I pay our coaches. We can make good things happen on the local level if we can avoid the diocesan bureaucracy."

"As you know, my parishioners are predominately farmers, and on occasion, when crops or commodity prices are bad, things get a little tight. It's awfully helpful to have independent resources at those times. My investments have come in handy"

Frank was curious about those extra funds but hesitated to inquire too much about Brennan's private matters. He thought he might be able to find someone in the community who was aware of Brennan's management style. Successful investors find it difficult to keep their successes private. He made a note to check around.

"You've just won your first state championship, is this your ultimate goal for all your sports programs?"

"Like I said previously, we strive for excellence in everything we do. I pay my coaches well and expect that they will compete for championships every year. They work hard because they know that the next job will mean a pay cut. We have periodic reviews where I sit down with them and their wives and get to know them intimately. I want the wives to understand that their husbands are making substantially more money than they could at any other school. That minimizes the problems at home when the coaches spend so much time on the job. One cannot get to know the wives well enough. They can make or break a good coach, so we don't want them carping about being lonely or ignored. The money really helps in this regard."

"So, that extra money for the coaches; does that come out of personal funds as well? Usually private schools pay less and count on other advantages to attract coaches, but you pay them more than they can get elsewhere. If I was a coach at Perpetual Help how much more would I make than my peers elsewhere?"

"Well Frank, that's confidential information. I've instructed my coaches to hold that information in confidence as well. Suffice it to say that Don Earnhardt had offers from institutions far more prestigious than Perpetual Help. I made him an offer he couldn't refuse, and he never regretted accepting it."

"Wow, you must be loaded!"

"The Lord has been good to me. I've done well"

Frank made a mental note to pursue this further. He remarked to himself, *"Is money really the key to his success?"*

"I understand that you have built very impressive support from some of the most prominent of New London citizens. Many pastors find this difficult because hard spiritual truths often cause significant discomfort when confronted. Does this not happen in New London?"

"Well, I put a lot of effort into cultivating important people. Sometimes rumors get started that the pastor cannot effectively deny. It helps to be able to go to these people and have them deal with the rumors. The more respected they are in the community the better. They become your most vocal supporters too, because their businesses benefit by the excitement a great school can generate in a community. Parents of boarders spend significant amounts in the community as they come and go, transporting the kids to and from school. Also, there is nothing like community pride to drive business to the local merchants."

"You have really got an impressive system. Do you mind if I talk to some of these individuals?"

"Not at all, they enjoy the notoriety."

"So, what kinds of rumors are you talking about?"

"I don't think we need to get into potentially divisive issues. Every pastor must confront rumors. It's the nature of the game."

"Frank, I think you have enough for a good story. I've got some personal business to attend to and need to go. I know that whatever you write will be very helpful to Perpetual Help School and I greatly appreciate what you are doing."

As Frank walked slowly to his car, his gut was telling him that there was much more to this story. Brennan's veiled reference to priests who were attracted to beautiful women was too provocative to be ignored. His apparent significant personal wealth, and his reluctance to talk about rumors, all sparked suspicion that begged follow up. He was decided to talk to some of the coaches and New London citizens. He thought to himself,

This could be a bigger story than I expected!

Chapter 5

Insights from an Old Rival

I have held my supporters back because I did not want a parish civil war and have the school destroyed in the process. But my supporter's patience is getting thin and if trouble makers continue I think they will have greater problems.

Sunday Bulletin March 14, 1971

Frank's mind was racing as he was driving the twenty-five miles to his home in Dickinson. *What if I uncover scandal here. I was just hoping for a great success story, but if Brennan has skeletons in his closet this could be humongous.*

Just then a pickup crested the hill in front of him his wheels just over the median. Frank had to crank his steering wheel hard right to avoid him. He came very close to losing control of his car. And the driver honked his horn as he went by, leaving Frank to curse him at the top of his lungs.

Relax, he thought as he tried to calm himself, *it's over.*

When he arrived home his wife met him at the door with the same limp hug that was beginning to bug him a little. He knew what she was thinking, and he felt it to be unfair. Sandy was sick of being poor and had zero confidence that the Brennan story was going to be much of a career booster. She was constantly pushing him to look for a new job.

"I had a strange phone call this morning that scared me to death," she said. "The caller refused to identify himself and he literally yelled into the phone that you better be careful what you write about Father Brennan. He said that Brennan has very powerful friends and they will do anything to protect him."

"You're kidding, why would anyone think that I have anything but the best intentions. I'm just covering a great sports story."

"Maybe you should drop the whole thing. The last thing we need is to make enemies. You are well recognized and highly thought of in the community. Why risk your reputation for a story that Brennan may not deserve anyway? I wish you would move onto a job that would pay better. I am so sick of being poor."

Frank's heart sank as he was again confronted by Sandy's constant negativity about his potential as a sports writer.

"Sandy, this could be a bigger story than I first imagined. Something is going on in New London that is bigger than their success in athletics. I'm not sure what it is yet, but I'm getting some bad vibes from some of the people and even Brennan himself. I need to see this to the end. There are a lot of journalists who make big money writing books. If you hang in there with me, maybe I can be one of them."

"Well for god's sake," responded Sandy, "be careful."

*****

Even though it was early in the afternoon, Frank was so wound up by the events of the day that he needed a stiff drink. Doug Bieber, one of his college buddies, owned a bar in Dickinson. It had been awhile since they visited. He had been a star athlete at Perpetual Help in the early 60's while Frank was being recruited by Brennan. They had been fierce opponents in high school and both were recruited by North Dakota State. He wondered if Doug might be able to shed some light on the conflicting messages he was getting from Brennan.

Doug's heartfelt and cheerful greeting lifted Frank's spirits as he sat down at the bar and ordered a triple scotch. He felt extra good whenever he was with Doug because they had been through so many athletic wars together. Both were rewarded handsomely for all the hard work they put in as young kids. They both played for very good teams. He was a bit jealous of Doug who was now a successful businessman.

After a bit of revelry and talk of the good old days, Frank asked Doug if he was aware of any negative rumors about Father Brennan.

"I was the best player on the 1962 basketball team. We took second in the state. I don't know how Brennan found out I was a good player, but sometime while I was in Junior High he began showing up at my games. He talked my dad into sending me to Perpetual Help. I was really ticked because

I wanted to stay in Dickinson and play with my friends, but once I realized that I was going to be on a very good team at Perpetual Help, I really got fired up and everything worked out. I never lived in New London and have lost contact with most of the people there. I've just heard a few rumors."

"I don't really have an opinion of Brennan, but one thing that sticks with me is the pep pills he gave us before big games. We weren't into drugs in those days, but I remember the boost I got when I took those pills. He called them pep pills, but I guess that they were probably speed. We didn't think much of it at the time, but they probably gave us an advantage. He only gave us the pills when we were playing the toughest teams, like Bowman for example."

Frank asked, "Why do you think he wanted to win so badly?"

"He just loved to stick it to the opposing team. He needed to feel superior. I'm not sure what his agenda was," Doug responded.

"I suppose you know that I was raised on a small ranch outside of Marmath. My dad moved there when I was three years old after playing for the Brooklyn Dodgers. He's a Hall of Famer, you know. He made enough money to buy the ranch and could do what he had always dreamed of doing; raising cattle and taking long rides over the prairie on his horse. In fact, he named his horse Duke after one of his best friends, Duke Snider."

"He was one of my all time, favorite players," Doug interjected.

"Dad taught me the same love of baseball and the ranch, and I got his athletic genes. Even though we lived in a remote area, I was fortunate that baseball was the entertainment of choice. All we needed to put together a game were bodies and an open field. Trust me, there was no shortage of open fields in Southwestern North Dakota."

'As a young kid, I watched every game I could, and always dreamed of someday being the star player. By the time I was 14 years old, I was the starting center fielder and best hitter on the team. The old guys I played with were mostly veterans of WWII. They were just happy to have survived and weren't too worried about who won the game. They would serve me up fat pitches that I would hit out of the park. They would just smile and encourage me. They wanted me to have the career of my dreams that none of them were able to have."

"I was bigger than all my friends and was recruited to play junior legion ball in New London. It was a long way from home, but my dad was so proud of me that he was willing to make the sacrifice to drive me to practice and games. He worked with me in his spare time and I got to be good enough to attract the attention of the colleges all over the country and even major league scouts, some of whom were dad's old friends."

"I also got Brennan's attention. I noticed that one of the faithful fans was a sickly-looking man who was always dressed in black. I didn't realize, at first, that he was a priest. He even showed up at practices. I asked my coach about him and was told that he was the local Catholic priest who ran Our Lady of Perpetual Help School. "In fact," he said, "he wants to talk to you about attending Perpetual Help.""

He bugged my dad for months trying to get him to send me to Perpetual Help. He said the boarding program was perfect for athletes looking for a great education and a platform to showcase their athletic abilities."

With that, Frank ordered another triple scotch and their discussion moved on to more reminiscing about the good times they had had together.

By the time Frank left Bieber's bar the sun had set, and Frank was anxious about getting home to work on his notes. The effects of the triple scotch had worn off, and he still had enough energy to work a few hours.

When he sat down in his office to begin writing his first thoughts about that day's interview he began to feel a strange presence in the room with him. He ignored it at first, thinking the alcohol must still be affecting him, but then he heard what he thought was a whisper that said,

"Next time we won't just scare you."

Frank jumped out of his chair frantically looking around the room afraid of what he might see. He thought he felt a cold breeze, but then silence. "What the hell?" He exclaimed aloud. After a few seconds he thought to himself,

Oh, what an idiot, this is ridiculous and resumed putting his first thoughts about the interview with Brennan on paper.

At the top of the first page he wrote,

"I have to talk to Therese Koch next."

Chapter 6

Therese

The walk out of the sisters and priests, requiring the hiring of extra lay people, will cost the school and parish about $27,000. So those who urged them to do so and those who had a part in it can be proud of themselves at what it is costing the school extra. We will make it though. It will take more than that to close Perpetual Help. The history of this event has not had its final chapters written yet.

Sunday Bulletin March 28, 1971

"If you're writing a glowing article about Brennan, I'm not sure I'm the right person to talk to, but sure, come on by tomorrow morning. I'll put some coffee on and treat you to one of my mom's magnificent caramel rolls."

As Frank put down the phone, he thought to himself, *nice lady, she doesn't sound all that angry, but she knows something.*

*****

Perpetual Help High School could not have produced a better student, a better citizen, or a better Catholic role model than Therese Koch. She was the oldest in a family of eight children; six girls and two boys, born and raised in New London by Garvin and Elsie Hunter. Elsie was a sister to Cleo and Floyd Sieger.

Therese was a special child and grew to be a loving mother to her children and companion to her husband, Arnold. Her high school years were stormy, because she fell in love with Arnold, already a grown man, eight years her senior, and a non-Catholic. Garvin and Elsie were adamantly opposed to the relationship. But, she was lucky to be in her senior year when Brennan arrived in New London. He was adjusting to his new assignment. This kept her conflicts with him to a minimum, and she left school with a strong relationship with him.

Arnold was from an active Lutheran family who was forced to convert to the Catholic Church to get Garvin and Elsie to agree to the marriage. He did so, graciously, despite strong opposition from his siblings. He enthusiastically supported Therese in her Church activities. He was a farmer of considerable skill and was growing his operation rapidly. Having been a native of New London, he had developed many strong friendships and was well liked and highly respected for the early success he had achieved.

Therese was active in the parish and was an advocate of many of the changes that Vatican II brought to the Catholic Church. This caused a degree of tension between her and Brennan who was a dogged conservative; he was one of the last to turn the altar around to face the congregation. But he respected her skills and desire to be a positive force in the parish.

She was a straight A student in high school and the first of eight Hunter children to graduate from college. She graduated with honors and was the lead singer in her college's annual opera performance. Her beautiful soprano voice would resonate throughout the church every Sunday as she sang with the choir. She taught at the public school briefly, and though a very tough taskmaster, was loved by her students. She was a parish leader and was admired by almost everyone in the community. People felt they could trust her, and at first, when they became disturbed with things happening in the parish, they felt comfortable in discussing them with her.

The Hunters and Siegers were a very close family. All but one of the six Sieger siblings still lived in New London. The single exception was Sister Mary Elizabeth, a Notre Dame nun, of whom the entire family was extremely proud. They celebrated most holidays together and they're family gatherings at Thanksgiving and Christmas were legendary. By the 1970's, when most of their children were married, the attendance at these gatherings reached upwards of 40 relatives. Their political discussions and Pinochle games were raucous affairs. The meals reflected their German Russian heritage and the pastries were to die for. All of them got along and loved their families. Everyone, along with their children, graduated from Perpetual Help High School. Paul, the family patriarch, gave the first $100 gift to Perpetual Help Parish to start the school.

By the late 1960's, however, a generational split was forming over the rumors about Father Joe Brennan. Therese was finding herself the focus of disagreements about the rumors about him that were running rampant in the community. She was having discussions with the new assistant pastor about the efficacy of the rumors and their obligation to find the truth. They met with the bishop about their concerns. At the same time, her uncles, Cleo and Floyd Sieger, were Brennan's biggest defenders. The growing conflict was never mentioned at family gatherings, but there was considerable tension below the surface.

*****

Frank walked up the curved sidewalk to the Koch home. It was larger than most in New London, but still relatively modest. It reflected a lifestyle better than the average New Londoner but was in no way ostentatious. It's emerald green exterior set it in contrast to the mostly white homes in the community.

He knocked lightly and a thin woman with her hair perfectly curled answered.

"Good morning. Mrs. Koch?"

She smiled brightly. "Mr. Nash, I presume."

He shifted his weight from one foot to the other. "Yes ma'am, Frank Nash. I appreciate your generosity with our time, and please, my friends just call me Frank."

"Come on in Frank and have a seat.

As he stepped into the house, he was greeted by the familiar smell of freshly baked bread."

I haven't forgotten the coffee and caramel rolls." Let me get them and we can talk."

Frank's eyes lit up when he saw the caramel roll.

"Whoa, if that tastes as good as it looks this meeting will be gratifying no matter where the conversation takes us."

"Trust me, my mama knows how to make her caramel rolls. She's famous for them."

They were warm, sweet and delicious.

"Absolutely scrumptious" Joe gushed, even better than Babe Miller's. Thanks a bunch."

"Therese, as I mentioned on the phone, I'm a reporter for the Dickinson Press and am doing an article on Father Joe Brennan and Perpetual Help School. You may have read some of my articles if you follow the "Saints". Several people told me to talk with you. May I ask you a few questions?"

Therese's eyes gave Frank the once over, and a slow smile spread across her face.

"Sure, I never thought about calling the press, but maybe it's the only way we can expose this man and hold him to account."

She took a bite of her own roll and washed it down with a sip of coffee and said,

"OK, where do you want me to start. I'm no longer a fan of Joe Brennan."

"I've been talking to people in the community about Brennan and a clear majority have nothing but good to say about him, but a couple of people have quietly suggested that I might get a unique perspective from you."

Therese rearranged the folds of her skirt in her lap. The air in the room seemed to have thinned out. Her hands moved around nervously, but her gaze never faltered.

"Despite having a great deal of respect for the way Brennan has grown Perpetual Help School, I am sorry to say that, as a priest, he is not a very good role model. He arrived at Perpetual Help with a glowing reputation. The Bishop personally introduced him to us and couldn't say enough good things about him. He also had a solid reputation among the clergy as an effective administrator and pastor. But very few people liked him at first. They respected him as a priest and, oddly, feared him in a way. He always gave you a piercing look that was quite intimidating. It was almost like he was judging every word you spoke, and all the while he had a slight grin that made you feel small."

"When he arrived, the parish physical plant was in drastic need of repair and replacement. There was no reserve in parish coffers, so he started badgering the people for money. I was in college in his early years but observed all this after I got married and settled back into the community. It was the same thing over and over. Every Sunday the sermon was all about money. He started by stressing tithing and asked for extraordinary sacrifices.

He played on the guilt that permeates the Catholic community. We live with so much fear of hell and damnation that even relatively poor farmers naturally feel uncomfortable if they neglect God's demands."

"He cajoled us with constant appeals for money. People were aware that the need was urgent, and many treated the Church as first priority even above the needs of their families and businesses. But it wasn't long before many of them began to resent him and began to complain bitterly. Every time one walked into the Golden West Bar someone was bitching about the priest. He told me that the complaining just came along with the territory. He felt as if people weren't complaining he wasn't doing his job."

Therese shifted uncomfortably in her seat as she continued. "Taking on the pastor of a Catholic parish doesn't make you a lot of friends."

"Believe me, I understand, Frank said, "but tell me about your experience with this."

"Well, first, Catholics view their priest as a direct representative of God, and as such they are to be respected even if they aren't perfect. They are given a great deal of latitude because they have sacrificed so much to serve the Church. One lady, who was a good friend before this scandal erupted, told me, after she asked me to stay away from her in the future, "Everything has come to us through the priest; all happiness, all graces, all heavenly gifts. Leave him alone."

Frank asked, "Why did you take this on then?"

"Because, I have a grander vision of the Church. Maybe if I hadn't gone to college I wouldn't realize how narrow-minded people can be. We are dealing with a scandal of potentially major proportion. We are finding evidence of sexual abuse, fraud, adultery, drug dealing, you name it. It is morally wrong to suspect these things and not either disprove them or, if found to be true, hold the person accountable. We give priests too much latitude. We see them as next to God and, so we overlook things we shouldn't."

"Our new assistant pastor became concerned when he began hearing rumors about Brennan that were highly uncomplimentary and felt that they could shatter the community. He set out to prove them false and set the record straight. Instead he found that it was even worse than the rumors suggested. He took his concerns to the bishop and got nowhere. In talking to other priests, he discovered that some of the former assistants had gone to the bishop with the same information, and in every case, were told to mind their own business and keep their mouths shut. They take a vow of obedience, you know."

Frank's pencil dulled as he feverishly took notes. "You wouldn't happen to have a pen handy, would you?" he asked.

After Therese returned with the pen, he went on.

"You have proof he's been involved in all those things?"

Frank smiled. His suspicions were being confirmed. "How many others are allied with you in the community?"

"It's a small group; less than ten, along with Father Tim Bryan, who started the whole thing. The bishop is furious with him, but he is a principled man and is ready to pursue this no matter the consequences. I doubt he will talk to you though. He wants to get results without any publicity."

Frank then asked, "Can you give me some idea of the extent of the problem?"

Therese replied, "Before I get to some of the details you need to know a couple of things. First, many of the victims have insisted that we keep their names confidential. Secondly, Arnold and I are getting very scared that this could get violent. We have been getting threatening letters and phone calls."

"Really? My wife got a strange call yesterday. She felt threatened. They told her I'd better watch what I write about Brennan. This is getting a bit scary."

They're all anonymous, of course. Let me show you a couple of them."

As he began reading the letters Frank's stomach began to churn and his shoulders drooped.

"How depressing," he remarked.

He read from the first letter.

"Mrs. Koch, you are from the devil himself. No one but you could say these things because you are possessed by the devil. Why don't you move out of the parish? Many would like that for sure. You cause nothing but trouble."

In the second letter, "You should be the one condemned, not Father. There are a lot of us for Father, and if you are not careful some of us are going to do something about you; even run you out of town. We could live in peace if you would let us, you devil you."

Therese then said, "We are getting very concerned about the whole situation. Arnold has been building his farming operation here for fifteen years and has been very successful, but we are already working on selling the entire kit and caboodle and moving out of state."

"You are a brave group," Frank said, "people do not like to hear dirt about their priests. You are right, we hold them in too high regard. We forget that they are human just like we are. The church itself is the biggest offender. They are more concerned with image than living up to the values they preach. It's really sad."

Frank's adrenalin increased as all doubt about the importance of the story he was contemplating, was removed. He never fancied himself to be an investigative reporter, but now knew he had to pursue this story to the end. His excitement was growing as Therese resumed.

"You should come to church on Sunday and listen to one of his sermons," she continued. "You would witness the very height of hypocrisy"

"Let me tell you about a few of the families who were impacted by Brennan."

Chapter 7

I Am Not Mentally Ill

Speaking of their loss in the finals of the 1971 state basketball tournament – The exposure of the school on TV for the last three days was good for us. It is publicity that you cannot buy and many people all over followed the team. People from Minnesota and North and South Dakota watched the games on TV. Even new London as a town gets some publicity from it, but for many people this is not desirable.

Sunday Bulletin March 28, 1971

Joe Brennan was not an impressive looking guy. For all his interest in sports, he wasn't very athletic despite having been a member of his high school basketball team for four years. In fact, everything about him screamed clumsy. He was fairly tall and bulky, but not a physically strong man. He looked like he had never worked out a day in his life. His skin was whiter than normal. He looked almost sickly. He had a gross, but somehow intimidating, limp. One leg was shorter than the other and when he came walking toward you his entire body rose and fell. It felt like he was erupting towards you with each step. That said, he had the swagger of someone you wouldn't want to lock eyes with, let alone cross. His arms are more ink than skin and his graying black hair was thinning so that from a distance you might mistake him for being bald. Beneath his pierced brows his eyes were direct, they did not blink as much as the average person. He didn't smile often.

He had a split personality. When he thought with his higher brain he could be engaging and inspirational. He could manifest love to everyone. But, more often, fear and shame would take hold of the primitive part of his brain and it was the boss, and he became a control freak. It was "them or us," "kill or be killed." It was if he was robbed of his better self, deprived of his ability to live his life, or to let God flow through his thoughts and deeds.

His obsession with sports as superintendent of Our Lady of Perpetual Help School might have led one to assume he had been a good athlete as a youth and that girls would have competed for his attention. But that was not

~ 33 ~

how it was growing up for Joe Brennan. He was shy and withdrawn. In his early teens, he developed diabetes and was on insulin the rest of his life. Although he was on the basketball team for four years, he seldom got to play.

Even before the onset of his diabetes, Joe never developed physically like the other boys. He was not very strong which made it difficult to do physical labor. He feared being ridiculed and stayed quiet and reserved when around others of his age. They picked on him and bullied him. Whenever things did not go his way he tended to start obsessing about this treatment. He always ended up repeating over and over "I'll show you bastards!"

He was rehashing all of this in his mind as he drove to Bismarck for a meeting with the Bishop. The phone call he had received ordering him to be in the bishop's office the next day angered him. He had to cancel a flight to Los Angeles for an urgent business meeting with his brother. He seldom flew anywhere because he had an intense fear of flying. But this meeting was important. His brother was threatening to walk away from the business because of a dispute over the disposition of one of their motel managers who was defrauding them. Delaying the meeting was going to have negative consequences, but the bishop had been adamant, and Joe wasn't about to use personal business matters as an excuse to postpone a meeting with him. The less the bishop knew about his personal business the better.

The bishop's personal secretary was about Joe's age. He always marveled at her beautiful body and wondered how she would be in bed. He winked at her as she showed him into the bishop's office.

Bishop Whacker walked toward him as he greeted him. He was smoking a Cuban cigar that one of his wealthy advisory board members gave him. Joe hated the cigars which he always thought smelled like Satan himself passing gas. The Bishop offered his ring to be kissed, and Joe bent down on one knee and dutifully did so.

God, I hate doing that, he thought to himself.

"I think you know why I asked you to come in for this meeting," Whacker began. "I am getting extreme pressure from a sizable number of the priests in the diocese to do something about your philandering; particularly from your assistant, Father Bryan. I've reminded everyone of them to keep their mouths shut and mind their own business. However, Father Bryan is being very persistent to the point I'm going to have to discipline him, but the pressure could force me to act."

"Your Excellency, I assume you haven't forgotten about your own indiscretions. I am warning you that if you pursue this too far everyone in America will find out about you and your boyfriend. If the public becomes aware of these revelations, whether about you or me, the Church will suffer. I may not be perfect, but I am a good priest. I run one of the best operations in the diocese. Kids from all over, who would otherwise not get a Catholic education, come to my school and thrive. The women who are accusing me are just disenchanted with their marriages. They can't wait to jump into bed with me. They act like it's a sacred act. One of them told me that it is an honor to have sex with me. As for myself, I think about sex obsessively. I don't know why, but I never act with malice aforethought, it just happens. I act without thinking."

"I am sorry to hear that you have this problem Joe, but that is an astonishing admission. It speaks to why I called this meeting. Bryan's group of parishioners is insisting that you need psychological counseling. To satisfy them I have arranged to have you examined by professionals at the Mayo Clinic. That's far enough from home that no one should get wind of it. You will start with an intensive session that will consume about a month of your summer vacation. The diocese will pay, and I've already arranged a substitute to take over your duties at Perpetual Help while you are gone. You need a good vacation anyway."

"What if I refuse? Psychiatrists are agents of the devil, heretics, antichrists. Why should I let them try to manipulate me? What a waste of time. Your Excellency, back off this. I swear I will expose you if you persist."

"I'm sorry Joe, but if you refuse, I have been authorized by the Vatican to begin formal procedures to remove you from the priesthood. Any retribution on your part will be considered as sour grapes. No one will believe it. I will use every asset at my disposal to make sure of that."

Joe's mind was racing as he left the meeting. He felt that all the effort he had put in to making Perpetual Help School an icon in the diocese was no longer appreciated. He reflected about all the other priests he knew who were sleeping with parishioners and even some who were molesting children and he thought, *why me?*

In the end, he decided the Bishop was right. He did need a vacation, and he was curious about the Mayo Clinic. It would be an adventure, and maybe it would get the "rebels," as he called them, to stop harassing him.

It will also give me some time to think about how I am going to stop the gossip and rumors. This has been my life's work. I am not going to let a few malcontents destroy my legacy. I'll show the bastards.

Chapter 8

A Bridge Too Far

Perpetual Help received a two rating from the Department of Education again this year. A lot of pressure must have been put on to take it away from us. A representative was in our school recently and knew all about our changes in faculty. So, we got over another hurdle in the revolution against Perpetual Help. If the revolution was just against me they would leave the school alone. Going to the Department of Education and other things does not look like a revolution just against me. I know some of you are near the explosion and action point, but we will wait just a trifle longer to see what develops.

Sunday Bulletin May 23, 1971

"My notes say that you are challenged a bit by your vow of celibacy, Father Brennan." Dr. Walter Drake was not big on small talk. Besides, he didn't much like the patient who was sitting across from him. The condescending smirk that was a semi-permanent part of his demeanor was unnerving. He seemed to lack any conscience about any of the charges outlined in the dossier he was referencing.

Father Brennan had arrived for the first meeting unshaven and looking like he had not slept the night before.

He curtly responded, "If you have a few patients who are priests, you know that celibacy is a joke. It's not humanly possible for a virile male, with the ego needed to serve as a priest, to avoid the urge to have a woman. We have easy access to all the sex we want. I'm told all the time that it's an honor to have sex with me. Women somehow seem to understand that we have needs, and they are more than willing to take care of them. I suppose there are a few celibate priests, but I'll bet they masturbate a lot."

The smirk on his face widened to a smile and he chuckled as he added, "there's nothing wrong with me Doc, I'm just a red blooded American male who found a gig that most men would die for. I'm just better at it than most.

I went downtown last night, and despite my deformity I had a woman stroking my dick within an hour."

Dr. Drake had to stifle his desire to lambaste him for manipulating the poor woman and acting so incredibly cavalierly. Instead, in the most sarcastic manner he could conjure up he calmly said,

"I'm sure there is nothing wrong with you, Father Brennan. It's surely normal for every Catholic priest to lack so much caution in his escapades with those who trust him implicitly, that multiples of them are willing to come forward and seek his removal as pastor. You don't feel like you are in an exclusive club? I call that a problem."

Don't let him manipulate you, said a voice in Brennan's head.

The voice had confounded him ever since he was in college. It came to him in his sleep and especially when he was in deep thought. It suggested solutions to stressful situations. He sometimes tried to ignore it, but often it was sweet music to his ears. He knew in his gut that it was Satan. He was so ever present that he had named him Bubby, after Beelzebub. The name seemed less threatening than conceding he might be possessed by the devil. That would condemn him to hell. Listening to counsel from Bubby, a kind of alter ego, was easier to rationalize. He could, at a time of his choosing, reject a being he pretended to be a mere friend and accomplice.

Doctor Drake continued, "Who is the real Joe Brennan? Who formed you as a person? Tell me, what was it like growing up for you?

"My father, died when I was six years old. My mother immediately anointed me the man in the family. On the day of his funeral, as he was being lowered into the grave, my mother turned to me and said,

"Joe, I will be depending on you. We've been left alone, and now, you must be the bread winner. Your brother and sister will need you."

"I was too young to even understand what she meant, but it was a burden."

My mother was devastated by our loss. We lived on a small ranch where we raised cattle and grew feed crops. Dad was never able to find water on our property and had to haul it from a neighbor's well for the entire time we lived there. The work load for two was overwhelming and now mom was alone. I guess she felt guilty because she had very little time to take care of us

~ 38 ~

kids. She was lonely, and often yelled at God proclaiming that she didn't deserve the life she had been dealt. Her angry outbursts are some of my most vivid memories."

"How did the outbursts make you feel?"

"I don't have any feelings about my mom. I felt sorry for her, but I tried to be around her as little as possible. She always made me mad because she demanded that I do everything. My brother and sister got away with murder, but I was always held accountable. I was so happy to get away from home. I sometimes think I went to the priesthood just to get her off my back. Irish mothers live and die for a priest in the family, you know."

"Most people wouldn't admit to a lack of feeling for their own mother."

"I don't understand why I am ambivalent about her. I always understood that things were tough for her. In the 1920's Southwestern North Dakota was isolated from the outside world. The roads were bad or nonexistent. The only dependable mode of transportation was the Northern Pacific rail line that ran 30 miles north of the ranch. The first 10 miles of road to get there was nothing but a wagon trail. The weather was unpredictable and harsh. Temperatures could be as high as 110 degrees in July and August. It could get as low as sixty below zero in mid-winter. The wind blew unmercifully. Calm days were rare. Mom would always tell about the day that she stepped out of the house to go feed the cattle and her nose froze shut before she got to the barn. Later the neighbor told her that the temperature was 30 below zero and the wind was blowing 45 miles per hour."

"There were no trees to stop the wind and the prairie stretched for miles as far as the eye could see. There were a few buttes that broke the monotony some. There were no building materials, so our house was a sod hut. Mom and Dad had plans to improve the place but after Dad died she gave up on that."

"The environment in Southwestern North Dakota was friendly to buffalo and rattlesnakes, but only the hardiest of us humans could tolerate it for long."

"Your mother seems like an admirable woman to me. It sounds like she went through a lot and did her best."

"There was a hard edge to her though, and her life was made even more intolerable by the drought and low farm prices in the 20's and 30's. Banks were weak and many failed, she couldn't get any credit. She went bankrupt and lost the ranch. We moved into Golva a nearby small town. The move taxed her to exhaustion. She was often depressed after that and would disappear for hours at a time. She said she took long walks and that the open prairie was the only thing that could calm her.

"We thought that she didn't want to be around us anymore. My brother and sister and I resented it. Fortunately, my uncle, was one of the few successful farmers in the area, and he owned a house in town that he gave her, at least we didn't have to take charity from friends."

"In the thirties, it wasn't uncommon for parents to send their children to orphanages because they weren't able to feed them," Doctor Drake interjected. "You were lucky that your family was able to stay together."

"I wish she would have sent us away."

Joe's voice cracked as he said this, and he momentarily became melancholic and his eyes reddened and teared up.

Dr. Drake took note of the uncharacteristic show of vulnerability.

"Tell me more about that."

"The day after we moved into our new place in Golva, mom told me I would have to take a job. The Funks, owned a store in town and needed someone to stock shelves and sweep the floors. She said we needed the money. I was scared because I didn't think I would be able to do the job, but she just told me that I would learn and that I just needed to grow up. We couldn't afford for me to be a kid anymore."

"I hated the job. Ralph Funk was downright mean to me. He was so pleasant around the customers, but he had no patience with me. He had a paddle hanging behind his desk in his office and threatened to use it on me if I wasn't perfect. He was a stickler for order and cleanliness. He would say to his wife, "that fucking kid can't do anything right." Whenever I messed up, he would cuss at me no matter who was around to hear it. He could string profanities together in almost symphonic fashion. I would go home crying almost every day. I pleaded with mom to let me quit. If I was too insistent, she would slap me on the head and tell me to "straighten up."

"She told me that without the money I was bringing home, we would be starving to death. I became determined to show her that I could do the work, but secretly I wanted to run away."

That's when I began hating her. About the only positive thing was that, despite the abuse, I picked up on things quickly. Before long I was running the cash register and counting the receipts at the end of the day. Funk let it up on me after that."

Brennan chuckled as he remembered how he first realized how smart he was.

"But I never had a chance to be a kid. I would have been better off in an orphanage. I don't remember ever getting a hug from mom until the day of my ordination. She only loved us when we made her look good."

"We might want to pursue your feelings about your mother more in-depth sometime later, but for the rest of today, tell me more about what it was like growing up in Golva, ND."

"I felt good about being given some responsibility in the store. Most of the kids thought it was cool that I could work the cash register, but they made fun of me anyway. They laughed at me because I was barely visible behind the counter. They called me the store midget. Fortunately, I didn't stay short forever."

"Kids made fun of me all the time. They said I thought I was too good for them because I would never play with them, but I always had school work to do after work. Mom made me study. Lots of time I wouldn't get to bed before 11pm. She always said they wouldn't let me into the seminary if I didn't have good grades. I always wondered what made her think I wanted to be a priest. I assumed she didn't care what I thought."

"I became obsessed with proving myself to her. Learning was fun and came easy for me. The other kids were jealous because I got the best grades. My mom and Mr. Funk always praised me for it."

"I never had many good friends growing up. The other boys bullied me. I had three cousins that were all about the same age, and they used to throw rocks at me on my way home from work. They would come into the store and steal candy bars and dare me to tell on them. I never did."

"It helped to be smarter than they were though. Even though I hated them I helped them with their homework. They were too dumb to figure out their math problems, so they came to me for help. I secretly wanted to kick them in the balls, but for some reason I couldn't turn them down."

"Everyone seeks approval in some way," said Dr. Drake. Do you think that your real motive was to find a way to dominate them, to pay them back for bullying you?"

"Naw, I thought they were losers, and I just wanted to show them I was in control. I did to them what they were doing to me. I made sure they understood that I would tell the teacher who really did their homework if they weren't careful. The bullying stopped after that, but I never stopped feeling like they were talking about me behind my back."

"As a matter of fact, I was smarter than most of my teachers. They couldn't get stuff into those kid's thick heads, but when I helped them they did better." After a while I felt nothing but contempt for those pricks. The girls were the same. I couldn't get one to look twice at me, yet they came to me for help with their homework. Not one of them would hang out with me. I spent a lot of time trying to figure out how I could get back at them. Sometimes I wonder if that's why I became a priest. I sort of enjoy being able to threaten them with hell and damnation. It makes them feel guilty about their extra marital affairs. They can't argue with a priest."

"So that's how you are getting back at your male tormenters, we need to talk more about this, but what about the women? The reason you are here is that you apparently don't have much use for your vow of abstinence. Jumping into bed with them would obviously create big problems in their marriages, is that really what this is all about, getting back at the women in your life because girls treated you badly?"

"Those stories about me are mostly lies. I have not been perfect, few priests have, but I don't have anything against women."

The minute these words came out of his mouth a vision of his mother popped into his head and "Bubby" burst into his consciousness. *Don't you dare tell him about your mother! He won't believe a word of it and he will think you are stark raving mad."*

"Joe? Joe?" Drake saw that Brennan had become completely oblivious to his surroundings. "Are you okay? We better stop for now. We will resume tomorrow."

"I'm okay, strange things happen to me occasionally, they are worse when I'm asleep."

*****

"Joe, come into the bedroom" his mother yelled.

"What do you want now," Joe yelled, as he barged into her room.

She was standing there completely naked. He recoiled and exclaimed,

"Mom!" and slammed the door shut behind him.

His mom reopened the door, grabbed him by the arm, pulled him into the bedroom and started ripping off his clothes. He resisted but she shrieked,

"I cannot go any longer without a man. You are the man in this house!"

After stripping him naked she threw him on the bed and began stimulating him.

*****

Joe bolted up out of his bed. As his feet hit the cold floor he realized he just had the dream again. At the same time, he heard the now familiar evil chuckle coming from an invisible echo chamber.

"Leave me alone, you bastard he yelled at "Bubby." I never had sex with my mother. Why do you torment me?"

The dream always depressed him, sometimes for days, so when Joe entered Drakes office for another dreaded session, he was still down. After a few pleasantries, Dr. Drake began,

"I've reread the dossier that I received from your bishop, and some of the things you talked about in reference to the bullying you dealt with as a young boy beg a few questions. Apparently, you overlooked sexual abuse in the boys' dorm at Perpetual Help School. The priest that perpetrated it is still there at your insistence. Is it possible that you are projecting anger towards your male students because of the way you were treated? Tell me about that."

Joe's shoulders fell, *Bullshit,* he thought, *I figured that I had put a lid on all of that when I got rid of the trouble makers in the dorm before they got too vocal.*

"Father Murphy needs help. We've had lengthy discussions about his problems. The bishop referred him to the Congregation for the Doctrine of the Faith. They're supposed to take care of these things, but nobody has heard a word. I don't have the authority to remove an assistant. That's up to the bishop. What would that have to do with me? Sure, we kept the lid on that one, but we were just looking out for the best interests of the school and more important, the Church. What's the big deal anyway? It's just sex. We preach against sex outside of marriage, sure, but no sin is committed more often. Priests are just as vulnerable as anyone else. We're human too, you know."

"You don't think there was any harm done to the victims?"

"Our kids are tough, mostly farm kids, they'll get over it. They are getting a great education. A little diddling by priest isn't going to kill them."

"You have a very cavalier attitude about sex. Nothing generates more powerful emotions than one's sexual nature. Did you not ever learn that after all the education you've been through?"

I had plenty sex education. They are almost obsessive about it in the seminary. I think it is overdone. We are sexual beings. It's how we procreate. Procreation is the real problem. Nothing keeps me away from women more than the fear of getting them pregnant. You can be damn sure that the times I have failed my vow of celibacy I've had a discussion with my partner to make sure she wasn't in her fertile period."

"Interesting. Is it your impression that all men feel the same way about these things?"

"I have no idea, nor do I care. We take extreme measures to discourage sex outside of marriage, but my experience in the confessional tells me that we are not very effective. I just smile and move on. Speaking of moving on, are we going to spend all of our time talking about sex?"

"You don't seem to be taking this very seriously. You are accused of massive sexual abuse, and you seem to have no guilt. This seems highly unusual for a man of God."

Being in a dark mood anyway, the idea that he was considered a man of God, caused Brennan to retreat into himself and fall into a long silence.

Man of God? Brennan repeated to himself, *I am so tired of having to live up to this fiction.*

He began thinking about the dream from the night before. *Could I really have had sex with my mother?* Then he heard Bubby's evil chuckle and he momentarily lost all touch with the world around him.

"You can't deny it any longer Joe," Bubby reminded him. "Remember her cries of ecstasy. It was though she loved you as her husband. You know it gave you pleasure."

Brennan erupted in anger, startling Dr. Drake to the point he feared for his own safety. He spewed obscenities unlike anything Drake had ever heard. But Drake never interrupted him.

"You forget about the rape of Adeline Funk, your boss's daughter too, don't you?" Bubby continued. "Well, get used to it, she helped make you the man you are."

It was like it was yesterday. Brennan could see Adeline's breasts which she exposed as she leaned over the homework she had asked him to help with. She was the prettiest and most popular girl in school. He knew her better than the others because she worked alongside of him in her father's store. He developed a liking for her even though she ridiculed him like all the other girls. She was terrible at Algebra.

Her dad hurried off to the local tavern for his usual nightcap as soon as the store closed. Since their books were with them, having come directly to the store from school, the two of them decided to start their homework before they went home. Adeline expressed great frustration because she could not understand how to solve linear equations. Since Joe had quickly mastered the subject he was happy to help.

When Adeline carelessly allowed her blouse to droop and reveal her developing breasts, Joe had visions of his mother as she hovered over the top of him, breasts hanging in his face. Without thinking, he grabbed Adeline and started to unbutton her blouse. When she began shouting at him to stop, he threw her to the floor, stripped off her clothes, and forced himself on her. The fury of Joe's assault so overwhelmed her that she quit resisting. The pain she felt when he entered her brought tears to her eyes. When it was over she was angry, confused and bewildered. When Joe got off her he admonished her for causing him to lose control and informed her that if she told anyone what had happened, he would tell everyone at school that she seduced him and that she was nothing but a slut.

"Remember the feeling of power that you experienced. That's what you want when a woman succumbs to you isn't it," said Bubby. "It made you crazy for more. You couldn't get any of the other girls, so you masturbated and even had sex with the sheep on your uncle's ranch, but your mother was always there for you."

When he came out of his stupor, Brenan gave a blank stare to Dr. Drake and said,

"We're done. I could care less what you report to the Bishop. I am not crazy, and I will not subject myself to this humiliation any longer."

Chapter 9

The Machinations of a Sex Addict

"MAYO CLINIC DISAGREES WITH LOCAL AREA EXPERTS: In the past few months you have heard many times that I was mentally sick and needed long extensive treatments, and some were so willing to help poor Father Brennan who was so sick and needed help. It was spread far and wide how mentally sick I was. At the specific request that I be examined I went to Mayo Clinic. After having three doctors put me through tests, they wrote to the Bishop and said that they could find nothing wrong with me mentally and that I needed no treatment. Either Mayo Clinic is behind the local experts or far ahead of them, but it is not with them."

Sunday Bulletin May 30, 1971

"Bless me Father for I have sinned. My last confession was yesterday."

"Yesterday? Young man, are you going to confession every day?"

"Yes Father, Satan stalks me every day and I can't resist him."

"What do you mean, stalks you?"

"He comes to me in my sleep, he mocks me when I try to pray, and he interrupts me when I try to study. He tells me the Ten Commandments are for ill-educated simpletons who can't think for themselves, and that I am too smart to believe such nonsense, and that I should seek my pleasures without guilt."

"It started when I got into high school. At first, I didn't understand what was happening. I mentioned it to our priest, Father Lack, in confession and he told me it was Satan tempting me. Father Lack knew how important it was to my mother that I become a priest and he said Satan works like that. He said there is nothing Satan hates more than another new priest. He was doing everything in his power to turn me away from the seminary."

"I had all these nightmares where Satan appeared as Saint Patrick. I don't know, maybe it was because my family were such strong Irish Catholics, but he would say that the Irish were stupid to fall for a church that was really a fiction created to amass power in Ireland."

He says if I leave the seminary and do his bidding he will grant me great wealth. He tempts me with visions of nude girls and I masturbate almost every day. I cannot help myself. I am trying to express true sorrow by daily confession, but it just keeps getting worse. I hate myself for being so weak."

"My son," the priest counseled, "you must pray every day. God will not abandon you. Create a holy space for prayer. Satan cannot enter holy places. Purify your soul, pray harder, do penance, fast often, and pray a novena to Our Lady of Perpetual Help. She will intercede for you. Jesus honors her entreaties. You can win this battle and you will become a better priest for having endured these attacks. This is your penance, and may God bless you and forgive you."

Joe suffered with these temptations throughout his time in the seminary. His daily confessions did not help. He became too weak and lackadaisical to do the penance his confessor ordered. Eventually, he stopped going to confession altogether. The temptations grew stronger as he neared ordination. He often thought he should leave and pursue the wealth with which Satan tempted him. His intelligence would serve him well in the business world. He thought that the priesthood would keep him poor the rest of his life.

But he felt he could not leave because of his mother's wishes. Irish mothers defined their self-worth by the number of priests they begat. Because of his sick sexual relationship with her he was contemptuous of her, but despite this he experienced an unyielding attachment and he could not get himself to disappoint her by leaving the seminary. Instead he worked out his insatiable drive for sex by living a nightlife that he hid from even his best friends.

Whenever they went out on the town, he would excuse himself by trekking off to the library to study. He never stayed long. After his friends were safely on their way, he raced to a tavern in one of the small towns that other students avoided. There he would find a woman, ply her with alcohol, then, have his way with her. He hated himself every time he did this, but the evil force that owned him was irrepressible. He excused his evil ways, even though he knew them to be mortal sins, by blaming Bubby, and he sloughed off any feelings of remorse for using religion to manipulate people. He agonized over why his fear of hell didn't stop him from pursuing sexual gratification, but his concern ended whenever he met the next willing female.

Despite his secret life, Joe seemed like a regular guy. His intelligence served him well in college much the same as it had in high school. His peers came to him with questions about their studies and he always seemed to have an insight that would help them. He was also fun to engage in theological discussions. His understanding of the Church exceeded that of any of his peers. Though he was extremely doctrinaire, they learned a lot from him. They didn't seem to mind his unwillingness to party with them. They just assumed he was more interested in academics than wine, women and song.

Visits from Satan bedeviled him throughout his life. When he was accused of being mentally ill, though he fought it with every fiber of his being, he wondered if this obsession with Satan was, in fact, a mental disorder.

*****

"Take control. Establish your authority. Put the fear of God in them."

Bubby voice was booming in his head, and Joe gave up resisting him.

"We are going to have a great run in New London. You will have no regrets if you listen only to me. These people are ignorant and uneducated. They've been programed to believe anything that comes out of a priest's mouth. Make them think you are building them up and they will never notice what you take for yourself."

How do I start?

"Your preaching, use your sermons. Every great leader ultimately controls his people through his rhetoric. I will guide you."

So, Joe plastered his Sunday sermons with messages of fear, damnation and shame that were the very opposite of the way he conducted his own life.

How can I do this, it is so hypocritical.

"Toughen up Joseph. This Catholic propaganda is all a fiction. How many times must I tell you that. It exists so that you can control those who will hasten your path to fame and fortune. You will get your reward soon enough."

The faint echoing giggle that followed was evidence enough of where the message emanated.

Your turning me into an animal!

But resistance was hopeless. His primal urges overwhelmed him. They seemed so natural and irresistible, so he bought what Satan was selling. In his mind he held all this "stuff" the Church was preaching in contempt.

At the same time, he taught that mortal sin confronted everyone and was punishable with eternal hellfire. It worked as Bubby predicted. He gained almost total control of his people. The guilt he stimulated served to enhance his image as priest and confessor. He convinced people that missing Sunday Mass, eating meat on Friday, and acting on "impure thoughts," would condemn them to hell. Near perfect attendance at Sunday Mass assured him a captive audience and served an agenda suited to his personal aggrandizement.

His most memorable sermon was his first at Our Lady of Perpetual Help. He used a variation of it often. It was plagiarized from the James Joyce novel, "A Portrait of the Artist as a Young Man." He had never read a more meaningful description of hell. Bubby assured him that it was the perfect way to introduce himself to his new congregation.

"As you know, Adam and Eve were our first parents. They were created by God in order that the seats of heaven left vacant by the fall of Lucifer and his rebellious angels might be filled again. Lucifer was a radiant and mighty angel; yet he fell. He fell, and with him a third of the host of heaven. These rebellious angels were hurled into hell. Lucifer fell because of the sin of pride, a sinful thought that offended the majesty of God for a single instant and God cast him out of heaven and into hell forever.

Adam and Eve were then created by God and placed in the Garden of Eden. Alas, my friends, they too fell. The devil, once a shining angel, now a foul fiend, came to them in the form of a serpent. He came to the woman, the weaker vessel, and pored the poison of his eloquence into her saying that if she and Adam would eat of the forbidden fruit they would become as God Himself. Eve yielded to the wiles of the arch tempter. She ate the apple and gave it to Adam who did not have the moral courage to resist her. They fell.

They were driven into the world, a world of sickness and striving, of cruelty and disappointment, of labor and hardship, to earn their bread by the sweat of their brow. But the all merciful God left them with hope. He promised that, in time, He would send down from heaven One who would redeem them, and once more make them children of God and heirs to the kingdom of heaven: and that One was to be Gods only begotten Son, the Second Person of The Most Blessed Trinity, the Eternal Word.

And he came, born of Mary the virgin mother. When he was grown, filled with love, He went forth and preached the gospel. Did they listen? Yes, they listened but could not hear. He was seized and bound like a common criminal, crowned with thorns, hustled through the streets by the Jewish rabble and the Roman soldiers, stripped of his garments and hanged on a cross.

Yet even then, in His hour of extreme agony, Our Merciful Redeemer had pity for mankind. He founded the holy Catholic Church against which, it is promised, the gates of hell shall not prevail. He promised that if men would obey the word of His church they would still enter into eternal life, but if after all that had been done for them, they still persisted in their wickedness their remained for them an eternity of torment in hell.

Hell is a quagmire, a dark and foul-smelling prison, an abode of demons and lost souls, filled with fire and smoke. The damned are heaped together in their awful prison, the walls of which are 4,000 miles thick, and they are so utterly bound and helpless that they are not even able to remove from their eye a worm that gnaws it.

They lie in exterior darkness. The fire of hell gives off no light. It is a never-ending storm of darkness, dark flames and dark smoke of burning brimstone, amid which the bodies are heaped one upon the other without even a glimpse of air.

The horror of this dark prison is increased by its awful stench. All the filth of the world all the refuse and scum of the world, shall run there like a vast reeking sewer when the terrible conflagration of the last day has purged the world. The bodies of the damned exhale such a pestilential odor that one of them alone would suffice to infect the entire world. Imagine some foul and putrid corpse that has laid rotting and decomposing in the grave, a jellylike mass of liquid corruption. Imagine such a corpse, a prey to flames devoured by the fire of burning brimstone and giving off dense choking fumes of nauseous loathsome decomposition. And then imagine this sickening stench multiplied a million-fold again from the millions upon millions of fetid carcasses massed together in the reeking darkness, a huge and rotting human fungus. Imagine all this and you will have some idea of the horror of the stench of hell.

But this stench is not the greatest physical torment to which the damned are subjected. The torment of fire is the greatest torment to which the tyrant has ever subjected his fellow creatures. The sulfurous brimstone which burns in hell is a substance which is especially designed to burn forever with unspeakable fury, and the fire in hell has a special property that it preserves that which it burns, and though it rages with incredible intensity, it rages forever. The lake of fire in hell is boundless, shoreless and bottomless. It is on record that the devil himself confessed that if a whole mountain were thrown into the burning ocean of hell, it would be burned up in an instant like a piece of wax. And this terrible fire will not affect the bodies of the damned only from without, but each lost soul will be a hell unto itself, the boundless fire raging in its very vitals. The lot of those retched beings is terrible! The blood seethes and boils in their veins, their brains boil in the skull, the heart glowing and bursting, the bowels a red-hot mass of burning pulp, the eyes flaming like molten balls.

It is a fire which proceeds directly from God's fury, working not on its own but as an instrument of divine vengeance. Every sense of the flesh and faculty of the soul is tortured. The eyes with impenetrable utter darkness, the nose with noisome odors, the ears with yells and howls, the taste with fowl matter, leprous corruption, nameless suffocating filth, the touch with red hot coals and spikes with cruel tongues of flame. And through the several torments of the senses, the immortal soul is tortured eternally in its very essence, amid the miles upon miles of glowing fires kindled by the offended majesty of the Omnipotent God, and fanned into everlasting and increasing fury, by the breath of the anger of the Godhead.

In hell the damned howl and scream at one another, their torture and rage intensified by the presence of beings tortured and raging like themselves. All sense of humanity is forgotten. The mouths of the damned are full of blasphemies against God and hatred for their fellow sufferers and of curses against those souls which were their accomplices in sin. There is nothing to compare to the fury of profanity that bursts from the parched lips and the aching throats of the damned in hell when they behold in their companions in misery those who aided and abetted them in sin, those whose words sowed the first seeds of evil thinking and evil living in their minds, those whose immodest suggestions led them on to sin, those whose eyes tempted and allured them from the path of virtue. They turn on these accomplices and upbraid them and curse them. But they are helpless and hopeless: it is too late now for repentance.[1]"

"My people, this is what awaits those who do not keep the Ten Commandments. Listen to the Church. You must keep its commandments, honor your priests and nuns, go to confession regularly, receive the Eucharist at least every Sunday and stay in the state of grace. If you do these things you will avoid the abomination of hell."

"But, you must also tithe 10%. The Church cannot survive without your financial support and God always takes care of those who give. Where would you be without the guidance of the Holy Father and his Holy Catholic Church? In Proverbs 3: 9–10, it says,

"Honor the Lord with your wealth and with the first fruits of all your produce; then your barns will be filled with plenty, and your vats will be bursting with wine."

And finally, encourage your children to nurture their vocations. Your priest is a man who holds the place of God; a man, who is invested with all of His powers. Our Lord said to his apostles, "Go," as My Father sent Me, I send you. All power has been given Me in Heaven and on earth. Go then, teach all nations. He, who listens to you, listens to Me; he who despises you despises Me."

"Well done" Bubby giggled.

The sermons impact exceeded Joe's expectations. The line for confessions was longer than any in Joe's experience.

"What you hear in there will serve you well," whispered the demon in his head.

You evil bastard, what are you suggesting?

"You shall see."

---

[1] James Joyce, *A Portrait of the Artist as a Young Man*, Dover Publications, 1994.

Chapter 10

Confidants

WE WISH TO REMIND YOU THAT the upset at the school this year cost the parish over $53,000 and therefore it is necessary that you do better in your Sunday envelopes than many of you have done and also pay your school bills when you can. The balance that is unpaid is going to be the Sister's salary for this past year, and they will need their money as soon as possible. However, I am not going to cover it with money from any other source except the parish and school. Maybe if some of you have to pay more to cover a shortfall you will not feel too good about the trouble this year.

Sunday Bulletin May 30, 1971

"In the name of the Father and of the Son and of the Holy Spirit, it's been six months since my last confession. Father, I need help. My marriage is in trouble and I have not had relations with my wife for two years. Last week I took out my frustration on my niece and forced her to have sex with me. Then I threatened her to keep her quiet. If my brother finds out what I did, I'm afraid he might shoot me."

"My child, it is good that you confessed this, but you will need spiritual direction. Call me this evening and we will make an appointment to talk in my office. For your penance, I will be asking you to take a special role in the parish and school. I will have a plan by the time we meet."

*****

The previous pastor was fired for mismanagement. It was a challenge to restore a semblance of financial viability especially given that Fr Moskowitz was extremely popular. Everywhere he went Brennan met parishioners who talked about how much they loved him. The welcoming words that followed always felt less than sincere, so when Brennan started investigating the financial condition of the parish he became understandably irritated.

Where in god's name, are the ledgers. The bishop said the finances were a disaster. I wonder if a set of books even exists.

~ 54 ~

He emptied cabinets and drawers trying to get a focus on the challenge in front of him. The rummaging created a cloud of dust and caused a fit of sneezing of the kind that always angered him. He was prone to dust allergies and life in rural North Dakota, where the fields blew with the all too frequent winds, tended to be dust filled. The sneezing fits often came at the worst time and he had no patience for them.

"God damn it" he yelled at the top of his lungs.

As usual, the profanity embarrassed him, and he mumbled to himself,

"I wish I could stop doing that. If someone overhears an outburst like that what would they think of me as a priest."

The words were barely out of his mouth when he heard a knock on the door. He was expecting Moskowitz's finance manager who he hoped would be able to enlighten him about the finances. A middle age man greeted him,

"Good morning Father, I'm Paul Grower.

Brennan was surprised by the figure that stood before him. He was accustomed to working with bruising hard-nosed German farmer types who would punch people in the face at the least provocation, but Grower was skinny and an unimpressive bookish type. When he spoke though he exuded confidence.

Reminds me of myself, Brennan thought.

The discussion that followed confirmed Brennan's worst fears.

"He simply wouldn't listen to me," Paul said referring to Father Moskowitz, "I tried to get him to establish a reserve, but he always said that that would require him to be asking for more money all the time and he just had too much concern for his people. He always said that they were burdened enough with the risks they faced every day. He worried about farm prices and weather conditions almost as much as they did."

"I told him that the rectory was going to fall down around his head, but that didn't faze him. He said he was just a humble man and didn't need anything fancy. So, we are faced with a sad state of affairs. I'm sorry you have to deal with this situation."

"Well Paul, don't feel bad. I'm up to the challenge. This won't be the first parish I revived. Let's get to work."

"I understand that you own the local hardware store. That must be a struggle in such a small town."

Paul smiled and said, "I have a good partner, I'm mister inside and Floyd Sieger is mister outside, and we treat people right. We have a base of very loyal customers whose needs often exceed their ability to pay. We are generous with our terms and give them plenty of time. We usually get paid eventually when the weather and farm prices cooperate. We're doing well."

"You might be looking for these," he continued as he produced the ledgers that contained the parish financial records."

"I've been looking all over for them"

"After a few frustrating meetings with Father Moskowitz at which he threw a bunch of receipts at me, I decided to just keep the ledgers with me. I would come up once a week to pick up the bills and have been keeping the books ever since. You should find them to be in good order."

"Well, that's a relief. I hope you will agree to continue your service."

"You can count on me Father, but I hope you will take more interest than Father Moskowitz did."

"Don't worry Paul, I have big plans for Our Lady of Perpetual Help. We are going to create the best parish and school in the entire diocese."

"That would be fun," said Paul. "But I wonder if you will be so confident after you see what I'm about to show you."

Chapter 11

Vicar of Christ as Master Intimidator

IN CASE SOME GET THEIR HOPES HIGH, the pastor is not leaving the parish, and so when he is gone now and then, it only means that he has other things to do. Because of the trouble this year, I will have to make a lot of contacts for students for next year and other school matters.

Sunday Bulletin June 6, 1971

His people had always been faithful to the Sacrament of Confession. They saw it as the only way to save their souls. But they were seldom comforted. Most were intimidated by the power of the man behind the partition in that dark, sometimes threatening place. The priest was God's instrument. He held the power to forgive and that intimidated them.

They fear you. You know that, don't you?

Brennan was kneeling at the foot of his bed saying the rosary when Bubby rudely interrupted him. He was excited about the impact his sermon had on the congregation, and despite knowing how diligent the average Catholic was about regular confession, he was amazed by the numbers who confessed at the end of Mass. He wanted to thank the Blessed Virgin for interceding for him. When Bubby wasn't present, he credited all his successes to the intercession of the Blessed Virgin. It irked him that Bubby had chosen to interrupt his prayer.

"Go away!"

"And let you continue the fiction that somehow this woman, who birthed a bastard son, should get credit for your successes when I'm the one pulling all the strings? You know very well who is making good things happen for you. Be careful or I'll run that limo you drive into a tree."

"You keep telling me this stuff is all a lie. You don't scare me," Brennan said aloud.

"Not to argue, but if you don't leverage that fear into the power and riches you seek, you are out of your mind."

"Oh really."

Bubby's face twisted into one of its most evil caricatures and he said,

"My friend Joe, you still think you can are in charge and play both sides. You will live a double life and have your women, your wealth, and your power while helping save the souls of your people. But you see, I am a jealous task master. Together we will gather souls for my realm. You and I will trick those naïve people into believing you are working for their salvation, but in the end, we will have played with their minds so that hatred and revenge consume them. Then you will have all that you desire in this life and I will have my wretched filthy dupes to torment for eternity."

"But I'm a priest. I am here to do God's work."

Oh yeah, what has that so-called God of yours ever done for you. He killed off your father when you were seven forcing you to take on a role of man of the family before you even understood what that meant. He gave you a psychotic mother who forced you to have sex with her. There is no sicker relationship between mother and son than that. So now you are a sex addict who cannot control his passions despite a lifetime of being taught how wrong that was supposed to be. There is no God! How could a loving God deal you such a fate?

"Oh, stop it. If there was no God, you couldn't exist. I'll find a way to get rid of you once I get what I need."

He had learned well while growing up. His mentor and childhood pastor, Father Lack, had preach with great fanfare and pomposity. Brennan used the same style to profound effect. He knew that he could use the pulpit to pursue almost any agenda. When addressing his new flock, he would ascend the three steps to the top of the podium in the ancient church he had inherited, and assume his best impression of medieval royalty.

The church reeked from restrooms so ancient their odor could only be masked, never eliminated. The wretched smells left no doubt of their origin. There was dust everywhere. Father Moskowitz seldom asked the people to help take care of their church. The janitor could not keep up. The pews were rickety, and the paint had mostly chipped away. The floors creaked and some of the studs were rotting. Yet the sanctuary retained a sense of the sacred that the people were reluctant to let go of, a magnificent altar, statues of saints as a backdrop, and cathedral ceilings painted with reproductions of Michelangelo's best from St. Peters Basilica.

But the need for a new church was obvious and Brennan reveled in his status of anointed savior. His message was righteous, and his pleadings fell on the ears of simple folks as he laid out the financial needs of the parish.

He preached, Sunday after Sunday, that any blessings they prayed for would be illusive if they did not tithe. God demanded his 10%.

His flock was not a wealthy constituency. They depended on favorable weather to harvest good crops and high prices to produce even a meager subsistence. Most of them never went to high school. Their education came largely from the pulpit and was otherwise directed by the Church. Fear of God was deeply ingrained in them, and when made to feel guilty enough, they gave generously. He never let them forget that parish needs were great, and God demanded that the tithe must be their first priority.

The cost of running a parish was high and he was not above threatening them when he thought he could get away with it. He withheld priestly services by making it clear that services were contingent on their cooperation. He intimated that children would not be baptized, nor daughters married, if their families were not paying their fair share. He never considered individual circumstances. One either paid up or suffered exposure in the Sunday bulletin. He kept records that he published every year. If the publishing of their meager contributions did not make them feel guilty enough, he shamed them. The demands made on everyone to raise their contributions were interminable.

He preached that God would bring grace to New London if the people would dig deep enough to finance a new church. If their commitment was generous enough, they would be proud to have one of the diocese most impressive monuments to the Almighty. He asserted that Our Lady of Perpetual Help Parish would be the envy of the entire diocese. He impressed upon them that they were special people destined for greatness.

This was an environment that took a special effort to sustain. He needed allies in the community who would support his agenda when the inevitable critics rebelled. Floyd Sieger's confessing of the sin of sexual abuse created an unexpected opportunity.

Brennan, heard the knock on his door at the same time as the familiar evil giggle penetrated his consciousness.

"Phase one," Bubby whispered.

His heart sank as a qualm of conscience almost deterred him.

I must remember that this is for the good of the church, he said to himself as he opened the door.

"It's good to finally meet you face to face Mr. Sieger."

Floyd Sieger stood in front of him looking like he had just come out of a coal mine. His face was covered with the dust that blew off the fields of black dirt around New London. They referred to the soil as black gold. It was some of the most fertile soil in the world and sprouted copious crops when conditions allowed.

"I apologize for the way I look, Father. I've been in the fields all day. These dang winds blow up a lot of dust."

"I didn't know that you were a farmer too. How do you manage to work both the farm and the hardware store?"

"I've got a large family, we manage," replied Floyd.

Floyd was in his early fifties and had been a member of Our Lady of Perpetual Help Parish since birth, but he had never seen the inside of the rectory.

"You live quite humbly, Father, I'm sorry."

"That's quite true, Mr. Sieger, maybe we can change that for the next pastor who serves here. But we aren't here to talk about my humble surroundings, you have some major life issues we need to address."

Over the next several minutes that were uncomfortable for both, they discussed the rape of Floyd's niece. As he learned the grim details of this and other aspects of Floyd's life, Brennan was reminded of his own past, as Bubby laughed and said,

"Sounds a lot like you. Give him his penance, and remember the plan."

Our Lady of Perpetual Help school, like all Catholic Schools, existed so that Catholic children received their religious training. Their uneducated parents weren't trusted to pass on the faith. Schools were needed to evangelize and keep the faith alive. Catholicism was a defensive and fear filled faith in the 1950's and 60's. Historically, there was a strong thread of anti-Catholicism throughout the country and the clergy attributed disagreement between peoples of different religions to anti-Catholic prejudice. Brennan was paranoid about this. He wanted to isolate his parishioners from the "anti-Catholic" haters. The school was the ideal place for this, but it was never enough to merely protect and spread the faith, he sought to marginalize and dominate all non-Catholics. He discouraged students from interacting with their non-Catholic friends, and absolutely prohibited dating them. Getting caught dating a non-Catholic was grounds for suspension from school.

He demanded excellence in every program; most visibly in extra-curricular activities, where domination would show those he felt hated the Church, the superiority of what he believed to be the "one true Church."

This meant that upgrading the church was not enough. All the facilities had to be upgraded. A new gymnasium was needed to replace the old bandbox, called the Memorial Hall, which was shared with the local Public School. Winning athletic programs needed the best facilities because even great coaches needed great athletes, and the small community of New London, could not supply the talent needed for a dominant athletic program. New facilities would act to attract recruits.

He was confident the people would give even more if they could see evidence that he was producing excellent results. Athletic teams that had always been very ordinary could become the envy of the entire Conference.

*****

"Floyd, this is what I want from you as penance for your sin. I have a mandate from the Bishop to remake Perpetual Help into the most successful Catholic school in the diocese, but I have a problem. He hasn't given me any money to work with. We must gather our own resources, and when people are asked to sacrifice too much, many times they rebel. This is where you come in. I want you to be my advocate. When you hear grumbling, try to reason with the person. I'm told you frequent the Golden West. Most disenchantment is voiced in the bars. Be persuasive. Find ways to keep people aligned with the needs of the Church. When I come under criticism, defend me. Go out and find a few others to help you. If you do this for me I assure you that I will stay fully committed."

"Father, my family helped build this parish, especially the school. Every one of my family graduated from Perpetual Help. We are some of the lucky few. Most certainly, I will help you whenever and wherever I can."

"And we won't forget your problem. When you need to talk come by the rectory. My door is always open."

Chapter 12

Cash Corrupts

Brennan's drive to succeed bore fruit. The Sunday collection grew gradually until it was large enough to begin setting aside funds in a reserve fund. Paul Grower had the issue on his agenda at one of their regular monthly meetings.

As they were getting down to business, Paul said, "Father, your constant harping about money is a pain in the butt, but I've got to admit that it has been very effective. You should be congratulated; Perpetual Help has never had extra money. It's time to develop an investment strategy. I'm looking around your office and I see mountains of cash just sitting out in the open. That's not only very dangerous, but not a very good investment strategy."

"That's easy for you to say, Paul, but we have a problem. Savings accounts at all parishes must be opened in the name of the Diocese.

The Bishop must approve all withdrawals. It is not unusual for him to raid successful parishes accounts to subsidize poorer parishes."

~ 63 ~

"Really, we've been poor for so long an issue like this has never come up." How does the bishop expect us to improve facilities if we can't count on using our own money?"

Joe, felt a light touch on his shoulder. It startled him because he knew that he was alone in the office with Paul. Then he heard the unwelcome voice in his head.

"Don't say too much," Bubby whispered, you are the one who counts the Sunday offertory. That cash has been a godsend, (so to speak) to you."

The reference to God made Joe smile to himself. His eyes brightened, and he let out an almost imperceptible chuckle. Paul took it as an ironic signal that they were up against a serious problem.

"Let him suggest a solution."

"I assume the bishop wants some of the same things we do. Wouldn't he discuss withdrawals from our funds with you beforehand?"

"Discussions with the bishop are pretty one sided when it comes to money. He has absolute control and we pastors have to honor our vow of obedience, so we don't win many disputes."

"Why does he have to know?"

"There's your chance, encourage him to expand on his thought."

Joe lowered his gaze and gritted his teeth.

Get lost you evil bastard, what you are implying is wrong.

"Wrong? By whose standards? We are way beyond that discussion."

"Paul, it wouldn't be all that unusual for a pastor to take discretionary action without the Bishop's knowledge, but it would be risky. Do you have a suggestion?"

"Let's just set up accounts in your name. You've done wonders in raising contributions. You can invest some of the money personally. No one has to know. Then if the bishop diverts money away from our needs, we can dig into our own reserves."

"BINGO!" exclaimed Bubby.

At this point it was easy for Brennan to accede to Bubby's temptations. The cash laying around the office hadn't all been going to pay parish expenses. His meager salary never seemed to be enough. He wanted some of the finer things in life. He was sick of the poverty in which he grew up. The Chrysler Imperial parked in his dilapidated garage wasn't affordable on his salary alone.

"Let me give that some thought and pray about it. We can discuss it again next time."

"Very good. You handled that brilliantly!"

As he showed Paul to the door a depression, that he always experienced when he allowed Bubby to control him, set in.

Paul noticed the change in his mood and asked, "Are you okay?"

"Get a grip you idiot. He suspects something is wrong."

"I'm fine Paul, sometimes I get a little overwhelmed. Managing a growing enterprise is a bit daunting, but I'm okay."

Unbeknownst to Paul or anyone else including the bishop there was more to "the plan" than quality facilities and a school with a dominant extra-curricular focus. The counting of the Offertory every Sunday evening was, indeed, a terrific opportunity. Given the amount of cash received and the absolute trust of his people, he could deposit money into his personal name without risk. It was easily justified as an emergency fund. The parish plan was to plow large sums of money into brick and mortar and there was no sure path to paying the bills when times got tough. Given the uncertain economics of farming, it was simply good management to create a contingency fund for when the crops were bad and the Sunday offering declined. New facilities and the need to keep an excellent coaching staff demanded more certain cash flow. This was all he needed to justify putting Perpetual Help's investments into accounts he controlled. The fact that it served a wider agenda was a bonus. If he could invest the money well enough he would be able to truly live the parallel life he had been building since adolescence.

Joe didn't notice the aura of satisfaction that enveloped Bubby. His grip on Joe was getting stronger. Easy access to the finer things in life would cause Brennan to stop resisting. The die was cast.

Chapter 13

The Master Plan

"We are getting a lot of publicity lately, and I wish they would put down how cheap our room, board, and tuition are so we could get more students. If we had a different name we might do better, but right now Our Lady of Perpetual Help in New London is a dirty phrase and being anti Perpetual Help is popular. But we are not done yet."

Sunday Bulletin October 31, 1971

Keeping a school economically viable was difficult in rural North Dakota. If the Sunday offertory declined, because the farmers were not doing well, salaries and utility bills still had to be paid. A boarding school with a great sports program was less likely to encounter cash shortages because boarders were paying tuition and room and board. Parishioners paid almost nothing to send their kids to the school, so their Sunday contributions were in effect a subsidy from those who had no kids in school. The subsidy was justified by the philosophy that schools were vital to the overall mission of the Church, and everyone was expected to pay their fair share.

Brennan knew that a top-notch sports program would attract students from a wide geographic area. Teams in very small public schools tended not to do very well so a lot of athletic talent went undiscovered. Farm families had plenty of work for their kids to do. They insisted on getting them home after school as soon as possible. Sports interfered with the evening chores. Often, farm kids did not go out for the teams.

But when they went to boarding school, all that changed. Sports were now a necessity to allow young men especially, to blow off steam and keep them occupied. When Brennan recruited students, he focused on families with athletic children. Frequently he came up against High School Activities Association rules forbidding recruitment of athletes. He simply ignored them.

Excellent sports programs would also address other pressing concerns. Pastors were always under pressure. Preaching about money all the time irritated their parishioners. When their kids were disciplined in school, they would complain, and could make his life miserable. Brennan needed a plan that minimized these problems. Focusing on excellence in extra- curricular activities was his remedy. The football and basketball programs were the main attraction.

So, when Brennan's teams began to dominate their opponents, his people became more forgiving and even began to idolize him. They may have hated his constant badgering of them for money but putting the local public schools to shame on the athletic field mitigated most of the criticism.

Good PR was also useful because of the strict interpretation of Catholic dogma. It was difficult to be a faithful Catholic. Guilt, shame, and fear dominated the message from the pulpit every Sunday. The world was changing in the 1950's and 60's as more young people went to college and came home questioning the old dictums. It distressed their parents when they challenged what they had learned in Catechism class. Brennan's mentor, Father Lack, had modeled behavior that when emulated, would be seen by older Catholics as routine, but would be challenged as cruel by their children.

Brennan never forgot the Sunday when, during Mass, Lack called out one of his childhood friends for dating a non-Catholic. Lack ordered her to stand up in front of the congregation while he read from the Catechism about the dangers of associating with Protestants, and then accused her of having sex with her boyfriend and insisting that she go to confession at once. He then talked so loud in the confessional that the entire congregation could hear every word. Brennan was prone to similar behavior.

So, it was not easy for a pastor to maintain good relations with parishioners. However, Catholics believed that the priest was God's instrument, and he was to be respected regardless of any human failures. St. Jean Marie Baptiste Vianney, the Cure of Ars is the patron saint of priests. This is what he said in writing about them.

".... everything has come to us through the priest; yes, all happiness, all graces, all heavenly gifts. If we had not the Sacrament of Orders, we should not have Our Lord. Who placed Him there, in that tabernacle? It was the priest. Who was it that received your soul, on its entrance into life? The priest. Who nourishes it, to give it strength to make its pilgrimage? The priest. Who will prepare it to appear before God, by washing that soul, for the last time, in the blood of Jesus Christ? The priest -- always the priest. And if that soul comes to the point of death, who will raise it up, who will restore it to calmness and peace? Again, the priest. You cannot recall one single blessing from God without finding, side by side with this recollection, the image of the priest."

Joe Brennan became a priest at a time when priests could do no wrong. This environment enabled Brennan to build a wall of protection around his activities when his dark side began to dominate him. Squirreling away money in his own accounts was just the beginning of the moral compromises that would control the rest of his life. He was living a lifestyle that he would have roundly condemned as a young man and which would have dishearten even his flawed mother and anyone else who knew him growing up. He had made a deal with the devil and had chosen wealth and power over God.

Chapter 14

Manna from Heaven

"The parents and the people who <u>want</u> music here at Perpetual Help are going to have to do a lot more financially than they have done if they expect to keep the music program going as it is now. Music in my book in running a school is a luxury financially, and if people do not want to pay for it, you cannot have it. We have operated the school for many years in the past without much music, and we have obtained the services of good music people to satisfy those who desired music. IF YOU WANT BAND, YOU ARE GOING TO HAVE TO SUPPORT IT FINANCIALLY AND SOON."

Sunday Bulletin December 9, 1971

"Ben, how are you? Good to hear from you." "Your call is timely. My parish construction project is just getting underway and budgets are looking to be almost unmanageable." "How is Mr. Kennedy doing with his oil investments in Alaska?"

Msgr. Benjamin Havok was a legend in the Archdiocese of Los Angeles. He was a power broker in the great postwar boom that was transforming Southern California and was turning the Archdiocese into a billion-dollar institution. It was becoming the wealthiest in the country.

He had a knack for making money that gave him influence from Rome to Hollywood. He bragged that he oversaw everything with a dollar sign in front of it. His work put him in close contact with business tycoons and leading Catholic families like the Kennedy's. He was to become one of the most powerful men in the city of Los Angeles.

Brennan knew Msgr. Havok far more intimately than did his closest confidants in California. They had spent a year together at Marquette University as graduate students and had become fast friends. Havok studied accounting in college and from his earliest years as a student was very astute in financial matters. The two became confidantes and communicated frequently over the years. They spent all their vacations with each other and their personalities were fused together because Havok was possessed by a sexual demon very similar to Brennan's. (Years after he died, allegations of sexual abuse ruined his reputation.) Brennan could leverage their relationship because Havok rubbed shoulders with some of the iconic lay figures in the Catholic Church in the United States including Joseph P. Kennedy.

"My friend," Havok pleaded, "you will not believe the money we are making. You need to jump on board. Do you have any ready cash you can invest?"

"Yes, a lot of cash is contributed in our Sunday envelopes. I've got plenty, but its parish money and my bishop doesn't look kindly on speculative investing. I've set some of it aside in personal accounts because, as you know, all of the parish accounts belong to the Diocese and there is no way I could get him to set aside money in designated accounts specifically for Perpetual Help Parish."

"Joe, we are literally transforming our Catholic School system out here with the money we are making. Land values are increasing rapidly and when we sell off our stock profits we use the money to get the best real estate deals. I see no reason you can't invest the money in your personal accounts and use it for your building program. You can literally explode your investment portfolio and pay your construction bills as they come due. Your bishop may not like it, but why does he have to know? God's work is far more important than a few rules. What is he going to say even if he finds out? There is no way he is going to expose that kind of information to the public. If you're successful, give him the credit. That will keep him happy."

"But are these trades legal? Kennedy has been known to be involved in some pretty shady deals."

"Kennedy is an icon in the church. He has connections as high up as the Vatican. In fact, he is a personal friend of the Pope. It is rumored that he is trying to get his son elected to the Presidency. I don't think we have anything to worry about. Mr. Kennedy wouldn't do anything to hurt the Church or his son's political future."

"Well, if it's good enough for Archbishop McIntyre it's good enough for me, but I have little experience in investing. I'll need your help."

"You've got it my friend! Here's the phone number of one of our stock broker friends in Minneapolis. He will help get you started. Stay in touch Joe, you're in for a hell of a run."

Joe's mind was racing as he hung up the phone. He had always kept the parish funds that he invested in his own name in a safe place. He was just beginning to consider investing in the stock market, and one of the first problems he encountered were the hucksters who were selling returns that were too good to be true. He didn't realize that there were insider deals that would make the parish rich. He could see that if the investments worked as well as Havok was claiming, the parish wouldn't even need all the money. How would he be able to continue making the case for tithing if he was overseeing a wealthy parish?

"You dummy."

Bubby again.

"I've got a master's degree Bubby. I'm not dumb."

"Nobody has to know how much money you have. Just make sure Paul and Floyd keep quiet. Let them in on the investment advice. If they're getting rich, they won't want to ruin a good thing."

The prospect of using some of the parish investments for himself was suddenly attainable. He justified it by claiming he was the one responsible for growing the sums beyond what the parish could ever possibly need. The thought of such wealth aroused him. Bubby's evil giggle was evidence of his approval.

*****

"Joseph, Joooseph, wake up!" Joe stirred lightly but ignored the familiar sound that tormented him almost every night. The visits from Satan always unnerved him. His inability to ignore them frustrated him greatly. "Jooseph, WAKE UP!" At that Joe bolted up and shouted,

"God Damn you, can't you leave me alone?"

At which Bubby let out a loud guffaw and said,

"Joe, you cannot live the double life you have lived and dismiss me so easily. We have a bargain Joe. I give you wealth and power and all the sexual pleasure anyone could want, and you give me your soul. It is too late to go back now Joe, we are in this for the long haul."

"Call the broker Joe. I will make sure your money will grow beyond your wildest dreams. You will be able to attract all the women you want. You will gain control over whomever you want to exercise power and to assure that all attacks against you fail."

Joe responded as he always did by calling out to the Blessed Virgin to "please keep him away from me," but her help was never enough.

Chapter 15

Opportunistic Investor

"Our thinking is that the school must be kept going to do its basic work, and if the people want either sports or music work at the school, then there is only one way to have them—put up the money. There is no money from the ordinary budget for either of them. So those that want them will have to show by dollar signs that they want these things."

Sunday Bulletin December 26, 1971

Hello, Joe? My name is Frank Amato; I have a note here from Ben Havok to call."

"Oh, thanks, I was just about to call you."

"What can I do for you?" Amato asked, pretending he didn't know.

"Monsignor Havok was telling me about an investment program that is making the Archdiocese of Los Angeles a boatload of money. He said you could help me do the same."

"How much money do you have?

"Well, I have virtually no personal funds, but I have some parish cash."

"Padre, I couldn't care less where the money is coming from. How much are we talking about?"

"I might be willing to start with $30,000 or so."

"God damn, I wish Havok would stop sending me a bunch of penny ante investors. We are making multimillions of dollars for him and all he can think of is his seminary pals. But, okay, bring me the money and I will get it into the market. You are a lucky man."

"Can't I just send you a check?

"Oh boy, aren't you the naive one. These are all cash deals. You bring the money to me in Minneapolis and hand it directly to me. That way I get to meet you and the deals are all off the radar screen. This stuff has to be held close to the vest or all the opportunity and momentum leaves the marketplace. This is the last conversation we will have over the phone, also. You never know when the wrong person might be listening. Kennedy has enemies. You can come by once a month or so and we can give you a report on the activity in your account. If you want to invest more, just bring the money with you."

This was the conversation that set Father Joe Brennan on a path that no one who knew of his humble past would ever believe. His preaching had a positive impact. There was a surplus in the Sunday Offertory each week with much of the money contributed in cash. Being in complete control of parish finances, and with Bubby providing all the justification for having the accounts in his personal name, the plan was in place. Monthly travel to Minneapolis was a minor inconvenience for the assurance that the Bishop would never become aware of the extra cash, and he would have full discretion to use it in any way that he pleased. He could tap his portfolio every now and then when he needed a little extra money to land the coach he wanted. He could pay many times what competing schools were paying. He almost always got his man.

Over the next three years he accumulated one of the largest fortunes in the history of North Dakota. He mined no metals, employed no people, harvested no crops, and invented nothing that changed the world. He simply tapped into a dark network of Wall Street thugs who were pumping and dumping oil stocks in Alaska, and who included some of America's most prominent citizens. When the oil scam ended, having exhausted its supply of naïve and greedy chump investors, it left the winners with fortunes and the losers bankrupt and humiliated.

The experience allowed Brennan to eventually become a sophisticated investor in his own right with enough money to take advantage of many and varied opportunities. His connection to very powerful people in the upper echelon of the church hierarchy enhanced his opportunities. His next big bonanza investment was even more cynical. In 1960 G. D. Searle and Company got approval from the FDA to sell the birth control pill. For years, Brennan had been hearing painful stories in the confessional from women about the difficulty of obeying the Churches rules on birth control and limiting the size of their families. Artificial birth control was the most frequently confessed sin amongst married women. The knowledge that Catholic women were undeterred by the prospect of committing a mortal sin and suffering eternal damnation, convinced Brennan that the pill would be incredibly profitable. Very soon after the FDA decision Brennan was the proud owner of 100,000 shares of G. D. Searle and Company valued at close to $2,000,000. Over the course of two short years Brennan tripled his money dumping his stock just prior to the end of the biggest run up in its stock price in history.

Brennan was not at a loss for what do with his money after his stock market successes. The Church had a long history of finding and acquiring the best real estate investment properties in America. With guidance from Havok, who told him that Kennedy was moving into real estate, Brennan became the proud owner of a large portfolio of hotels and motels geographically diversified around the western United States.

Henceforward his teams would have great coaches funded without regard to the weather or the price of commodities. When Don Earnhardt looked for a coaching job after a stellar football career at Johnstown State, he was shocked to learn that he would earn three times what he was being afford elsewhere to sign a contract at Perpetual Help School. He had hoped to get on the fast track in a high-profile position at one of the big eastern North Dakota schools. The little farm town of New London was not his style, but he could not resist the extra money. The overwhelming commitment to excellence that Brennan professed excited him.

The hiring of Earnhardt was preceded by the arrival of Ted Holbrook who was already transforming the basketball program. Brennan's first decision upon arriving in New London was to convince the current coach, Cleo Sieger, that it was not productive to continue coaching in the community in which he had grown up. Cleo had been an excellent representative as Perpetual Help coach and a loyal graduate as well, but preoccupation with his farming operation often detracted from his coaching job. Winning seasons had been rare. Brennan's persona as priest and pastor worked to his advantage with Sieger, who loved the Church, and who was reluctant to ever question a priest. He readily offered his resignation.

Holbrook immediately turned the program around. The team went from being a perennial patsy that could seldom get beyond the consolation round at the district tournament to a solid threat to advance to the regional tournament every year. Holbrook was also well paid.

Earnhardt left Our Lady of Perpetual Help School after only three years, with a 25-game winning streak, which was extended by later coaches to 38 games. He would become the future head coach at North Dakota State University where he compiled a stunning win-loss record. He eventually became head coach of the New England Patriots. Ted Holbrook left Perpetual Help to become head basketball coach at St. John's University in Collegeville, MN.

Earnhardt and Holbrook were the first integral ingredients in the Bubby inspired plan to build an empire for Brennan that would serve a wider agenda already formulating in the back of Brennan's mind. He would need cover for an emerging lifestyle that would ruin Brennan if not concealed.

Chapter 16

Nash Tragedy

"Sister Francine is being transferred at the end of January. She probably would have been transferred last year if it had not been for the trouble. Her leaving reminds us of a certain word—a parasite—one who lives off of others. Many of our parents and students have lived off the sacrifices and prayers of Sister Francine."

Sunday Bulletin January 23, 1972

"My God!" Frank exclaimed as he and Sandy walked out of Sunday Mass at Our Lady of Perpetual Help.

He had decided to take Therese's advice and hear one of Brennan's sermons for himself.

"If I didn't know better, I'd swear he was a reincarnation of Jonathon Edwards."

"Who?" asked Sandy.

"In one of my American History classes in college, I wrote a term paper on the Great Awakening of the early 1700's. Edwards gave one of the most famous sermons of the time. It was pure fire and brimstone. Brennan must have studied Edwards in the seminary. Well, maybe not. Edwards was a fundamentalist Christian and a notorious anti-Catholic, but there were a lot of similarities. I thought that Vatican II had moved us away from all that."

"No wonder he raises so much money," Sandy remarked, "He almost had me dropping a $20 bill into the offertory."

"I need to spend some more time with Father Brennan. After hearing this tirade, and what Therese Koch told me, I realize that my article is going to take on a whole different tone. Based on his sermon, I suspect that he is more a master manipulator than a brilliant administrator. He might be running a successful Catholic school, but he is apparently not an honorable man. The least I can do though is get his side of the story."

"I'm beginning to think you are onto something big Frank, but please be careful. I'm not sure the Church is ready to hear anything negative about one of its priests."

*****

Getting the busy Brennan to commit to another meeting proved more difficult than Frank had hoped. His long absence during the summer of 1970 frustrated Frank who was unaware that he had been ordered to get counseling by the Bishop. When Brennan finally returned to New London for the beginning of school in the fall Frank called him for a follow up interview.

When Brennan realized it was Frank Nash on the line he jumped him about his not having published his article saying,

"Frank, I thought you were going to publish your article about me last spring. What happened?"

"I decided that it would be a better article if I included impressions of people in the community. I found a variety of opinions and wanted to get your reaction."

Brennan stiffened, and Bubby quickly inserted himself.

"He heard gossip!"

What do I do?

"Don't worry, you have your Mafia."

"What the hell are you talking about? What Mafia?

"You haven't been reading L'Osservatore Romano"

"The Vatican News? What would they have to do with the Mafia?"

There have been rumblings about priest abuse in Italy and the secular press is charging the Vatican of using Mafia tactics to suppress criticism. This is so delicious. I wish I had thought of that myself. The gates of hell are being thrown wide open. Many of your friends will be joining you there. I think I must announce a new Holiday for the folks. We could celebrate with burning ember sandwiches."

~ 78 ~

The loud echoing peal of laughter that followed no longer scared Joe, but it did annoy him.

"Well trust me, there is no such thing as a Vatican Mafia and I've never heard of something so outrageous as Mafia in New London. And I am not going to hell. I'll make amends"

Call it what you want Joe, but you have supporters who will go to great lengths to protect you.

"So, you are saying I should go ahead and meet with Nash and summon my supporters if things don't go well?"

"Brilliant idea."

With that said, Bubby went silent.

"Are you there?" Nash's voice startled Brennan out of the trance he had been in.

"Sorry, my morning coffee boiled over," he lied, "I won't be able to meet with you until after Thanksgiving. That weekend is notoriously slow around Perpetual Help, but beforehand I am going to be very busy with school business. By then we should have another undefeated football season behind us. I hope to see you at a few games."

Sandy and I are planning to be in Billings with her family for Thanksgiving. Would you by any chance have business to do there around that time?"

"As a matter of fact, I have ongoing reasons to get to Billings now and then. Sure, lets plan that."

"Thanks, and you can count on me being at least a couple of your games. Just doing my job you know."

*****

Frank and Sandy left for Billings as the sun was coming up. It was a classic North Dakota fall day with clear skies and a fabulous sunrise. The air felt prairie fresh and new with a gentle breeze disguising the unknown danger that awaited them. They stopped for a moment and watched as ribbons of golden sunlight spilled onto the prairie. The rolling hills were silhouetted against the brilliant gold sky. The dew drops glowed with their own golden radiance.

Sandy was filled with the anticipation of being with her family for the holiday. Franks was excited too, but he could not set aside the prospect of a wide-ranging interview with Brennan. He feared that things could get ugly when he asked about the families he had learned about.

They picked up the morning paper that was in the driveway every morning but did not think to take it along to read. Nor were they inclined to listen to the radio as they left Dickinson. Frank could think of nothing but discussing his upcoming interview with Sandy, so when they left home in the almost calm weather and bright sunshine they were unaware of the weather forecast.

As they drove West, the weather turned cloudy, and the wind came up. They paid very little attention. Weather in this part of the country unexpectedly changed often so they saw little reason for alarm. Soon a light snow began to fall. At first it was of no worry, but as it increased in intensity along with the wind, Sandy became alarmed. She interrupted Frank's discussion of the upcoming interview and snapped on the radio. Irritated, Frank turned it off.

"How can we talk with all that noise?" he asked.

"Aren't you worried about this weather?" Sandy responded. "I was just hoping to catch a weather forecast."

"Come on, this is nothing. We'll drive through it eventually."

Frank was just getting into detail about some of the victim families, so Sandy did not protest further. An hour passed with Frank talking nonstop and Sandy hoping that Frank had been right about driving through the storm. Evidence of that was absent, however, and she insisted on turning on the radio to get a weather report. What they heard alarmed them. The forecasters were proclaiming the storm to be potentially the worst Thanksgiving season blizzard in Montana history.

"We need to turn around and go back before this gets worse," insisted Sandy.

"We are almost half way there. What sense does it make to go back? We're close to Miles City; we can stop there if it keeps getting worse."

The words were barely out of his mouth when the wind picked up and visibility dropped to near zero. Frank had to strain to see the center line on the road. The dense white swirl obliterated the usual traffic signs.

"We should have checked the forecast. It's getting so cold the heater can hardly keep up."

The white out eliminated all evidence of the road as it suddenly disappeared. They were stuck in a swirling storm of screaming silver. The wind raged without end, only reducing its ferocity long enough to gather strength for another attack. Frank did not notice the slight curve before the car careened off into the ditch.

Attempts to get back on the road proved futile as the wheels of the car disappeared into an emerging snowdrift.

"My God" Frank exclaimed, "I hope we're not the only car on the road. This storm has to stop soon, or we could be in real trouble."

He instinctively checked the gas gauge and found some solace in the fact that it still showed half full. Sandy wasn't so easily comforted. The radio was almost exclusively reporting on the storm. They were now saying that it could be a twenty-four-hour event and that winds were exceeding forty miles an hour. Even if it quit snowing the wind and the cold alone were life threatening.

"We've got to save our gas, oh my God please don't let us freeze to death," she yelled.

As the day progressed the storm intensified. Not one other car came by, and Frank could only assume that the road had become impassible and been closed. They would have to wait it out. As daylight turned to dusk, grim reality was setting in. By 4 PM he could see that they were going to have to hunker down for the night and their fuel would not last. He was thankful they typically carried heavy winter clothing in the trunk for just such an eventuality, but he feared that it would not be enough to stave off freezing if they were not rescued soon. The sky had cleared, but the wind was howling. The temperature dropped to what he thought had to be at least 15 below zero and was bound to get even lower as the night progressed. The car was almost buried, and it became difficult to open the doors. They needed to take extraordinary steps just to stay alive. Frank noticed wooden fence posts protruding from the snow banks.

He said, "I wonder if I can make a fire with them."

Sandy responded, "What good are fence posts? Where would we burn them, a fire outside does us no good."

It slowly dawned on them that the fire had to be inside the car. They were able to remove the back seat with extreme effort, but still faced the problem of lighting the fence posts on fire, then controlling the flames, so that the entire car did not burn. He had matches in his emergency kit and could siphon a little gas out of the gas tank to solve the first problem, but large flames could get out of control and the smoke could kill them. They also had to remove the carpet so that the bare metal was all that would be exposed to the fire. The hard work kept them warm for the moment.

By the time they finished preparing it was pitch dark and their gas tank was empty. They would have to tend the fire and fight the smoke if they were to survive the night. Sandy remembered the rosary that she carried in her purse but had not used for years. Together they prayed for help.

Who would have ever thought I would resort to praying a rosary, Frank thought.

As the next day dawned, Frank was exhausted from staying awake all night to tend the fire. It had gone out a couple of hours earlier and the cold was beginning to have its affect. His feet and hands were frozen, and he had been unable to stave off the sleep of the freezing man. Sandy was sleeping next to him. He did not notice her shallow breathing.

By mid-morning the wind subsided and, as luck would have it, one of the local farmers had ventured out to open roads so he could tend to his livestock and he found them. He had all he could do to get them out of the car.

When Frank awakened, he was in the Billings Hospital with no memory of how he had gotten there. All he could think of was how thankful he was to be warm again.

"Where is my wife?" he asked the nurse, who had entered the room at the first sight of Frank's awakening.

"Mr. Nash, I'm sorry, she did not make it.

"What are talking about? She was sleeping right next to me!"

"I'm so sorry, but you were very lucky yourself. Your extremities will take some time to heal. We have contacted your wife's family. They should be arriving soon"

Frank lay in the hospital bed; the sudden loss tore him apart his mind numbed by anguish and confusion.

"I'm sorry to say, there was nothing we could do," were the words of Dr. Matthews who had followed the nurse into the room.

This can't be, he thought to himself. *Why Sandy and not me? I killed her. Why wasn't I more careful? One moment she was sitting beside me - yelling, shouting at me to slow down, to pull over. Then the frantic, failed, effort to keep ourselves warm. Now all that's left is her lifeless frozen body. How could I do this?*

That night, death did not just take Sandy, but Frank's spirit too. They were going to have kids. The son he hoped for was to be the athlete of his dreams. Now he would never be. He was alone, his lover and mother of the family they had just recently hoped to start was gone. Interviewing Father Brennan was the farthest thing from his mind.

The farmer who rescued Frank mentioned his experience to a friend who repeated the story to a journalist. Frank's first visitor was from the Billings Gazette. Then the local TV station picked up the story. Even though blizzards were a common occurrence in Montana, a freezing death was rare. The story was a compelling one and the news spread nationwide.

Chapter 17

No Longer Just a Symbolic Father

LENTEN RULES:

"Ash Wednesday and Good Friday are days of both fast and abstaining.

All Fridays of Lent are days of abstaining.

By Divine Law, as recorded in the Scriptures, the life of a Christian must be a life of penance.

Anyone who neglects all forms of penance violates Divine Law and is guilty of serious sin."

Sunday Bulletin February 20, 1972

Brennan had just finished packing and was not aware of the record storm that had stopped all travel through central Montana. But as he went to turn off the radio the announcer was talking about the storm and caught his attention. They mentioned the Nash's ordeal. When he heard Frank's name, he picked up the phone and called the Billings Hospital and asked for Frank. Frank was not taking any calls.

When Brennan left New London for Billings, the skies had cleared, and the winds had calmed. It was extremely cold, but that never inhibited Joe Brennan when he was on a mission. He would be in Billings within a matter of hours. He always celebrated the liberal attitude of the state of Montana about its speed limit. His brand-new Chrysler Imperial cruised nicely at 90 miles an hour and Brennan loved the thrill of the open road. And he was always in a hurry.

These trips had become more frequent as his wealth piled up. It was when he did his best thinking. He would become totally lost in thought as the humming tires of the Imperial put him in a near trance. The changing topography of one of the most beautiful states in the union made no impression on him.

It was a fruitful place for Bubby as well. Joe struggled mightily with a conscience that had been well formed growing up, and which led him to pray the rosary every day. Bubby ignored his prayer activity because it made Brennan feel good and prevented him from perceiving the full implication of Bubby's mastery over him. Brennan's behavior was antithetical to everything he had learned in school, in church, or in seminary so it was convenient for him to have an excuse for his double life. He was happy to have Bubby's companionship on these long drives across mostly empty highways. He could justify anything simply by insisting he was incapable of resisting "Bubby." He was persuasive, and Brennan felt he had provided the means to grow his wealth. Despite a troubled conscience, Joe could not give that up.

Brennan was compulsively in conversation with Bubby. Even though he continued his regular rosaries, his devotion to the Blessed Virgin had little substance. He had become so corrupted that he was able to continue to preach with conviction while his lifestyle was dictating who he really was. His need for sexual gratification consumed him. He knew, by every standard, that he was committing mortal sins, but, his experience with his mother held him hostage. He often thought about her on these long drives and he would alternate between visions of her naked, and anger at himself for continuing to think nostalgically about his experience. His mother had triggered an insatiable need for sex that he never fully understood.

"Bubby" was always somewhere in his consciousness and would assure him that there was nothing to be angry about. Was it wrong if your own mother had modeled your behavior? It no longer seemed logical that there could be a God that prohibited sex outside of marriage yet allowed one's own mother to demand sex from her adolescent son. This whole God thing seemed flawed, but he acknowledged that it sure worked to protect his lifestyle. What other career could have presented opportunities for, not only unlimited access to vulnerable women, whom he viewed as naïve and stupid, but to inside information from some of the most sophisticated investors in the world. He would not be having an audience with a Pope anytime soon, but Joe Kennedy was personal friends with one. Most people were not able to luck into a network bolstered by the likes of Joe Kennedy. If he had not been a priest it would have been nearly impossible to get access to information that would make him wealthy beyond his imagination.

He had prospered only because of Bubby. The methods he used to build his empire had not come from God; they were fed to him in his dreams by Bubby. Often, the dreams seemed more real than life itself. Bubby was his most reliable confidante even though he could be a bully at times. He was downright scary whenever Brennan hesitated to do his bidding. Doing as he was told always worked better.

Yet, he often wondered whether he was just a weak and manipulative tool of an evil presence? In his heart, he knew he was corrupt, and even criminal, but the passions that overwhelmed him, controlled him.

These thoughts passed through his mind almost every time he took a long trip. An eerie soft cackle accompanied them, as "Bubby" embedded himself further into his consciousness.

This time the drive proved to be very fatiguing, and near the end Brennan was fighting sleep. Bubby would never let him down though. Suddenly the image of Nevada Black jumped came to mind. She had been his first triumph at Perpetual Help. Dealing with her father scared him and triggered the need to build a wall of protection around himself. The upcoming meeting with Frank Nash would not be happening if that wall had not included the sports empire he built. His thoughts drifted to the day that an angry Dr. Norman Black showed up at his house to confront him about the seduction of his daughter.

At the time, he did not have the confidence that he had gained over years of cavorting with "Bubby." Black threatened to go to the Bishop and the Mother House in Mankato and anyone else who had enough power to hold him to account. He was angry that he had put himself in position to lose everything that he had accomplished to that point in his life.

At first, he could only stutter and stammer. He begged Norman to buy the ridiculous notion that priests were human beings too, and that his daughter had presented an opportunity that a lot of men would have been unable to resist. He was embarrassed and humiliated by what he had done, and needed a quick fix.

He had visited Benjamin Havok before his rape of Nevada and shortly after Havok became the chief financial manager of the Archdiocese of Los Angeles. Havok introduced him to Tommy Lee, the heir to several General Motors auto dealerships who was selling cars to the clergy at deep discounts. Brennan had bought his cars from him ever since their first meeting. They became personal friends after Lee invited him to share his box seats at Dodger games. He attended regularly when he was in LA in the summer time.

Tommy Lee was a two-time loser in marriage and it was affecting his standing in social circles. A trophy wife was a major asset in staying connected to those who mattered, and Tommy could not keep a wife. Multiple divorce settlements also beset him financially.

When Norman Black threatened to destroy Brennan's career over an ill-advised sexual encounter with his daughter he thought of Tommy Lee. Tommy needed a wife he could count on. Norman Black needed a husband for his daughter. Nevada Black was pregnant with Brennan's child.

Brennan guessed that Black was just as concerned with his daughter's future as he was outraged at the identity of her child's father. Pregnancy outside of marriage had destroyed the lives of many an indiscreet female. The fact that a priest was the father would likely place an even greater burden on a woman. The assumed seducing of a priest would be an unforgivable sin. Norman would likely do anything to protect his daughter.

"Mr. Black," Brennan began after initially fearing a physical confrontation, "what I did was inexcusable, and I am sorry for the hurt that your family must feel, but I think I may be able to make things right for Nevada and her baby, and at the same time enable you to avoid the embarrassment that goes with an illegitimate grandchild. Give me a few days to see if I can find a solution that will benefit everyone. I have a very wealthy friend in Los Angeles who has just lost his wife. He may be open to an introduction to Nevada. Some of my friends have been very generous in their business relationships with him. He might be willing to do me a favor."

Brennan was right about Norman Black's mindset. Without hesitation, he agreed to listen to a mutually beneficial solution. His anger dissipated once he had hope that his family's reputation could be preserved.

*****

"Tommy?" "This is Father Joe Brennan. I am in desperate need of help."

Thus, began the conversation that led to the marriage of Tommy Lee, the West Coast auto magnate, and Nevada Black the daughter of a small-town chiropractor. The baby would be well taken care of in a home that Nevada could have only dreamed of as a small-town North Dakota girl. Tommy was demanding and sometimes condescending, but overall Nevada would be happy. She avoided the stigma of bearing a child out of wedlock and even became somewhat of a celebrity in New London. She never explained how her relationship had started with Tommy Lee, but people were happy for her nonetheless. Nevada was a beautiful young woman and perfect for Tommy's needs. She became a big hit in Tommy's social circles. Tommy would make sure that Nevada would not be his fourth failure as a husband. Her child would carry his name and inherit much of his wealth.

Chapter 18

Trunk Full of Cash

"It seems our people have just about eliminated weekday Mass on their Lenten schedule. With all the Catholics in town and country, people who live close to town who could come once in a while during the week, it seems that the spirit of lent and fervor for the Mass has about disappeared. I CAN HARDLY BELIEVE THAT WE CATHOLICS OF TODAY ARE WISER AND HOLIER THAN THE CATHOLICS OF YEARS AGO, WHO WENT TO WEEKDAY MASS DURING LENT AND HAD TO FAST BY THE STRICT RULES. The fruits, no doubt, will show up in time, if not soon."

Sunday Bulletin March 5, 1972

"What are you doing here? You have got to stop dropping in on me without warning."

Margaret Bryan was surprised when she opened the door to her apartment to find Joe standing on her doorstep. It was 7:30 AM and she was still in her nightgown. Brennan noted his good fortune and saw no need to formally greet her. He grabbed her, and in an almost violent embrace, picked her up and carried her into her bedroom.

"It has been way too long!"

When it was over, Margaret felt like she had been raped.

"You could at least leave me with some dignity," she cried.

"Sorry, but I just can't go so long without sex. Don't be complaining. You live a pretty nice lifestyle thanks to me."

Margaret stifled her emotions. She remembered how Brennan had rescued her from her marriage with Jack Bryan in which violent sex was the least of her concerns.

"What brings you to Billings?"

He told her about the reporter who had been bugging him for an interview ever since the state tournament, and mentioned he was the individual who made the news the other day when he got stuck in the blizzard.

Margaret said, "I thought I recognized his name!" Are you sure you want to subject yourself to an interview? Aren't you afraid that with all the rumors running rampant about us that he might quiz you about them?"

Brennan responded," I've known he and his dad for many years, and I've got friends that will disabuse him of the need to follow up any rumors. The publicity will be really good for the school. Recruiting has been getting more difficult and we need the exposure to attract the kids. I can control it, it will be fine. I've already met with him once and it went well. I haven't been able to get hold of him though and it's doubtful we will be meeting. You heard that his wife froze to death, right? I was coming out here anyway. I have other business and I needed to see you."

The meeting with Nash would never happen.

*****

"God damn you," Brennan screamed as he tossed the vial of pills he was holding at his dealer.

"The last time I gave one of these to someone she almost died. What are you trying to do to me? Everything I've tried to build in New London will disappear overnight if they ever find out I'm giving drugs to high school kids. It was damn lucky that she was so drunk that she never became aware that she was given anything other than alcohol. Are you trying to get me arrested? We just finished the football season. One of my players could have collapsed on the field if he had gotten a bad dose of speed!"

Brennan was livid as he confronted the man that he had trusted for years to supply him with the drugs he wanted.

"I guarantee you, if this ever happens again, I will destroy you. I will find a way to get you arrested, prosecuted and put away for life."

"Don't you be giving me any of your high and mighty bullshit," his drug supplier responded, "I'll take you down with me and be laughing my ass off as you rot in the cell next to me."

Brennan's self-assured comeback was evidence of why he could lead his double life in a small town like New London.

"No one will believe a Catholic priest would deal drugs. And trust me; my bishop will move mountains to prevent negative publicity about one of his priests."

However, with each passing day he worried more about being exposed. He was fighting a losing battle with "Bubby." He had to be sure that the drugs he was using to alter women's behaviors and support his voracious sexual appetite were of the purest variety.

He left this confrontation with his dealer determined to find someone more reliable, but his anger subsided as quickly as it had surfaced, as he began thinking of returning to Margaret's apartment. She was a reliable mistress and would give him all the sex he needed without drugs. He smiled with anticipation of having her twice in one day.

Margaret greeted him as he arrived wearing one of her sexiest outfits. She was aware of his over the top sexual appetite and thought it prudent to be prepared. Her lifestyle depended on being as accommodating as possible and, he was not in Billings all that often. When he was not around she was free to live her life anyway she wanted.

Brennan's eyes brightened as he saw how attractive she could be when she wanted to. Even though she was never quite able to satisfy him with her love making, he still obsessed about her body. He was vaguely aware that his needs were insatiable, so he never blamed her for being inadequate.

After two hours of aggressive sex, he took her to dinner at Jake's. He wanted Margaret to feel good about the day and she always appreciated dining at Billings best restaurants. The Billings elites favored Jake's. It featured dark walnut tables with flowers on each one, live piano music, a flagstone tile floor, a lounge area with soft leather couches, oval coffee tables with splendidly proportioned cabriole legs, and tea served from silver trays in white teapots. Margaret fell in love with the place the first time she saw it.

"Jack would have made fun of this place," she chuckled.

"Not his style I'm sure. There will be far nicer places than Jake's in your future. I promise you that," responded Brennan.

As they were making their way to Jake's, Brennan, as was typical, was in a hurry, and ignored the speed limit. When Margaret, uncomfortable with his reckless driving, asked him to slow down he just smiled. Speed exhilarated him, and he never paid attention to appeals for caution about traffic laws. As they approached the restaurant, he sped up to avoid hitting a red light and miscalculated by a split second. As the light turned red just before he entered the intersection he saw the cop who was sitting in the intersection.

He thought to himself, *"Oh god, another ticket. There go my insurance rates again."* In a matter of seconds there were red lights flashing in his rear-view mirror. He was accustomed to cops shoving their face through the driver's side window and asking for his driver's license. It was so routine that he never thought about the roll of cash sitting in the cup holder.

The sight of cash lying out in the open instantly created suspicion. The officer asked Brennan to step out of the car and place his hands on the roof top. Simultaneously, he called for backup. Before Brennan knew it, there were three cop cars surrounding him with lights flashing. He didn't panic, but his stomach was churning. He knew that they would search his car.

Once the officer felt that the situation was secure, he demanded that Brennan open his trunk. Brennan thought about refusing and claiming that they had no right to search his car without a warrant, but he thought better of it, hoping that the police would treat a clergyman with deference.

When the police officer opened the trunk he blurted out, "Holy shit!" as he counted 10 grocery bags full of cash.

He turned to Brennan and said "You say you're a priest? Where did all this cash come from? And who is your friend?"

He did not wait for an answer. Instead he ordered Brennan to stay where he was, and to keep his hands on top of the car. He needed to consult with his fellow officers to figure out whether the money was contraband and subject to confiscation. After discussing it, the three officers decided to check with the Police Department in New London to verify Brennan's identity.

"Dilly, you better take this call, it sounds like the Billings police have Father Brennan in a fix. I don't need this hassle," deputy Jerry Cando yelled, desperately trying to avoid any connection to another incident involving Brennan.

Billy Clark had been chief of police for a long time and had no respect for the Reverend Brennan. He had long ago quit going to Mass. He was a convert anyway and never rigidly Catholic, so he was not afraid of confronting the man he called the "Good Pastor."

He grabbed the phone, and without any of the typical niceties asked,

"What the hell did he do now?"

The officer on the other end was a bit startled and he responded,

'Who am I speaking to?"

"This is Chief of Police Billy Clark, what can I do for you?"

What did you mean, what did he do now?"

"Oh, this isn't the first call I've gotten about him. There are constant rumors around here that Brennan is sleeping with coach's wives and molesting high school girls. There are even rumors of him having fathered children. Very few people believe any of it but calls like this make me wonder. This is the third call from out of town cops we've received in the last five years."

"Well, we have a guy out here who just ran a red light and claims to be the pastor of a church in New London. He sure doesn't look like a priest. He has a woman with him who acts like his girlfriend and we found a boatload of cash in the truck of his car."

Chief Clark asked, "what kind of a car is he driving?"

"A big honking Chrysler Imperial," came the response.

"That's what he drives. Does he have a limp?"

"That he does. It must, in fact, be your Pastor."

"Give him a scare and let him go."

The officer replied that they would have to think about that, thanked Billy for the help and hung up.

Despite having verified Brennan's identity, the officers could not agree on what to do. Two of them were Catholics themselves and arresting a priest just seemed wrong to them. The officer who first confronted Brennan was not so sure. There was something he did not like about this man, and the offhand comments about the rumors surrounding him made him uncomfortable.

He said, "We have the authority to grab the cash and make him prove that it's his, I think we should at least do that."

"But priests are God's servants," the others protested, "If we didn't have priests, we wouldn't know God. It's a grievous sin to not show respect for a priest!"

"Forget it; we won't have anything to do with this. Let's take a vote."

"OK, OK, I'm outnumbered. I'll let him go."

As he drove away, Brennan was beside himself with anger for being so careless. He snapped at Margaret,

"Why are you looking at me that way?"

"I'm not stupid," he yelled at the top of his lungs.

His anger made her cry. It was so demeaning. Whenever he yelled, it made her feel worthless. It was times like this when she wondered if priests were really that Godly and doubted that she truly loved him, or maybe just wanted his money. He had promised to send her kids to college. It was impossible for her to give that up, so she just shut up whenever he yelled at her.

As they resumed their journey to Jake's, a picture of a smirking Bubby jumped into Joe's head.

"GOD DAMMIT," he screamed as he slammed his fist into the steering wheel.

Chapter 19

Scrutinizing the Rumors

One thing that disturbs me about sports in our state is that it is no longer sports – but has turned to hate in so many cases. Perpetual Help does not object to having almost everyone against us for winning, since we have been winning so much, but hating us for it is carrying it a bit too far. The difficult thing about a lot of this hatred is that it comes from Catholics who say that they love Christ and the Church. We do not ask them to like Our Lady of Perpetual Help School, but I don't know how they justify as Catholics, hatred of an institution, Our Lady of Perpetual Help School is doing a lot more for Christ than they are doing and perhaps ever will come close to doing for Christ. Hatred makes people blind to many things."

Sunday Bulletin March 12, 1972

THUMP.... THUMP.... THUMP was all that Frank was aware of as he lingered over Sandy's grave while the graveyard attendants covered her. Her funeral had been delayed while he recovered from the frostbite that had almost killed him as well. It had warmed, and this last day with Sandy would be a short-lived return to fall, the last of the leaves rustling in a slight breeze.

The tears he never thought he had, were streaming down his cheeks. He sobbed uncontrollably. In that moment of loss his world was collapsing. Where there was once light, there were only shadows. The pain coming and going like waves of snirt, the frigid snow and dirt only residents of the great plains know about. He called out for her, but the connection was gone... she was gone... he knew that his time to be alone had come.

Loss was the side of loving he had never been warned about.... that when you lose your lover, your heart is buried with them. When the dirt hits the casket, it buries your soul too. There is no coming back, and so the world becomes as if made of shadows and every breath feels hollow in the chest. Joe Brennan could not have been farther from his mind.

Frank, you've got to write the story…. Frank, you've got to write the story!

"Sandy? Oh my God, is that you? As he came to full consciousness, Frank gradually realized it had been a dream. But it had been so real. Was it time to return to the investigation of Brennan? He had thought very little about it these last months since burying Sandy.

He took the dream as an omen and decided to resume his inquiry. He would meet first with Brennan's two biggest supporters. He had been somewhat intrigued to find that they were not only big financial supporters, but that they were also his biggest defenders. Based on his conversations with Therese Koch, he found it difficult to understand how anyone could defend Brennan. Therese suspected that Floyd Sieger and Phil Grower had something to do with the threatening letters she and Arnold had received which made the upcoming meeting even more intriguing.

The weather, always a major item of discussion in farm country, had not been cooperating this spring and had been impervious to the prayers of the famers. Crops were barely poking above ground and it was already early June. The prayers of the congregation, though multitudinous, were not changing the pitiful sight of the crops. There was great concern amongst, not just the farmers, but also the small businesses of the type run by Sieger and Grower. They suffered financial hardship whenever crops were bad. This year the sun had ideas of its own and seemed to relish scorching the land. There was no prospect for the heavenly relief of rain any time soon. Everything was hot to the touch and the prairie was tinder-dry, ready to burn on any careless spark. Non-stop worry replaced the usual joy of the start of summer.

Frank hoped that Sieger and Grower weren't too stressed to engage in productive conversation. People tended to be friendlier when the spring planting was sprouting in all its splendor, and prospects for a good harvest were in evidence. Frank need not have worried. His subjects were eager to talk, though not about the dark side of the man who some were referring to as the" Big Dad."

Sieger and Grower greeted him warmly. They were eager to hear what Nash had in mind. Both had children who had graduated from the high school and Sieger's son had been a star football player during the Earnhardt era.

Sieger never missed an athletic event at the school, and Grower was respected as Brennan's chief financial manager.

Sieger promptly jump started the conversation by saying, "We really appreciate your efforts in publicizing the excellences of our pastor and school, but you need to be warned ahead of time that you are likely to hear some pretty vicious rumors as you go about your interviews."

"I remember you mentioning that when we talked briefly at the Golden West. I have, in fact, been hearing some things."

"Paul and I both want you to know that there is absolutely no truth to them. There is a contingent of people in this community who are extremely jealous of our success and they do everything in their power to bring us down. We are here to tell you that none of the rumors are true. Father Brennan has been a godsend to this town and your story can be very helpful in putting the naysayers in their place."

Grower added, "New London was just another farm town on the North Dakota prairie until Father Brennan arrived. We've always been proud of elevator row and the distinction of being the largest primary grain market in the world, but few people outside of New London are even aware of that. Since Brennan arrived we've become the envy of every community in Southwestern North Dakota. People are jealous of our school and sports programs. We love our pastor. He has put us on the map."

Frank, wondering aloud, asked, "What do you think drives Brennan to be so successful?"

"Discipline," shouted Sieger!

The loud retort startled Frank.

"Tell me what you mean. Therese Koch has been getting threatening letters. I have no idea if Brennan has anything to do with them, but if so, that would be an interesting interpretation of discipline."

"I hope you're not putting any stock in what you hear from Therese Koch. She's one of the rebels who is spreading lies about Brennan," Sieger responded. "She is my niece, and I have been talking to her mother about her. We'll get her under control."

Frank noted Sieger's anger and wrote himself a reminder to ask Therese about her relationship with her uncle.

"Let's talk more about the discipline. Tell me how that is all working out."

Grower said, "Our kids are the best behaved anywhere. It is a joy as a parent to have the backing of the pastor. When kids get out of line, he holds them accountable"

"Sometimes he goes too far," interjected Sieger, "he can be too hard on the kids."

"Floyd and I agree that parents sometimes object to the way that their kids are being treated, especially when they get suspended from school, and that they are so upset with Father that they are inclined to believe, and even start rumors."

. "Some of the families pull their kids out of school and send them to the public school," said Sieger, "that really upsets Father, so he uses his Sunday sermons to admonish them for babying their kids and not supporting Catholic Schools. He never names them by name, but he understands everyone knows who he is talking about. Everybody knows everyone else's business in a small town like New London."

"Floyd and I view these things as minor in comparison to the excellence that Perpetual Help School exhibits in every aspect, whether in sports, drama, speech, music, you name it."

"I'm a bit taken aback," Nash responded, "I always assumed Brennan was a man with great vision who was a skilled manager of people. You make it sound like he operates by intimidation. That isn't how great leaders surround themselves with excellence."

"Don't forget that he is a priest, said Sieger, "They are God's representative and have full authority over their parishioners. They lead from moral authority. It's a sin to defy them. Their leadership style can't be judged by secular standards."

"We get more vocations to the priesthood and the convent than any other parish in the diocese, said Grower, "people, including the young, must see him is a good role model. Why else would they follow in his footsteps?"

The rumors are too persistent to be dismissed as attempts at revenge by people with grievances, Frank thought. *Therese Koch doesn't strike me as someone seeking revenge.*

So, he asked, "Can you tell me more about school rules?"

Both men thought that Brennan's rules were essential to the success of a Catholic School planted amid a largely Protestant community like New London. There was no disagreement as they laid out a litany of rules many of which Nash thought were outrageous. Every student was expected to be at daily Mass. When they missed, he called the parents and accused them of indifference to the church and bad parenting.

Dating of non-Catholics was forbidden. It could lead to mixed marriages, or worse, with individuals leaving the Church. He preached constantly about this, declared it to be a mortal sin, and did everything in his power to prevent it. He taught that marrying a non-Catholic would condemn one to hell. He warned students who violated his rules, and ultimately suspended them from school, if they did not break up. Not surprisingly, young people who were not Catholic viewed this as an insult. They resented it, and many carried that resentment with them for the rest of their lives.

Steady dating, defined as going out with the same person more than three consecutive times, was strictly forbidden. He issued warnings that, when ignored, were followed by suspensions. They related the story of one such couple who were suspended three of the four years they were in high school. Had Brennan not been in a very serious car accident which kept him away from the school for almost a full year, it would have likely been four suspensions in four years. Some of the kids just would not let him walk all over them. But they paid the consequences.

Frank was aware that the Catholic Church often applied strict discipline in its pastoral relationships, but he thought that much of what he heard pointed to a heartlessness that seemed counterproductive to building a faith community. There seemed to be very little autonomy to make good choices. He thought the prospect of living under such a regime would be very stifling. As he remembered his dad's decision to not send him to Perpetual Help School, he made a mental note to thank him the next time they were together.

"Wow!" Nash remarked, "how is he so sure he has accurate information when confronting students?"

"He makes them all go to weekly confession. He knows everything, Sieger laughed.

Frank left the meeting with Sieger and Grower greatly disturbed. *I've got to get back with Therese Koch,* he thought.

He had extra time before he had to leave town, so he decided to randomly connect with some of the kids at the school. He assumed that the track team would be practicing after school and since most of the athletes knew him from his sports reporting, they would be willing to answer questions before their workout.

*****

The story that unfolded confirmed Frank's delight in having not attended Perpetual Help. The kids were eager to talk. They did so with obvious contempt.

Brennan taught the upper-class religion courses. This enabled him to keep strict control over student's lives. To make sure that they never missed Mass on Sunday, they had to outline his Sunday sermons. He would read selected papers and comment on them in front of the class. He sought to embarrass those who did poorly and questioned them about whether they had really been at Mass.

When he learned that a couple was dating steadily, he would ask the class what he should do about it. He was not in doubt, but rather it was his way of embarrassing students and frightening everyone into compliance. He loved to create stress for the individuals involved while they awaited their discipline. Some found him to be just plain mean.

He made a point to attend every athletic contest and used his religion class to embarrass athletes who did not live up to his expectations. His coaches hated this but could do nothing about it. He controlled them just like the kids. He even criticized the coaches in religion class and the Sunday bulletin.

When asked about how Brennan seemed to know everything they did by the next day, students seemed mystified. They assumed that he must have spies in the community. This was a big concern because it sowed a significant amount of suspicion and destroyed trust even among friends. Few felt safe with even their closest friends, although that didn't stop them from constantly gossiping about him.

~ 100 ~

It was clear that few of the kids had any love for Brennan, so it was not a surprise that rumors about the priest were a favorite topic of conversation among them. They were cautious about talking to Frank though because they feared that if overheard by the wrong person their conversations might get back to Floyd Sieger and he would confront their parents.

Their fears were justified because a number of these confrontations had occurred in the past and they sometimes ended in fist fights, especially if Sieger had been drinking. However, just as there were some who defied his rules regardless of the consequences, Nash got some of the bravest of the young people to talk about what they had heard.

Two of the girls reported that they caught him window peaking.

Nash said, "That's surely nonsense."

He tried to express skepticism about such outrageous statements, but the girls insisted they had personally witnessed this on more than one occasion. They said that following him around at night was one of their pastimes. They reminded him that there wasn't much for kids to do at night in small towns. Given all the rumors, following the priest around was exciting.

Frank could learn only so much in the brief time he had before track practice, so he decided to return to New London the next day and approach some of the kids he heard Brennan had targeted. He would interview as many students as necessary to get a full sampling of opinions.

I wonder if this story might be too controversial to publish in a small-town newspaper, he thought.

Chapter 20

The Rape of Sheila Kronk

"THE WEEDAY ATTENDANCE BY THE PEOPLE LIVING IN TOWN HAS NOT BEEN GOOD THIS LENT. The younger married people have been especially lax in this matter. You were asked at the beginning of lent to do this a couple of times a week. However most of you turned deaf ears to the suggestion. I KNOW YOU GO OTHER PLACES IN THE EVENING. You parents are not only not concerned about appeasing God's anger for sins of the past year but also not concerned about any good example for your family. I think this is downright <u>laziness</u> and <u>indifference</u> to Christ's action and prayer in the sacrifice of the Mass. Lent is going to pay dividends someday, but not the kind you will desire at that time."

Sunday Bulletin March19, 1972

The quest to talk to the kids who lived under what he now saw to be the iron fist of the man called "Big Dad," led him to seek out Carl Hunter and Sheila Kronk, the two unfortunate, assumed to be lovers, who he harassed for going steady. It wasn't hard to connect with either of them because they walked to and from school together every day. Both were happy to talk with him. Hunter was a potential track star when he was a freshman, but he was more interested in Sheila than the demanding work necessary to excel in track. Carl's friends told Nash that he would rather be with Sheila than to practice track. Frank was familiar with Carl. He had reported on many of the Perpetual Help basketball games and had written a complementary story on Hunter after he led the team to one of its big tournament wins. After briefly introducing himself, Frank asked if he could set up a meeting. They happened to be walking past the hardware store that Carl's dad owned so Carl suggested that they step inside to talk right away.

When Hunter realized the conversation would be about Big Dad, he was eager to talk. He was not a big Brennan fan, to say the least, and it didn't take long for him to make that obvious.

"Tell me about your relationship with Father Brennan," Frank said.

"He's a jerk."

"That's putting it mildly," interjected Sheila

"I've been told the two of you have been suspended from school a few times. They say you are going steady and Brennan forbids it. Your kind of gutsy being seen walking together.

"We're seniors, school is almost over. We're not afraid of him anymore. Maybe you're wondering why Sheila and I won't stop seeing each other."

"Let me start by saying that we like each other a lot and Big Dad is not going to run our lives. He has been on us since the day we first stepped foot into Perpetual Help, and for me, it hasn't just been about Sheila. He doesn't like the way I play basketball and he is constantly harping about how I am wasting my talent. He even told me that my life will suck if I don't become a priest. Fat chance of that, if he is the shining example of what the priesthood is supposed to be."

Frank was taken aback at Hunter's anger. His first reaction though, was, "Big Dad? That's what you call him, huh? Good Lord, where did that come from?"

"He's been called that ever since I can remember. I don't know who came up with it, but you can be sure that it's not a term of endearment.

"Why do you think Brennan is so adamant about steady dating? It seems perfectly normal to me that guys and gals that go to school together would form exclusive friendships and would want to be together a lot"

"He just wants to control everybody. He thinks I'm going to get her pregnant. Having sex with Sheila is the sickest thing I have ever been accused of. To top it off, he just had a baby with Darlene Brandt.

Frank thought to himself, *oh my God, what did I just fall into?*"

"Sheila won't even hold hands with me." Hunter quickly added. We've gone together for four years and I've never even kissed her."

Frank could see that Sheila was uncomfortable with the conversation. Her face had turned beet red.

"That stuff can wait. We are soul mates. We spend hours and hours talking with each other. I wouldn't trade our time together for the approval of anyone, much less Big Dad."

"But Sheila, he's done something to you that you won't talk about. You've been acting differently since the last time we were suspended from school. All of a sudden, you seem distant. It's almost like you don't want to be with me anymore."

"Hunter, this is not the place to talk about our relationship. I've got to go. Dad needs me at the store."

With that, Sheila walked across the street to her dad's grocery store.

"I hope you will talk with Sheila again, said Hunter, "she is hiding something."

"Oh yes," Frank assured him. "I will be very anxious to talk with Sheila, but I've got a few more questions first. What makes you so sure that Father Brennan got Darlene Brandt pregnant?"

"Everybody knows that. We just hear things all the time," Carl responded adamantly.

"One night a group of us were hanging around, just talking, with nothing else to do, and Darlene's sister, Donnie, mentioned that she woke up one night at 2 a.m. and Big Dad was standing in her bedroom doorway. She was totally creeped out. But don't talk to her about it. The family is very angry, and they deny everything. They left town over a year ago, anyway. Brennan gave her dad a job running some of his motels in Dallas. Everybody thinks the job was a bribe to keep the Brandt's from talking."

"You need to talk to some of my sisters too. Therese is part of a small group who confronted the bishop about what is going on. She says they have some affidavits from some of his victims. She knows way more than I do. My sister, Arlene, was in the convent and when she decided to leave Big Dad paid her a visit. He tried to talk her out of leaving. They went out to dinner together and he invited her to his motel room to pray the rosary. She was always wary of him and had heard rumors too. She wisely declined.

Another of my sisters was dating one of our football stars and when he tried to break them up she became obstinate. You don't mess with Violet if she thinks she is being wronged. When she basically told him to go to hell, he smacked her in the face right in front of the religion class."

"He treats everybody like that. What makes it worse is that the parents always back him up. Sometimes they get worse punishment at home. Nobody questions him, at least, not until lately."

"I hope you talk to Sheila again. She's been alone with him in his office. Every time he kicks a girl out of school he pulls her into his office in the rectory. The last time Sheila came out a different person. Ask her about that."

As he walked away from the meeting with Hunter, Frank had a sick feeling in his stomach. He could not believe what he was hearing.

He wondered, *how could a Catholic priest in a town of just over 1,000 people live such a perverted life for almost 20 years? Surely the bishop had to be aware of these rumors. Hadn't assistant pastors heard the rumors and confronted Brennan, or at least reported them to the bishop?"*

It was getting late and Frank was determined to continue his investigation, so instead of going home only to return the next day, he decided to check into the hotel. When he got to his room he picked up the phone to call Sandy. Then it hit him, she's gone, and all the pain flowed over him again. His world had become blacker than ever before, loneliness crippling his every move. Amidst the raw pain, he suddenly felt a frigid breeze in the room. It pulled him out of the depression that was setting in and he thought, *where have I felt that before,* and then he heard that now familiar faint cackle. It echoed slightly throughout the room and was followed by the evilest voice he ever imagined.

"I warned you Frank, your Sandy didn't have to die. You killed her by continuing to pursue this, so called, story of yours. Worse is on the horizon. Go home. Throw those notes in the trash. I will not let you destroy Father Brennan."

This time it was impossible to dismiss the voice, but at first Frank thought he must be mad.

This can't be real, he thought, *demons don't make life and death decisions, only God can do that.*

Even in his state of near depression and confusion though, he knew one thing and that was that the devil, if that is who this evil presence is, could not enter holy places. He sat on his bed and began to say the rosary; on his fingers. His upbringing had alienated him against the rosary, so he had no beads, but he couldn't think of anything else to do.

The repeating of the HAIL MARY gradually put him in trance like state. As he was finishing the cold breeze had subsided and the demon was gone.

So there, you bastard, there's more of the same in store for you if you ever tempt me again.

In a brief time, he had discovered so much disturbing information that he began worrying that word would spread, and people would stop talking for fear of alienating Brennan's enforcers. He was already overhearing bar talk about his interviews when people didn't realize who he was. The talk was that he was about to hear from Lloyd Sieger and the confrontation would not be pretty. Now he was having these delusions of an evil presence that threatened him; a being that he had never really believed in. He decided it had to be an omen that, if evil was resisting it, the story had to be told. He needed to work fast and needed to talk to Sheila Kronk again.

Frank was thankful when Sheila agreed to talk and invited him into the produce department in the back of her dad's grocery store where no one would see them. Carl had mentioned that Frank would be looking for her. She wanted to make sure that no one saw her talking to him. She feared people would bring pressure on her Dad. He was not a fighter, and no one was more absolutist than he about the sanctity of the priesthood. She was pretty sure that he wouldn't stand a chance against Sieger if confronted at the Golden West where he occasionally stopped for a beer after work.

Frank began by telling Sheila, "I appreciated your taking the risk to talk to me," he said, "I am just beginning to realize how delicate the situation with Father Brennan is in New London. I was all set to write a story that was very complimentary of Father and the excellent job he was doing at Perpetual Help. I am blown away at the negativity and the anger I am uncovering in my interviews. Carl sounded very angry and seemed almost vengeful. He spoke highly about you though. He really likes you."

Sheila felt a knot in her stomach at the mention of her relationship with Carl. Their four years together were about to end. She too felt they had been soul mates and they shared every detail of their lives with each other. However, since her last meeting in Brennan's office something had happened that she could never tell anyone, especially Carl.

*****

"Miss Kronk, please come to the front of the room."

"Mr. Hunter, stand next to her."

Brennan left the two high school seniors standing in front of the class for what seemed like an hour before he finally spoke again.

"What should be done with these two?" he began. "They have been suspended from school twice for going steady. They are lucky I was not here last year. Believe me, I would have expelled them had I not had the accident. Three strikes and you are out, you know. In eighteen years at Perpetual Help I have never experienced the disrespect and defiance that these two have shown."

The class stirred uncomfortably and became grimly silent.

"What do you two see in each other? What is it that keeps you so defiant of authority? And why haven't you been confessing your sins? Don't tell me that you haven't committed mortal sin together, yet I don't recall one incident where either of you have confessed it."

Sheila was dumbstruck and too embarrassed to look up, but Carl was easily angered whenever he experienced the slightest injustice, and Brennan's accusation triggered an outburst of the magnitude no one had ever seen when "Big Dad" confronted someone. He literally screamed at the top of his lungs in denial that anything immoral had happened between them. No one had ever heard Carl Hunter utter even one word of profanity, so the shock was audible when they heard him scream,

"God damn you, you evil sonofabitch! Sheila Kronk is as pure as a girl could possibly be. All we ever do is talk. I've hardly ever even put my arm around her. I love her and respect those limits. You defile a beautiful human being. Damn you to hell; you are a miserable example of a priest!"

Brennan was confounded at such disrespect. He was not used to being challenged.

All he could think to say was, "get out of my sight, both of you! I'll deal with you later. You will be lucky to ever set foot in this school again!"

The two of them walked out of the classroom together and Sheila turned to Carl with the most beautiful smile he had ever seen and gave him a tender hug. It was the first time she had ever allowed Carl an intimate embrace.

When they exited the school building she let out a loud laugh and said, "That was awesome Carl, I love you more than ever."

The two of them knew from experience that they would be hearing from their parents and that their unavoidable conference with Brennan would not be pleasant.

The very next day Carl was in Brennan's office at school. The meeting was short, but the verdict was much less severe than Carl had expected. Brennan simply said that he was lucky to be a senior because, otherwise, he would no longer be welcome at Perpetual Help. He told him to get out of his sight and to not come back for a week.

It was spring time and Arnold Koch was in the middle of springs work. He welcomed the free help whenever Carl got suspended. He always pretended that working on the farm was punishment, but in his heart, he knew that Carl was being treated unfairly, and he got progressively angrier as he became increasingly aware that Brennan was preying on women in the community. Carl welcomed the week off from school and didn't consider a week of farm work to be much of a punishment. He rather enjoyed working on the farm.

Sheila did not get off so lightly. Brennan called her into his office in the rectory the following Saturday. She could not have been less prepared for what happened. When she knocked on his door he yelled at her to come in. She found him sitting at his desk with a Cheshire grin on his face. She had expected the usual cruel smirk and was at first bewildered. Her bewilderment quickly became panic. His grin turned into an almost demonic sneer. He fiendishly declared that she may get away with a "holier than thou" front with Carl Hunter but he knew who she really was.

He said, "You are a very patient whore aren't you Miss Kronk? Well I know girls like you. They take pleasure in tormenting their men, denying them sexual gratification and turning them into pliable eunuchs. I am about to show you how a real man handles women like you. If you know what's good for your reputation you will not resist."

Sheila Kronk was not easily intimidated. Since she held Brennan in contempt, she was under no illusions about the rumors that went around about him. She had been told, in confidence, by several of his victims about how he had abused them. Her awareness was, in fact, one of the reasons she so stubbornly held on to her relationship with Carl. She was not about to submit to Brennan's threats, so she challenged him.

"Father (she reflexively used this term of respect) I know your game. The town mafia may have the power to stop the rumors about you, and you have all the adults in town under your thumb, but the girls you have talked into bed with you are friends of mine. I know their stories. I'm wise to you and outraged by your hypocrisy. The Catholic Church will lose every one of the students who have gone to Perpetual Help since you've been here. Sorry, there will be a few exceptions. Those whose families have been so thoroughly brainwashed that they can't think for themselves, or are corrupted by your bribery, will stay in the fold. But the rest will leave. Most of them already know that all the stuff you preach is pure B.S. They judge the Church by the example they see. They've already made their judgments. You can still intimidate us with your control over our parents, but once we get out of this hell hole of a small town we'll be done with you and your phony religion. Carl Hunter has been a perfect gentleman and has respected the limits I've put on our relationship. I value our friendship more than I can say and I am not about to cheat on him with the biggest hypocrite I've ever known. You preach that sex outside of marriage is a mortal sin, and guess what, I believe that. I'm not about to risk going to hell for the likes of you. Threaten me all you want, but you will have to rape me if you want sex from me."

Brennan was stunned. No adolescent had ever talked to him that way. For the first time he was inclined to back off, but then "Bubby" inserted his evil presence. The sudden transformation shook Sheila. Brennan's eyes suddenly turned red and rolled back into his head and she heard a soft roar and gibberish she couldn't understand. It lasted only briefly but it terrified her. Then she noticed that Brennan's demeanor had changed. He seemed to have dropped all pretenses that he was a priest and had developed an almost demonic presence. "Don't you dare talk to me that way," he howled, "do you think they will call it rape? They'll never believe your story. I have them in my grip. I've built the finest educational system ever seen in the diocese, maybe even in the country. Our football and basketball teams are the envy of every community in the state. We have state championships in wrestling and honors in every activity we've competed in on the state level. Do you actually believe that anyone is going to believe that I raped you?"

With that, he got up from behind his desk and revealed for the first time that he was naked below the waste. As he moved toward Sheila to grab her he yelled the same threats he made in the beginning then added a bribe. As he did so, his voice returned to the condescending tone he always used to intimidate students.

"Sheila, I have a lot of money. I know your father's business is only marginal. He has a large family. If he has to pay, you will not be going to college. I can pay for your education. Do this for me and I will see that you are cared for. God has granted me the power to forgive sin. You won't be going to hell. Think about it."

"You fool!" I've kept Carl Hunter at bay, demanding he respect me for who I am, and never allowed myself to so much as hug him, and you expect me to have sex with you, so I can go to college? You are possessed by the devil! Stay away from me! I'm getting out of here"

She turned to leave, but Brennan beat her to the door and locked it.

"Not so fast," he sneered.

Sheila saw the demonic look reappear and panicked. She slapped Brennan with all her might then clenched her fist to slug him again, but he caught her arm and slung her to the floor.

Sheila's brain went into overdrive. Before she could stop herself, she began kicking with quick and powerful force. Then the voice of caution whispered, "he's a priest, must I submit?

Half her brain gave her reasons to doubt, and the other bombarded her with memories of religion classes. Thoughts of her punishment for flunking a test on the role of the priest, turned her brain into a mental soup of conflicting instructions. She had been forced to write 100 times,

"Who is the priest? He stands with angels, gives glory with archangels, shares Christ's priesthood, refashions creation and, even greater, is divinized and divinizes. Only the priest receives the mission and sacred power to act in the person of Christ."

No, I will not let him have me

She strained to protest but nothing came out, till she screamed, hoping someone would hear her. Suddenly, her body convulsed with raw sobs and she shook like a leaf. Fright consumed every cell in her body swelling them with terror. Then she went limp. He was too strong.

When he penetrated her, it felt like a nail bomb exploding inside of her. With every second she felt the rise of her blood pressure, but she knew that this was the least of her worries.

What did I do to deserve this? What if Carl finds out?

Oh my God, this is all my fault. I should have broken up with Carl the first time I was warned.

When he screamed in ecstasy, she vomited.

He looked down at her with revulsion and shouted, "You pathetic bitch! Get out of my sight."

Then he gathered her clothes, threw them at her and pushed her into the front porch where in the grip of silent panic, her heart racing, she dressed then ran aimlessly, afraid to go home.

*****

Breaking up with Carl seemed the only safe way to make sure that he never discovered her secret. She was no longer a virgin. Carl would know she had been unfaithful the first time they ever made love to each other. But she couldn't get herself to tell Carl of her decision because she truly did love him. She had always assumed that they would someday be married. In the fall she would be going off to college. There would be long periods of separation. That would be the time to give Carl the news.

For now, she resolved to ignore the sick feeling in her stomach because there were some things she really wanted Nash to know. It took all her strength to avoid breaking into tears when Nash began the meeting by asking how Sheila felt about Brennan and how the three suspensions had affected her. She was filled with anger and guilt. She was ashamed, so she just ignored the question and launched into a litany of wrongs she felt Brennan had done to her friends, the school and the community. This guy, Nash, didn't have to know her full story. Carl would be sure to find out if she told him everything

"This is the first story I heard when we moved to New London four years ago," Sheila began. "I hear now that the family is going to move out of town. Darlene Baumgartner is one of my best friends"

Chapter 21

The Baumgartner's

"IS IT A HOLY WEEK IF WE RUSH SOME PLACE AND SPEND THE TIME VISITING FOR AN EASTER VACATION? IS IT A HOLY WEEK IF WE USE THE TIME ON GOOD FRIDAY FOR SHOPPING INSTEAD OF MORNING ADORATION AND AFTERNOON SERVICES? Let us make it a Holy Week by going to Mass on the weekdays this week and by increasing our fasting, and taking part in the main services at Church."

Sunday Bulletin March 26, 1972

Matt Baumgartner was one of the friendlier of New London's citizens. He had virtually no enemies and was a respected business man. His family had been in New London for two generations. He had built a successful bulk fuel business that served the surrounding farms and was known to be a man of high integrity. He and his wife Virginia were raising five children. The first four had been daughters and Matt lobbied Virginia hard to make sure the next one would be a boy. He didn't really want any more kids, but he was very happy to have finally had a son. He knew all the lobbying in the world wouldn't produce a son but had felt that a little light-hearted pressure would make Virginia less resistant to just one more child. The fifth one was a charm. Limiting family size was very difficult for a practicing Catholic especially in a small town like New London where constant gossip made it difficult to keep family affairs private. Once Matt got his baby boy, he scheduled a vasectomy in Deerfield, a town far enough away to be certain that no rumors would start. He had his boy and five was enough.

Matt routinely ate lunch at home and on this gorgeous Monday noon he was in a particularly good mood as he drove up Main Street listening to a Dean Martin song on the radio. As he turned into his driveway, he noticed that they had an unexpected guest. Father Brennan's Chrysler was parked in the driveway. While backing back out to park on the street, he noticed his daughter, Brenda, standing near the front room window talking to Brennan and Virginia, who appeared to be very upset. He thought to himself, *oh my God, did Brenda do something to get herself suspended from school?*

As he walked through the door, he found Brenda in tears and Virginia beside herself in anger. Brenda had not gone to school that morning because she decided she could no longer avoid telling her mother about her experience with Brennan the previous Saturday. She had been called into his office because Brennan thought that she was dating a non-Catholic. She was prepared to deal with Brennan's typical harangue about non-Catholics and fully expected to be forced into an immediate confession to confess her "mortal sin," but was unprepared when Brennan Sat next to her on his couch and began to grope her.

Choking back tears she was confronting Brennan.

"You put your hand on my leg and began moving it up between my legs. I yelled at you to stop, but you grabbed me and threw me to the floor. You started tearing at my clothes and tried to take off my panties. I only got away because I kicked you in the balls. I hurt you bad enough to let me loose."

Then, looking at Matt, she said, "As I was running out the door he yelled after me that if I told anyone he would ruin your business."

Matt looked at Brennan with distain, and muttered almost in a whisper, "You son-of-a-bitch!

Virginia had never seen Matt look that way, his eyes had a deadness, a stillness. He had developed a hardness. It was as if all his resentment towards Brennan for constantly preaching fire and brimstone and harping about money from the pulpit and harassing his children about their relationships had exploded into consciousness at one time.

"You preach morality in religion classes and you harangue us every Sunday about birth control and faithfulness to our wives and all the temptations you fantasize we have. You forbid dating of non-Catholics and steady dating. You preach to these kids incessantly, warning them about premarital sex, and you yourself are attacking my daughter?"

He lunged toward Brennan and would have beaten him, but Virginia grabbed him and persuaded him to stop before he was able to do any damage. Brennan recoiled and cowering while falling to his knees. He recovered his composure quickly though and reiterated his warning,

"Back off Baumgartner, I was serious about running you out of business. It would be no loss to New London or Perpetual Help. You refuse to tithe while expecting us to educate your children for the pittance you

~ 114 ~

contribute. I have supporters who resent your lack of commitment. They will do whatever I tell them.

Matt yelled back saying,

"By the time I get through with you they will be hauling your ass out on a rail. When the Bishop hears about this he'll have you run out of the priesthood."

Brennan just laughed and said, "The bishop knows me better than anybody. He knows this school would close if it wasn't for me. I know how to make things work. I won't be going anywhere."

At that, Matt ordered him out of his house, shoving him down the front steps and warning him that he had not heard the last of this.

*****

"You're not going to receive your diploma? What the hell happened now?" Matt Baumgartner looked at Darlene with a combination of anger, disgust, and empathy. His children had grown up with positive values that he and Virginia had modeled to them. Nobody is perfect though, and Darlene tended to test his patience now and then. She was very outspoken and often voiced her dislike of Brennan. She had heard all the rumors and she and her friends had been window peaking. She rebelled against everything preached by Brennan. His attack on Brenda had relieved her of the last scintilla of respect she had for priests in general and Brennan, in particular.

She explained, "A bunch of us went out to Haman Dam last week to celebrate graduation. We drank some beer and just had a fun time. One of "Big Dad's" snitches ratted us out. God, I wish I knew who that was. He is going to hold my diploma as punishment. I have to meet with him in his office tomorrow."

Matt was not happy to hear that Brennan was harassing another one of his daughters.

He said, "Be careful. Do not let him touch you or intimidate you. You are graduating, and he will no longer have any control over you. I will kick his ass if he tries anything. I just can't wait to get out of this town. Fortunately, I think I have a buyer for the business. I wish you luck. Wish me luck too."

~ 115 ~

The conversation with Brennan went exactly as Darlene expected. He spent ten minutes telling her what a bad person she was and trying to convince her that she would get nowhere in life because she had not learned to obey the rules. He also suggested that her father would be punished because he had too little respect for priests. Darlene was so accustomed to Brennan's harangues that none of what he was saying had an impact on her. All she was interested in was getting her diploma and getting out of his presence.

She asked, "what do I have to do to get my diploma?" His demeanor suddenly changed to that evil look she had seen so often in religion class.

"You know what you have to do," was his response. Given Brennan's history with her family, Darlene knew at once what he was referring to. She leapt out of her chair and very calmly looked him in the eye and said,

"Drop dead. You are out of luck, Mr. Big Dad. After what you did to my sister, do you honestly think I am going to jump into bed with you? Keep your fucking diploma."

With that she stormed out of his office. She slammed the door behind her and didn't hear him say, "You can forget your college scholarship. I will see that Fairmont College learns who they have mistakenly offered to subsidize."

*****

By now Frank Nash was getting angry.

"This is child abuse!"

He asked Sheila, "How much more of this stuff is out there? Sheila responded, "I'll tell you one more story and that's it. I'll already be in trouble when the likes of Sieger and Grower and their cronies find out I've been talking to you. You'd better be careful too, Sieger will kick your butt if he thinks you're going to write anything negative about "Big Dad.""

"A few years ago, we got a new coach. His name was Jack Bryan. I was a 9th grader when he left town, so I suppose he came here about five years ago. He had a big family, seven kids, I think. One of them, Rick, was a good basketball player. He made all state even though he wore a leg brace because of an accident. Jack wasn't well liked because he had a drinking problem and was very hard on his players. Rumors were all over town that Brennan had an affair with Bryan's wife. The only ones who believed it were the young people. Bryan's kids would talk about what was going on all the time, but the adults wouldn't believe it. Brennan's defenders were always complaining that anti-school people, and the Protestants in town who hated Catholics, started the rumors. Last summer one of Carl's sisters got married and Rick was at the wedding. He got very drunk. He took a scoop shovel and went up to Big Dad's place and knocked out every window in the house. Somehow, he got them all replaced by the end of the next day. No one in town ever knew what happened, but Rick bragged about it and we sneaked up to Big Dad's and checked. He has new windows. Most adults are oblivious."

"Carl probably told you that Therese Koch, one of his sisters, is involved with a group who has uncovered a lot of stories. They are trying to get him removed. I think one of our former assistant pastors is involved too. That's about the extent of what I am able to tell you for now."

With that Frank got up to leave and said, "Sheila, I appreciate your time. Thanks so much for talking to me. I've spent some time with Mrs. Koch. She's the one that gave me the first heads up that Father Brennan was not the man that he portrayed himself to be."

"One more thing before I go. Carl says that you are a different person since the last time you were suspended. He thinks something must have happened in Brennan's office. Did Brennan do anything to you? I promise to keep it confidential." Sheila's face turned white even as she vigorously asserted that all her meetings with Big Dad had been pretty much the same. There was nothing but a talking to. Nash glanced into her eyes before he turned and walked out. He suspected she was hiding something.

Frank returned home after his meeting with Sheila. It was supper time, but he wasn't hungry. He went directly to his office to find the notes he took when he talked with Therese Koch. The sun was rising before he laid them aside.

Chapter 22

Coach Thomas

"A perusal of the financial statements shows that many people did not give much to Our Lady of Perpetual Help for 1971. Many would show the same thing if you went back several years.

WOULD WE HAVE A PARISH CHURCH—just a parish (no school by any means) if these people were our support? Do they have money for other things?

Thirty people and their donations were listed!

To expect a parish any place to exist on this kind of money is ridiculous. $450 from thirty parishioners would be quite a parish. I have not included some of our poor people nor DISTINGUISHED OBJECTORS in this list. These people use Perpetual Help but they do not do for Perpetual Help. CHRIST GAVE HIS LIFE FOR US. MANY OF US DO NOT WANT TO GIVE VERY MUCH MATERIALLY BACK TO CHRIST. NO CHURCH HAS FOUND A WAY TO OFFER SALVATION AS A FREE COMMODITY. SOME HAVE GONE TO TITHING, WHAT HAVE YOU GONE TO?"

Sunday Bulletin April 2 1972

Dan Thomas was born in Beach ND, a small town in the western part of the state. He was a cousin to Joe Brennan who was several years his senior. Dan was an outstanding athlete who led his Beach High School basketball team to two state championships. He was in the 9th grade when Joe Brennan was ordained to the priesthood. He acted as an altar server at the celebration Mass. Dan and Joe had not been close personally. Dan was one of the many young people who thought Joe was arrogant and condescending, but the community was excited about the ordination, so when his father informed him that he had been asked, Dan was honored to help celebrate the occasion. Regardless, it would have been a waste of time to argue about it with his dad.

Ralph Thomas was not one to take his kids opinions into account when a family principle was involved.

The celebration was as big an event as anything in anyone's memory in Beach, ND. There was no bigger honor that could befall a Catholic family than to have a son ordained to the priesthood. Every important citizen in the community showed up. The Catholic mayor gave a short talk.

In his speech he said, "There is no greater honor that can be bestowed on the Catholic Community here in Beach than the ordination of one of our own to the priesthood. A priest is a man who holds the place of God–a man, who is invested with all the powers of God. "Go," said Our Lord to the priest; "as My Father sent Me, I send you. All power has been given Me in Heaven and on earth. Go then, teach all nations. . ... He, who listens to you, listens to Me; he who despises you despises Me."

There was almost no one in the crowd who thought these words were extreme. The Mayor was simply reflecting the honor bestowed on every priest in the Roman Catholic Church. Joe Brennan smiled broadly as he listened to the speech.

At the end of the celebration he stood for hours in the receiving line accepting congratulations from the throngs that showed up, many of whom he barely knew. Dan Thomas observed all this in amazement and thought to himself that his cousin Joe didn't deserve all the accolades. He had heard the rumor of his rape of Adeline Funk. It came up every time the name of Joe Brennan was mentioned at Beach High School. None of the adults in the community ever wanted to address it. They were too proud of their seminarian. Dan kept his thoughts to himself though. He was too young to share opinions amongst adults.

Dan's athletic prowess at Beach High School created an opportunity to continue his education in college, a rarity for a small-town kid. His father had lofty expectations for him and pushed him to work hard and make the best of his opportunity. This was not a burden for Dan. He had learned the value of hard work. It was the reason he had so much success in sports. He was not that much more talented than the others, he just outworked everybody. He was, in fact, an over achiever. Western Montana College gave him a scholarship to play basketball and the Yellow Jackets quickly realized that this small-town ND boy was a bigger prize then they first imagined. He would be a key part in building a powerhouse basketball program that would survive his graduation by many years.

Dan's dedication to sports delayed the normal interaction with girls while he was in high school, but things changed in his sophomore year in college. He always accused his teammates of caring more about their next score at the sorority houses than about winning ballgames. But then he met Vonnie Dowling, a freshman From Billings Central High School. She had been a cheerleader for four years and the senior prom queen. She would be his first and only girlfriend.

She was not only beautiful, but smart and athletic. Something radiated from within that made her irresistible. Guys pursued her, and girls courted her friendship. She was all about simplicity, making things easy, helping him to relax and be happy with what he had. He wondered if that was why her skin seemed to glow. Her inner beauty lit her eyes and softened her features. When she smiled and laughed he couldn't help but smile along too. To be in her company made him feel that he too was someone. She radiated an intelligent beauty.

It was love at first sight, and Dan knew from the start that he was going to marry her. He never neglected Yellow Jacket basketball, but he was with her every day that he was not out of town on a basketball trip. They met for lunch whenever their schedules allowed. On days that was impossible they studied together in the library.

Vonnie quickly fell in love too. She found him to be thoughtful and considerate and was proud to be able to claim him as her own. Her girlfriends were all jealous.

They were married within a month of Vonnie's graduation.

Dan had stayed on at Western as a graduate assistant to await Vonnie's graduation. Head coaching jobs were difficult to come by unless you had experience, but Dan was well known as a college star and was sought after by many of the head coaches at the bigger high schools. Missoula High was the biggest school in the state and Dan had several productive interviews with the key people there. They had asked him to come in for a final interview. He was confident that the job was his for the taking. Unexpectedly things changed.

Two days prior to his trip to Missoula the phone rang as Dan and Vonnie were finishing their supper. It was Cousin Joe Brennan calling.

"Dan, this is Father Joe Brennan."

"What a surprise Joe! I haven't heard from you since your ordination. What's up?"

"I'm at Perpetual Help in New London now and am looking for a basketball coach."

"Perpetual Help huh? We used to beat the crap out of them every year. Why would anyone want to go there? It sounds like a place coaches go to die."

"I see that you haven't been keeping up with North Dakota Sports. I hired one of my college friends a couple of years ago and he's turned everything around. We've been in the regional tournament the last two years. He's moving on to coach at St. John's. You might remember that I graduated from there."

"Interesting, how can I help?"

"Dan, I've stayed in the background, but I've been watching your progress as a player and now grad assistant. I've even been to a few of your games this past year. I didn't want you to know I was there because I wanted a completely objective view of your work. I make my own assessments when evaluating coaches and want to observe everything both on and off the court. I particularly like to see how other people react to them before and after the ball games. Their girlfriends are important too."

Brennan claimed that you could tell a lot about a person by the type of woman he attracted. Vonnie Darling met his criteria for the perfect coach's wife.

"I hear you are considering the assistant coaching job at Missoula High School."

"How did you find that out?"

"It's my job to know these things. How much are they willing to pay?"

"Not nearly enough. Teachers and coaches aren't paid very well in Montana schools, but I want to coach badly and with Vonnie getting a job there, as well, we would be ok."

Then Brennan asked, "What would it take to get you to come to Our Lady of Perpetual Help?"

Dan was not inclined to go back to small town living, and he indicated that no amount of money would get him to go to New London.

Brennan responded, "I'll pay you five times what Missoula High School is offering."

Dan was so shocked he almost dropped the phone. "Are you serious?" he asked.

"Dead serious," came the response.

He never made decisions without discussing them with Vonnie, but the shock of such an outrageously generous offer caused him to respond on the spot.

"Well, that makes a difference, there is no way I can turn down that kind of money."

He knew what the head coach at Western was making, and he would be making more than his college coach. How Brennan could afford to pay an inexperienced coach that much money did not concern him. Nor could he know that there would be future consequences for such generosity.

Chapter 23

Please, Don't Shoot Me!

"PARENTS MUST BECOME MORE RESPONSIBLE FOR THEIR CHILDREN. Events the last 10 days alone indicate that parents are not making their children come in at decent hours. <u>DECENT HOURS</u> HAVE TO BE SET BY THE PARENTS, and the parents have to insist that these hours be kept. Last Friday and Saturday night indicate that the young people are doing pretty well as they please."

Sunday Bulletin May 21, 1972

In fact, Thomas had not followed class B basketball back home while in college, so he was happy to know that the basketball program had been served so well by his predecessor, Coach Ed Holbrook. The team, coming back for his first season, included several veteran players who had gone to the regional semi-finals the previous season. He guided them to their first state tournament where they took second place. It could have easily been their first championship save for their conference rival, Mott High School, who beat them five times including in the state championship game. Unfortunately for Thomas, it would be the last time he coached a state tournament team. Events off the court would cancel the joy a young coach should have felt from such a memorable accomplishment.

Brennan arranged for one of the nicest homes in town for them to live in. Vonnie was pregnant with her first child and was happy that her child would have a comfortable place in which to grow up, and that they would have few financial limitations. Her family had been relatively prosperous, and a meager life style was the only concern she had about marrying a high school coach. Her dream was that Dan would rapidly advance to a college head coaching job and money concerns would drop into the background. The big money contract and the lovely home in New London felt like a gift from God.

Brennan noticed Vonnie's apparent desire to live amongst the wealthy few with the accompanying boost in image it represented and could not resist the opportunity it embodied. Few people could equal his financial resources.

Spreading a little money around always worked to his benefit, so as Sheila was unpacking belongings on the Thomas's first day in New London, Brennan paid her a visit. Dan was getting oriented at school.

Brennan was fully aware of the power of his image as priest. The truth was; few priests deserved it. He knew dozens of them who thought nothing of using it to their advantage when they proved too weak and who then abandoned their vow of celibacy. He was shocked to have discovered that even his mentor, Father Lack, had strayed.

There was an old adage among priests that if you were going to stray from your vows, you should do so at least 500 miles from home. It turned out that Father Lack was a true believer in that principle. He was a frequent visitor at brothels in Reno Nevada. Brennan didn't think that was a very creative approach, but he smiled whenever he pictured the old guy romping in the hay with some prostitute.

Vonnie's obsession with her image made her an easy mark. People who loved money were always persuadable. When he found Vonnie struggling to move some of the heavy furniture, he offered to help. That led to some friendly banter that soon evolved into a suggestion to take a rest and get to know each other better.

Very early in the conversation, Brennan mentioned, "It is hard to be a celibate priest in an out of the way, small town where every move is scrutinized."

Vonnie was bewildered by the brazenness of such a conversation with a person he barely knew, but she thought maybe it was okay for her to be a sounding board for a lonely priest who needed someone to talk to. However, his next words caused her near panic.

Brennan's demeanor suddenly changed, and a strange noise seemed to emanate from him. It sounded like a growl. Then his eyes momentarily rolled back and all she could see was the whites of his eyes. When he spoke the first words sounded like an echo.

"Jesus blesses those select few women who help his priests deal with their physical needs. In larger communities, there are groups of women who consider it an honor to have relations with a priest. You might benefit in many ways if you would have sex with me."

Then came an almost imperceptible, but evil sounding, chuckle. Bubby had taken over.

Vonnie didn't know whether to scream, call the police, or just throw him out of the house. Because of his status, she opted for the latter.

"Father, please leave."

"You realize, don't you, that I have resources considerably beyond the salary I am paying your husband?"

"You're asking me to be your prostitute! With all due respect, would you please leave. I love my husband and am pregnant with his child. I am not a slut, and you are scaring me. Please leave before I call the police!"

As he was leaving, he demanded of her, "do not say anything to Dan. His career could end before it begins. And don't be so naïve as to think that I am paying him all that money just to come here to coach. You were part of the bargain. If he wasn't married to you I would have never hired him. Good coaches are a dime a dozen. Priests work hard and sacrifice everything for those we serve. What would be wrong with helping a good man cope and getting paid on top of it? Think about it."

Brennan had acted too quickly, but he had correctly assessed Vonnie's vulnerability. There were future opportunities to revisit the issue and Vonnie eventually succumbed.

Her baby was born during that first magical season at Perpetual Help· after which she became increasingly impressionable regarding Brennan. When he suggested that a big bonus was in prospect because of Dan's good work, but that he might sweeten the pot a little if she reconsidered his proposal, she slept with him for the first time.

The relationship quickly overwhelmed her. She found Brennan's sexual appetite to be sordid to the extreme. He was never satisfied with one orgasm. He insisted that she continually stimulate him until he could come a second time; and sometimes a third. Dan worked long hours coaching basketball as well as serving as assistant in football and track, but their liaisons were so protracted that she feared getting caught.

In the fall of their second year in New London Dan took ill during football practice and decided to go home early. He caught Brennan on top of Vonnie on the living room floor, his roman collar askew around his neck and nothing else on except his black socks. Dan Thomas was an even tempered young man, but this scene triggered an uncontrollable rage.

"Sheila, no! This can't be happening!

Then, looking at Brennan, he screamed, "You bastard!"

He rushed the couple and began to beat them without mercy, first Brennan, then, Vonnie. Brennan pleaded with him to stop,

"You can't do this to a priest!"

Dan at first hesitated, then after a few more blows to Brennan, he stopped, sat on the floor and wept uncontrollably.

Awakened from his nap by the commotion downstairs, his six-month-old son, cried too.

Dan's breakdown gave Brennan his opportunity to escape. Once he was gone, Dan regained his composure, got up from the floor and stared at his still half-naked wife.

He said softly, "Would you please get dressed? You disgust me."

Vonnie turned her back to him, bent over to pick up her cloths and started sobbing.

"I am so sorry," she said, "he promised to double the bonus he gave you after the basketball season and give you an even bigger raise for next year. He begged me to allow him to love a woman. He struggles so hard with celibacy. I just wanted to help him. He has been good to us."

Don looked at her in disbelief and said, "Vonnie how did you hide this side of yourself from me? I don't even know you. I thought we had the perfect marriage. You were my first and only girlfriend, and I have been faithful and dedicated to you since the day I first laid eyes on you. How could you do this to me?"

"As for that mother fucker of a so-called priest, he hasn't heard the end of this. He can take his money and shove it."

With that, he stormed out of the door, went to the garage where he stored his hunting rifles and handgun, unlocked the gun cabinet, pulled out his handgun, loaded it with six shells, shoved it into his belt and began walking the three blocks toward the rectory.

By then Vonnie had dressed. She ran out of the house desperate to talk to Dan to try to explain that what he had seen had nothing to do with how she felt about him. Before she could say a word, she saw the gun.

She screamed, "Nooo, what are you doing, no, no, please stop."

She grabbed at his arm trying to stop him, but he just shucked her off, and when she ran at him again, he back handed her so hard he knocked her to the ground.

By then the neighbors were looking out to see what all the commotion was about. Fearing their situation would be exposed, Vonnie ran into the house to call the police.

Vonnie's heart sank when Jerry Cando answered the phone. He was ridiculed in the community as "Jerry the Cop" because of his ham-handed ways. He had no police training and held his job only because small North Dakota towns could not afford trained professionals.

Jerry was best remembered for the time when he discovered a man trying to rob the bank. While the robber was going in the back door, instead of confronting him, Jerry went in the front door making enough noise to make sure that he was heard. The robber went back out the back door and escaped. As the story goes Jerry felt like the real escapee. He could brag about stopping a robbery and escaping with his life.

As luck would have it, Jerry was just coming on duty and was the only one available.

Vonnie was too upset to worry much that the keystone cop, Jerry, was her only hope to stop Dan from shooting Brennan.

She yelled into the phone, "My husband is on his way up to Father Brennan's office to kill him."

At first, Jerry thought he must be dealing with a mad woman, because these things just did not happen in a town like New London.

"What kind of joke is this? Who is this? You can be arrested for prank calls like this."

"Vonnie Thomas, the wife of the Perpetual Help basketball coach. Please stop him, he's going to shoot him!"

Vonnie's desperation convinced him to investigate so he jumped into his car and rushed to the church rectory. Deep down, he knew that he was hopelessly out of his league as a cop. He had no idea what he was going to do when he arrived. He drove up just in time to see Dan kick in the door and barge into Brennan's office.

When Brennan saw Dan rushing toward him, his usually pale complexion turned an even whiter shade of white. With Dan's gun aimed directly at his head he backed away, stumbled over his couch and fell to the floor. At that moment, almost paralyzed by fear himself, Jerry leaped through the door and yelled,

"Mr. Thomas; stop!"

He pointed his own gun at Dan, and remembering that he never carried it loaded, was relieved to see that Thomas hesitated. Getting arrested would have consequences he had not considered in his moment of passion. He threw his gun at Brennan, looked down at him in disgust, spit on him, and walked out.

Dan was never prosecuted for attempted murder. Brennan pleaded with Jerry to keep the incident quiet saying he would not press charges in any case. Brennan's world would surely crumble if word of this incident and its proximate cause ever spread into the community. Being easily persuadable and lacking training, Jerry decided that there was little risk to the community from the highly respected Dan Thomas. He decided to tell no one; not even chief of police, Billy Clark.

*****

Therese began weeping softly as she finished the story of the Thomas family.

"They were such a neat couple," she said through her tears. "We miss them so much; they were such beautiful and talented people."

Frank said, "You know he is currently coaching at Sheridan Community College, right?"

Therese responded, "I don't pay too much attention to sports, but it seems to me that someone told me that."

Frank said, "He's done an excellent job there, and rumor has it that he is being groomed for an administrative position that could lead to the Presidency of the College. Things are turning out well for him, but what a tragic story. There were other stories as well, obviously."

"Yes, the Thomas story was sad," Therese went on, "but in many ways, it was far worse for the Bryans."

Chapter 24

Coach Bryan

"A boy in the grade school was reported being drunk, and this is not the first time. What time does he go home?

Some freshman boys were able to obtain beer, wine and whiskey from older ones. Certain country places are well known as party places for young people where they have kegs of beer, plenty of wine and whiskey. Cannot anything be done to control this? Or do you feel better if they are not in town and not in the country?"

Sunday Bulletin May 21, 1972

Jack Bryan was born in 1926, the seventh of 10 children, eight of them boys. His father, Sean, was a hard-drinking Irishman who labored long hours in the copper mines of Montana. His sons tended to the wild side, and Sean struggled to make them the kind of boys he could be proud of. He was a tough disciplinarian, so the strap often came off the hook in the kitchen. As they grew older, the boys developed a camaraderie that made them legends in their hometown of Great Falls. They would challenge each other to see who could get the worst whipping from their dad without showing any pain, and they stood behind each other when any one of them got into a fight. When you fought one of the Bryans, you fought them all. And they all became hard drinkers like their father. In their heyday, no one messed with the Bryan brothers.

Their toughness also made them stand out athletes. They excelled in football, basketball, and baseball. For many years the Great Falls St. Mary's High School Teams dominated Montana athletics largely because of the Bryans. The records they set would have been even more impressive if they hadn't shared the same flaw. It was not unusual for the St. Mary's teams to show up short handed. The Bryan's drinking issues often relegated them to the sidelines. The coaches didn't take their drinking lightly, so suspensions were frequent.

Sean was proud of his boys, but the conflicts at home over their drinking and fighting angered him. He became tougher and meaner and his relationship with them deteriorated over time.

Jack, being the second youngest of the boys was the toughest of them all. He spent most of his childhood and adolescence trying to prove he could be as tough as his brothers. While they loved each other dearly, the older boys relentlessly goaded on young Jack. They introduced him to whiskey before he became a teenager and made fun of him if he wouldn't guzzle it with them. Jack adapted quickly though, and his brothers came to respect him enormously. They were also proud of his athletic skills. Jack was the best athlete in the family and would eventually be able to choose amongst college scholarship offers in all three of his sports. He always dreamed of playing for Notre Dame, so he accepted a football scholarship there, but World War II ended his dream of playing for the Irish. He enlisted in the Navy right out of high school and served admirably. He received the Navy Cross for the rescue of the entire crew of a torpedo boat that had come under attack by a Japanese Zero.

When he returned to Montana after the war, he opted to enroll at Montana State, where he would later be elected to the Grizzlies Sports Hall of Fame.

It was at Montana State that Jack met Margaret Ackerman. She was a cheerleader and member of the dance team that performed at Grizzly basketball games. She was attracted to Jack, like a lot of the other cheerleaders, because he was well known and a great athlete. He could also party with the best of them, so their times together were great fun. Their love life was often reckless and reflected their overindulgence in alcohol. Margaret got pregnant in their junior year. Jack's parents were adamant that they get married immediately. Ricky Bryan was born three months after the wedding.

Billings Central High School had their eye on Jack even before he graduated from Montana State. His athletic success in college made him a great prospect to take over for their longstanding football and basketball coach Chuck Stern. Stern had kept them in the top tier of Montana High School sports and was about to retire. Excellent sports teams were considered essential in keeping Catholic High Schools in every part of the country in the spotlight, and Jack Bryan fit the mold for what Billings Central needed to stay on top. He came from a good Irish Catholic family and starred at a state university. He would be perfect for the Ram's program.

Jack excelled as head football and basketball coach at Billings Central for 10 years, but his success on the field was not matched on the home front. The partying, drinking and carousing that made college so much fun was not conducive to success in his career and marriage. The often-misguided upbringing he had received as a young man did him little good in handling his own children.

Yet Jack loved being from a big family and wanted to have as many kids as Margaret would agree to. Margaret wanted a career. She graduated in the top of her class in nursing and hoped to pursue her career while raising only a couple of children. With Ricky being born so early in their marriage, she had been hard pressed to finish college. She delayed a second child until she got established in her first job, but Jack and Margaret could never agree on limiting their family. Margaret found herself pregnant so often that a career became very difficult.

Jack's drinking increasingly became a problem as well. He did not seem able to deal with the ebb and flow of life, so he began to drink every day, then throughout the day to alleviate his problems.

He was very tough on his athletes. He thought it would make them better men and serve them well as adults. However, the kid's parents often objected. When confronted by a parent or a school administrator, Jack would try to use his Irish humor to assuage their concern, but internally he became angry when parents opposed him. A good stiff drink at the local pub on the way home from practice always seemed to help him deal with his frustrations. Over time, one drink became three, then five, then more. By the time he got home he was in no condition to be a father to his children.

The alcohol also fed Jack's adolescent pattern of challenging anyone who questioned his motivations. He and his brothers never took a hazing without confronting their adversary, and so it was for Jack in the bars after practice. He would start a fight without regard to the size of his opponent. Some days he would arrive home with bruises to his face. Sometimes he needed stitches. When he showed up at school the next day, the halls would be abuzz with speculation. Jack was amused by all the attention, but Margaret was in a panic over fear that he could lose his job.

Drink also made Jack mean and antagonistic at home. Margaret became desperate to protect the children from their drunken father. In doing so, she risked an angry outburst aimed at her. Occasionally Jack would strike her. In the morning, after he sobered up, he would be apologetic and try to make things right, but Margaret would not take it forever. She decided to seek a divorce.

The drinking also affected his work. As his problems at home escalated he began to start drinking even before leaving for work in the morning. When he went to school with alcohol on his breath his demise as the coach of the Billings Central Rams began. He tried to hide the alcohol on his breath, but when his behavior aggravated the problem, he was soon let go.

Jack was unable to face Margaret with the news and didn't go home for a week. He stayed drunk the entire time. When he finally went home, he found Margaret packing. She did not know where she was going. All she knew was that she needed to get the kids away from their father and the chaos that seemed to forever surround him.

In ten years at Billings Central Jack's football teams had been undefeated four times, and his career record was 72-8. His basketball teams were in the state tournament nine times and won three state titles. Despite all his success he was a broken man.

*****

Jack began a desperate search for work, but his reputation had spread, and despite his record, his drinking problem overrode every other consideration. Alone, angry, and confused and after another blow out with Margaret, Jack left Billings and headed south to Greybull, Wyoming He had no idea what the future held for him. He stopped there and took a room at a rundown motel. He spent his days at the Silver Spur, one of the many dives in Greybull. When the bar closed at night, Jack was often passed out in one of the booths. The bartender never saw Jack when he was sober and had no idea he was formerly a successful coach. When he found him passed out, he just threw him out into the street. When he came back to work the next day, Jack was always gone only to reappear in the early afternoon. This went on for weeks, and then Father Joe Brennan showed up in Greybull.

Chapter 25

Empty Promises

"A freshman girl was seen walking the streets at 5:30 AM –no doubt having not been home all night. —with another girl who was perhaps not home either—but a freshman girl—where does she belong at 5:30 in the morning unless starting to milk cows or getting breakfast.?"

Sunday Bulletin May 21, 1972

Brennan was on the rebound from his affair with Vonnie Thomas and his confrontation with Dan. He needed a new head coach. Dan filed for divorce after several more confrontations. Brennan was lucky to be alive, but he had survived a crisis and was again out to continue building his legacy. He was seeking another superstar coach who would keep his Perpetual Help teams dominant and his supporters under control.

Brennan's good friend, Father John Congdon, ran Billings Central High School. They visited occasionally when Brennan was in Billings, and on their last visit, Brennan mentioned that he needed a new coach.

"We just fired the best coach I've ever had," Congdon mentioned."

"I heard you dismissed Bryan," Brennan responded. "I'm guessing it was because of his drinking problem. I keep track of all the top coaches in the area and am aware that he is a drunk. Has he turned up anywhere? I haven't heard that he is coaching any more. That would be too bad. If he could get control of his drinking, you couldn't find a better man. What has become of his family?"

"His family is still in Billings. They still attend Mass at my parish. Margaret says that Jack is living in Greybull, Wyoming and she is very worried that he will drink himself to death. She hadn't heard from him in weeks the last time we talked."

"She is at her wits end trying to care for seven children and hold down a nursing job as well. I would knock walls down to be able to help them reconcile and get Jack into treatment. That damn Irish blood is an absolute killer when it comes to alcohol. Jack is a particularly hard case. Unfortunately, unless he decides to seek help, there is nothing I can do."

The conversation with Father Congdon got Brennan thinking that he might have the key to getting Bryan into treatment. He would be able to offer extraordinary pay as an incentive to go to New London and start a new life. Once sober and with new hope of reconciliation with his family, he could be a productive coach again. It would be quite a coup. Had it not been for the alcoholism, there might have been no way to attract a quality coach with Bryan's experience. He decided to call on Margaret Bryan to see if she could find Jack. Father Congdon agreed to introduce them and set an appointment for the next evening after Margaret got off work.

The conversation with Margaret did not go well. She was angry and fed up with Jack and the divorce was almost final. She had no interest in reconciliation.

"He is a drunk, plain and simple. His breakfast is whiskey with a rum chaser. He is slurring his words by lunchtime and passed out by the afternoon. What little food he eats is in the form of chips and pickled wieners. The only time he was home was when they cut him off at the bar and he was still able to stumble into bed. I'm waiting for the day he kills somebody on the road. I can't get him to stop driving when he drinks. He leaves empty whiskey bottles around the house. Wherever a bottle was after he emptied it, that was where it stayed. His temper terrifies me. He detests himself and anyone who shows him kindness. When he thinks he is alone he cries with regret for all the mistakes he's made."

All she would consent to do was to tell Brennan where to find Jack.

The next morning Brennan left Billings for Greybull. Greybull was a small town, so he was sure he would be able to find Jack. He started with the bars. He had to check only a couple. He walked into the Silver Spur and there was a man he assumed was Jack sitting at the bar with a bottle of whiskey in front of him. Joe, the bartender, had become so accustomed to seeing him that he no longer bothered to serve him like a regular customer. He just put the bottle in front of Jack and let him pour his own.

He looked older than his true age. Years of drinking had robbed him of his youth. His eyes had a strange sunken look and were so bloodshot he appeared to have pinkeye. His cheeks glowed under broken veins, his actions were labored. But, it was early afternoon, so Jack was still lucid.

Brennan greeted him with a slap on the back that Jack took as a friendly Greybull greeting. Hoping for a little companionship, he offered Brennan a drink. Brennan gracefully declined and said,

"Jack, my name is Father Joe Brennan, I am the Superintendent of Our Lady of Perpetual Help School in New London, North Dakota. Your wife Margaret told me I might find you in Greybull."

"I'm surprised she cares," responded Jack, "she threw me out of my own home. I have been wondering if I would ever see her and the kids again."

"She is angry Jack but working and taking care of seven kids is wearing on her. Maybe we can figure out a way to help both you and your family. I need a coach. I've never had an opportunity to have even a serious discussion with someone with a record like yours. I will pay you very well to coach football and basketball at Perpetual Help. I know it is a step down for you, but in your condition, it may be the best you can do. We are building a great program. You may have heard that we came within a hairs breath of a state title in basketball this past year and our football teams have been second to none the last five years or so."

"I have one condition though. You will have to get treatment for your drinking. It will help get Margaret and the kids back. Then you can come to Perpetual Help and start a new life. I will do everything I can to help you; even pay for family counseling."

"Jack, we can win a bunch of championships together. I've watched a few of your son Ricky's junior high games and I am confident that he is an all-state player in the making. Every coach with a kid that good wants to coach him. This will give you a second chance."

Jack was happy to hear that Brennan knew about Ricky.

"How in hell do you know about my kid?" he asked.

"Jack, I need to win ball games. I do my homework. I go through a Chrysler, like that one outside, every other year. I'm familiar with, and have watched, almost every good Catholic athlete in three states. I try to get every one of them to come to Perpetual Help. Occasionally, I get a really good one. That's how we build winning teams at Perpetual Help. Combined with the best coaches in the state we win a lot. You and Ricky can be a part of that. What do you say?"

Jack asked, "Recruiting is against the rules, isn't it? I don't need the hassle of making a commitment to coach; then have the state come down on me for recruiting."

"Well Jack, rules are made to be broken, plus, I focus on the value of a Catholic education. I impress upon the parents that it is their duty to pass their faith onto their children, and that sports are secondary. They will get a great religious education and a have a chance to play on a winning team, maybe even get a college scholarship. How could it get any better than that? The parents usually agree. I don't think the rules ought to prevent these kids from getting a Catholic education. My conscience is clear."

Jack thought about all of this, and after downing a couple of straight shots, said, "Where do I go for treatment? If it all goes well, and Margaret agrees to give things another go, I'll come to Perpetual Help."

Brennan said, "I'll get things all set up and get back to you."

As he walked out of the bar, Jack grabbed the bottle of whiskey in front of him and guzzled it thinking,

One last drunk. God almighty, please don't let me blow this one.

*****

Jack went into rehab highly motivated to start a new life as husband, father, and coach. To the delight of his family, he emerged a new man. Reconciliation gave him new energy and a determination to make things work this time. He took over a Perpetual Help football program that had been dominant since Don Earnhardt took over the program. The record the previous four years included only two losses and Brennan made sure Jack understood that winning was not optional.

The basketball program had progressed more slowly, but the previous year's second place finish at the state tournament was now the standard by which Brennan would measure every coach. Fortunately for Jack, expectations for his first year were tempered by the fact that the previous year's graduating class included some of the best athletes ever to play at Perpetual Help. Jack would need to rebuild before Perpetual Help could resume its journey to the top.

He had no way of knowing though that fate would end all hopes of the successful fresh start with his family.

Chapter 26

Impaired for Life

GRADUATION NIGHT was a mockery for many parents of what control they should have over their children. They let non-graduates run all hours of the night and booze, instead of demanding that they be home at a reasonable hour. The 1972 graduates will be able to pat themselves on the back because of the events of graduation night. Perpetual Help is changing the time and circumstances of graduation starting next year. No more of this kind of stuff."

Sunday Bulletin May 21, 1972

Despite dominating the community in so many ways, Brennan still cast a somewhat mysterious shadow in New London because he was often absent for weeks at a time. People wondered where he always went. His absence in the late summer of 1962 would extend far longer than normal. Toward dusk on a late August evening he was on another of his long road trips racing down a Minnesota freeway at his usual twenty miles per hour above the speed limit.

His frequent companion, Bubby, was again dominating the conversation he was having with himself as the miles droned by.

"So, your feeling guilty about your affair with Vonnie Thomas, I see."

"You know it was wrong and it would never have happened if you would leave me alone. In fact, buzz off. Please God, release me from this evil presence."

"Evil is as evil does comrade. I'm here to stay, your God has no power over me. Maybe you need a little reminder"

Suddenly the trailer that was being pulled by a pickup truck in front of him decoupled and careened wildly back and forth across the freeway. He was driving too fast to avoid it. Braking did not help. It was like falling off a cliff with just enough time to regret his tiff with Bubby but not enough time to fully grasp what was happening. There wasn't a thing he could do by accelerating, braking, or swerving. He was trapped in a steel prison. As the front of the car hit the trailer, inertia became his enemy. His body jerked to the dashboard, his face collided with the windshield. His nose crumpled and broke.

He sat there screaming, glued to the wheel of his wrecked car. Screaming at his steering wheel, at himself, at the very fate that seemed avoidable if only he had not insulted Bubby. Most importantly he screamed at the idiot driver of the truck that had lost its trailer.

He wondered why he was still alive, then he began to taste the coppery blood pooling in his mouth. He could feel it grazing his teeth and soaking his tongue. He felt the aches and cracking in his bones. Each crack felt like rocks burrowing into his skin. He sucked in cramped air and felt his lungs caving in on themselves. He saw spots in the corners of his vision, making his head feel like the only thing inside of it was static. A buzzing noise, filled his ears. He felt like he was there for hours, fading and waking and fading and waking. His agony seemed to be the only thing keeping him alive. It was the only thing he could feel anymore. That's when he looked at his legs. His right leg was thrust upward and protruded grossly from its hip socket. Blood soaked his car seat. Then he passed out.

When the ambulance arrived, Brennan was near death. The paramedics revived him and stabilized him on the way to the hospital, but the collision had caused multiple injuries and almost destroyed his right leg. There would be many months of rehabilitation before Brennan could return to New London.

*****

The students at Perpetual Help High School were too well behaved to openly celebrate the absence of "Big Dad," but they let out a collective sigh of relief when they heard the news about the accident. In his absence, religion classes resumed being about religion again. Students temporarily stopped worrying about being friends with their public school and non-Catholic contemporaries. Openly dating a non-Catholic no longer carried the fear of suspension from school. The same applied to steady dating. Carl Hunter and Sheila Kronk were able to finish an entire school year without getting suspended. Life was good for the young people in New London.

The parish seemed to function just fine, and the Notre Dame nuns loved the freedom of not being under constant scrutiny by Brennan. There was a sense of serenity at school on the part of both the students and the nuns that promised to make school fun again.

Things were also good for Jack Bryan. He was yet to experience the difficulties of serving as head coach under the scrutiny of Joe Brennan. He had an entire school year to introduce his own system and restore the basketball team's path to dominance. His football team lost two games, which was two too many by Brennan's standards, but they still won the conference championship. The basketball team was a tougher proposition, having lost all five starters from the previous year, but Jack was able to develop a group of talented underclassmen that would produce Perpetual Help's best team ever the following year. Unfortunately for Jack and his children, this year would be the only year where performance on the field would decide success or failure or indeed, their whole future as a family.

Chapter 27

No Help Without Conditions

"Young men not 21 are selling liquor to our high school students. But this town is so structured that you cannot do anything about it. People over 21 supplied plenty of liquor on graduation night. I could take a lot of people in and around New London to court for selling to minors and in some cases selling drugs to high school students. It is not my work to do that, but the parents who might care. But if you do not know what your students are doing or if you know and do not do anything about it, then why DON'T WE LET THE YOUNG PEOPLE HAVE A LIQUOR LICENSE FOR THE TEEN CENTER AND AT LEAST HAVE SOME CENTRALIZED SUPERVISION OVER THEIR DRINKING?

THIS PERMISSIVENESS BY THE PARENTS RIGHT NOW IS QUITE RIDICULOUS.

Sunday Bulletin May 21, 1972

When the news of Brennan's accident reached New London, one of the first to show concern was Margaret Bryan. She had let it be known how grateful she was for the help she and Jack received from Brennan. The new job was important to their fresh start, but the presence of a sober Jack, determined to make things work, seemed almost miraculous. Margaret attributed all these positive changes to Brennan. When she heard of the severity of the accident and the prognosis of a lengthy rehab she asked Jack if she could go to Minnesota, to help care for Brennan. Her experience in the Billings Hospital had been a mixed bag of compassionate nurses giving great care, and many dysfunctional individuals projecting their unhappiness on their patients. She had not really missed her job.

But, she felt so grateful to Brennan for all that he had done for her family that she thought she could repay him by being his care coordinator and making his recovery as easy as possible. Jack did not object and made arrangements for child care while Margaret was away.

Brennan was confined to the Little Falls, MN hospital. It was small enough to appreciate the extra help Margaret offered and so readily agreed to give her a small stipend in return for taking full responsibility for Brennan's care.

In Billings, Margaret had been a person of uncommon gifts. She was like a star gymnast, making something so impossible for others appear easy and natural. On the ward, she had a calming effect. Nurse Bryan never hurt her patients, never became impatient or belittled their pains, physical or otherwise. She spoke to them like they were people who mattered, not just withered old bones too stubborn to die. Her speech had a liberal dose of terms of endearment: "honey, sweetie, sweetheart and love." With just her presence their pain medications seemed to work better, their appetites improved, and they slept more deeply. Joe Brennan would be the undeserving beneficiary of full time care by this amazing professional.

Margaret's intentions were pure. She would be serving the greater good represented by the Church while repaying her new friend for saving her family. But, like the majority of Catholics, she was naïve regarding the human failings of many priests. One of the things she had memorized for a test in her theology class in college would forever influence her. She vividly remembered a quote from St. Bernard whose Bavarian village had been given over to days of feasting and festivities in gratitude that a young man from among them had been made a priest.

He said, "A (priest is a) man who holds the place of God–a man, who is invested with all the powers of God."

"Go," said Our Lord to the priest; "as My Father sent Me, I send you. All power has been given Me in Heaven and on earth. Go then, teach all nations. . ... He who listens to you, listens to Me; he who despises you despises Me."

When the priest remits sins, he does not say, "God pardons you;" he says, "I absolve you." "At the Consecration, he does not say, "This is the Body of Our Lord;" he says, "This is My Body."

Father Brennan was a minister of God, and as such, deserved personal attention from someone who cared deeply for him.

But, despite her eagerness to serve, she felt uncomfortable from the beginning with the way that Brennan looked at her. He started making sexual comments, jokes, and gestures, that she felt were not at all pastoral. He would 'accidentally' brush up against her or grasp her hand longer than was usual when she helped him in and out of bed. One day he hugged her, not a perfunctory gesture showing appreciation. It lingered, his stubble glazed her cheeks, and he brushed his lips on hers. His hand traveled the distance from her shoulders to her buttocks. He touched her in intimate places that, at first, she dismissed as accidental, but were too frequent to be ignored.

At first, she tolerated the advances, but the day he ran his hand up her leg as she was preparing him for the day's rehab session she rebelled. She pulled away from him, her knees knocking against each other. There were other people present in the room and although she was not sure if anyone had noticed, she rushed out of the room feigning illness to give herself time to recover her composure and decide how to deal with the situation. When the rehab session was over, and all the other personnel were gone, she reentered the room to confront Brennan.

"Father Brennan, you're a priest and I am a married woman with seven children. What do you think you are doing making sexual advances towards me?"

Brennan's answer shocked her but also appealed in a strange way to her sense of compassion and respect for the sacrifices made by all priests.

He said, "Margaret, celibacy is a cross that every priest must bear. It is a burden most of us are unable to manage. I have a compulsive need for sex that is so strong I am unable to resist attraction to a woman. I have never understood why these feelings manifest so strongly in me. I feel possessed by a demon. Some of my priest friends have told me to seek counseling. I am more inclined to simply ask God for forgiveness. You have been so compassionate in caring for me and I have developed extra strong feelings for you. I want you to be my lover. No one will ever find out, and I'm betting that your love life with Jack is not very satisfying. It is hard for me to ignore things I hear in the confessional, so I apologize for throwing this back at you, but maybe we can help each other."

"Father!" she exclaimed, "New London is an extremely small town. Even if I could justify being your mistress, there is no way that it would remain a secret! I could never keep it from Jack."

"Margaret, "you have not been around New London long enough to know this, but I have insulated myself from rumors. Some of New London's most prominent citizens will defend me without fail. The community is becoming increasingly endeared to the success the school has had in every department. Success in sports creates a loyalty among the people that serves to put virtually any rumor to rest. My people have a personal stake in the success I've had in new London. They believe that I bring God's blessings to Perpetual Help and support me implicitly. Plus, every Catholic believes that their priests are next to God. They refuse to believe that a priest could violate his vows. You have nothing to fear."

"Father, other than the time one of Jack's drunken teammates forced himself on me, I've only been with Jack. Despite all our troubles, I have been faithful to him. Please don't ask me to do this."

"Margaret, I would prefer that you act willingly, but I never intended to help you and your family without conditions. This is one of them. It comes with other benefits though. I have a lot of money and I can use it for your family. You will want your kids to go to college, but who will pay. I can do that. There will be special things that you want but can't afford. I can get them for you."

"What if Jack finds out?"

"Don't worry, I can handle him. He has never treated you well. You don't owe him anything."

With that, Margaret, her frustration with her difficult relationship with Jack overwhelming her better instincts, closed the door to Brennan's room, pulled the curtains, and began to disrobe.

Chapter 28

Outed

Brennan's recovery and rehab took the better part of a full year. He emerged from the hospital with a severe limp that would change forever how people remembered him. It would become the focus of significant ridicule amongst the students of Perpetual Help. His infirmity also altered the appearance of invincibility that had always characterized him. He became less of an authority figure and students ceased to fear him. He lost the ability to intimidate. The grudging respect, that students granted him previously, evaporated. He lost his implicit aura of the God-Priest and they now felt free to make fun of him.

Some even began to confront him when disciplined. This sometimes ended in physical violence since Brennan could not abide any challenge to his authority. When confronted by one of the Hunter girls, who felt he had unfairly attacked her in religion class, he slapped her so hard she fell to the floor. He bruised her lip and drew blood. Her parents were not happy. Their kids had often been singled out for Brennan's sick idea of discipline. This would have severe future consequences for Brennan as the story of his abuses became better known. Therese Koch was born Therese Hunter.

The Bryan family, along with most of the adult parishioners, continued as before. Jack was blissfully unaware of the relationship that had developed between Margaret and Brennan. He was never happier at home and was having remarkable success as head football and basketball coach. His team's records were much better than expected given the huge loss of talent from the previous year's graduating class, and he was poised for even better results in the year to come.

Jacks second year at Perpetual Help felt like a return of the good old days at Billings Central. He was back with his family, had his drinking under control and his teams were winning. It was one of his most gratifying years as a coach. His system was in place and his players knew what to expect. His basketball team embraced his toughness and responded with a determination and an "I'll show you" attitude that translated into an aggressive style of play and resulted in the best record in school history. The senior class had been playing together since sixth grade and had lost only one basketball game through their sophomore year. Their junior year had been a disappointment and they were determined to return to dominance.

The football team had to adjust to some radical changes. Jack's style was old school. He believed that confronting a team's strength and winning every individual battle was the key to winning consistently. He avoided adopting the modern offensives sets that had become popular. The less time he needed to commit to learning the new methods the better able he was to devote time to his first love.

He coached basketball for love of the game and football to earn a little extra money. He loved to win though and was even tougher on his football players. They were equally tough on their opponents. Perpetual Help's winning tradition motivated the players as well. They well remembered the days when Don Earnhardt's teams were walking all over the Badlands Conference every year.

Jack was beginning to feel the same excitement that had been his trademark. He made a concerted effort to keep control over his drinking and his relationship with his children, especially Ricky, was never better.

Tragically, all his hopes were destroyed before the end of the football season. Margaret was unable to sustain the fiction of her faithfulness to Jack. She was good at play acting for short periods of time while she was back home from Little Falls, but once life returned to normal, and she was home full time, every encounter with Brennan triggered a fear inside of her that manifest as part depression and part reticence to show affection for Jack. He would eventually notice. He started asking questions that Margaret could not answer persuasively, and their relationship began to disintegrate again. After keeping his drinking under control for the previous year, Jack began reverting to past behaviors. When he got drunk, he confronted Margaret aggressively about his suspicions. While he was never physically violent, she became concerned that his anger was hurting the kids. She sought counseling from the only person she had confidence in; Father Brennan.

Brennan's first reaction was panic. He yelled at her and berated her for not being more careful to conceal their relationship. He admonished her to get a grip and to take whatever measures were necessary to act more naturally. But she began to experience panic attacks. The stress of the pressure exerted by both men in her life increasingly troubled her. She called Brennan whenever things overwhelmed her.

These encounters confused her, and she began seriously considering breaking off the relationship with Brennan. Luckily, Jack did not yet suspect that she was having an affair.

Margaret sought constant reassurance from Brennan that all was okay. If a phone conversation was not enough to calm her, he would sometimes drive over to her house. Jack was teaching or coaching so he was unaware of the meetings, but the two youngest Bryan children were present. They were too young to understand what was going on, but the visits became so frequent that they acquired a familiarity with Brennan. They did not like his angry interactions with their mother and it was not long before they began to express their feelings.

During a rare family dinner together one of the children mentioned how "yucky" he felt when "uncle father" patted his head and told him to be a good boy. Jack had not heard anyone refer to Brennan as "uncle father" so he asked Margaret what it meant.

"How do they know him that well?"

Margaret was taken off guard and her answer raised suspicions that her relationship with Brennan had become problematic. Once the children were in bed he confronted her. Margaret panicked, and admitted she had a relationship with Brennan, but promised to break it off at once. Jack was devastated. He could not suppress his anger.

He raced out the door running as fast as he could to the rectory where he expected to find Brennan. But Brennan was on one of his frequent trips out of town. Had Jack not had time to cool off he would have given him a beating.

~ 148 ~

The reputation that the Bryan boys had in Great Falls did not come about without good reason. One did not give offense to one of the Bryan brothers without consequences.

Unable to confront Brennan, he walked downtown to the Empire Bar, ordered a fifth of whiskey and stayed till closing. By then he was in a drunken stupor. When he next confronted Margaret he tried to beat her, but she was able to keep him at bay. Stumbling drunk was not conducive to fighting anyone, even a woman. He threw a few pots and glasses at her but did no physical damage. He passed out on the floor amidst the broken glass. When he woke up in the morning the hangover suppressed his anger, but he returned to the sullen man who had earlier been unable to function as husband and father.

There would be no more happy times in the Bryan household. Margaret, being under Brennan's spell, never tried to sever her relationship with him. Jack would be forced to live with a vexing resentment that would characterize the rest of their time together.

Jack's visits to the Empire Bar became more frequent and sometimes ended in fights. He was a bit of a wise ass and not everyone could take his ribbings. Jack showed up at school, more than once, with evidence that he had fared poorly the previous evening. He got a reputation as a dangerous but bumbling drunk. As time passed, patrons learned to avoid him after he had a few drinks. No one would get near him when they saw him sitting at the bar.

Despite the downward spiral of his personal life, Jack was still effective as a coach. The football team finished with an 8-0 record and a conference championship, and the basketball team had the best record in school history. Brennan was always an irritating presence, but Jack was determined to be the coach that his players deserved. He would have to settle his score with Brennan after the season.

The affair with his wife was not the only challenge Jack had with Brennan. He added to the raging fire with his constant carping about coaching decisions in his Sunday bulletins. This was a regular practice that angered all his coaches, most of whom ignored it, thinking that the extra money they were making made up for the criticism. But money did not matter anymore to Jack. To him, these periodic critiques were fuel for the fire.

Matters escalated to a blow out when Brennan walked into the locker room before the regional championship game and started handing out what he called pep pills. Perpetual Help was about to play the Fort Yates Warriors for the third time. They had split two earlier games, and Fort Yates ranked second in the state just behind top ranked Perpetual Help. Brennan's hot pursuit of a state championship meant that anything was acceptable, so long as it could be concealed and not sully his reputation, or that of his school. At the time, few knew what pep pills were, so nobody was alarmed. The players were oblivious, but Jack knew they were illegal. Brennan wanted a competitive advantage and giving his players pep pills seemed to be well worth any potential risk.

Jack exploded when he saw what was happening. He slapped the bottle of pills out of Brennan's hand and yelled,

"Get out of my locker room before I call the cops. While we're waiting I will personally kick your ass!"

Brennan protested saying, "Jack, I run Perpetual Help School and I will decide what is in the best interest of my students, back off or you will be looking for a job."

With that, Jack grabbed Brennan in a bear hug and threw him out of the locker room yelling, "You've got too many secrets to threaten me my friend. Don't you ever walk into my locker room again, because if you do, I'll be doing some talking."

What was already expected to be a tough game for Perpetual Help, was made hopelessly impossible by the pre-game events that destroyed the concentration of the players. Perpetual Help could never get control of the game and lost badly.

The loss stacked on top of the revelation of Brennan's affair with Margaret and the confrontation in the locker room all signaled the end of Jack's career in New London. Because he knew so much of Brennan's dark side, Jack was able to stay at Perpetual Help for another year. Had he been in control of the situation, he would have left, but he was unsure that his family would come with him. There was no certainty that he could even get another coaching job.

Margaret sided with Brennan after the locker room confrontation and seemed inexplicably unable to break her relationship with him. Jack was forced to live with a wife who continued in a damaging relationship with a priest, who seemed to be in absolute control of her. He was unable to prevent

Brennan from entering his home with his children present and engage in sexual activity in the upstairs bedroom. Brennan was throwing all caution to the wind, risking everything in the hope that Jack would not risk his job and family by outing him to the community.

However, Jack would only take so much and soon did become a threat to go public. Brennan was at wits end trying to figure out how to protect himself. He told Margaret they had to do something about Jack. He suggested they use his drinking problem to get him committed to a mental institution. By this point, Margaret was completely under Brennan's control, and she readily agreed. Arrangements were made to have the authorities pick up Jack, and forcefully take him to an institution. They arranged for the county sheriff and a professional from the mental institution to come to the Bryan home with proper papers and take him away.

The chaos he had been living with for the past year made Jack wary of everything out of the ordinary. Margaret called him at school and begged him to be home at a certain time to have a conference with Brennan.

"He wants to see if he can work out an accommodation so that you can leave Perpetual Help in good graces with a substantial cash settlement in return for your agreement to keep quiet about our relationship."

Jack intuitively realized something was up. Brennan would never ask a teacher to walk out of the classroom for personal reasons unless the situation was urgent. His fears drove him into action. He got into his car, drove off with no belongings and little money, and disappeared. No one heard from him again for seven years.

Chapter 29

Using Ricky

I would not be surprised that Sister Francis Marie has done as much or more praying that we would find the necessary teachers and coaches than all the wrestlers and football players together. I hope I am wrong, but this is just my surmise. I feel a sense of "we don't care, for we will get someone. There is a lot of difference between someone the students would settle for if it took praying and the someone who is needed to do the good job. I FIND THE YOUNG PEOPLES WORDS ABOUT THEIR INTEREST IN PERPETUAL HELP AND THEIR SUPPORT GIVEN BY PRAYER AND CHURCH SUPPORT ENVELOPES MYSTIFYING."

Sunday Bulletin June 25, 1972

Our Lady of Perpetual Help please intercede for me. I want to do the work of Jesus, but what I want to do I do not do, but what I hate, I do. I have the desire to do what is good, but I cannot carry it out. I do not do the good I want to do, but the evil I do not want to do—this I keep on doing. It is not I who does it, but it is sin living in me that does it.

The familiar evil giggle interrupted Brennan's prayer.

"You fool, you ask for help from the mother of a non-existent being. I know you are a weak man, but this is borderline insanity. You're getting everything you could possibly want, and you go crying to some mythical mother of god?"

"God damn you. Get away from me. I just destroyed the family of a man who I was trying to help. You made me want his wife. I cannot do the good a priest is ordained to do. Please, I beg of you, leave me alone. I want to be a good priest. I'm going to say the rosary"

"Good luck with that. I've given you notoriety, and money, and power, and all the beautiful women you want. You're not going to get rid of me so easily. Say your rosary. Keep fooling yourself that you can cover your evil with prayer. When your done we have work to do. And don't push me. Your next accident will be your last."

*****

"Floyd, get with Paul and come see me immediately."

"I'm in the middle of a plumbing project. We've got pipes backed up. I can't just walk away from a customer."

"Get Paul and be in my office in 30 minutes if you know what is good for you. I have a problem that could get out of hand very fast if it is not addressed immediately."

Luckily Paul had just closed the store and was finishing some bookwork when Floyd called. They were in Brennan's office well within the 30-minute deadline.

"Father, what is so important that you can't wait until tomorrow to deal with it?"

"Jack Bryan just walked away from his job. He drove off without a word. While I was trying to get an explanation from his wife I got a phone call from Leona Baumgartner saying Bryan's daughter accused me of fucking her mother. That's exactly how it was said. We have a crisis on our hands that needs to be gotten under control. You need to stifle the inevitable rumors."

"Why would a kid say something like that? Is it true?" asked Floyd.

"Why would you even ask, Floyd? You, of all people, know that we men sometimes don't live up to our values. What difference does it make? If people start believing this kind of stuff, I will be forced to leave. What do you think would happen to your school if I wasn't around? Trust me, it won't last five years, so I'm not asking for your help, I am ordering you to shut down whatever rumors crop up!"

*****

With the help of his newly created "Catholic Mafia" the misbegotten couple used Jack's disappearance to give them the cover they needed to protect Brennan. Jack was known to be unpredictable at best. Many people assumed his drinking had gotten the best of him. Opinions differed, but Brennan never said a word other than a short announcement of the change in coaches in the Sunday bulletin. Only Floyd and Paul's hand-picked few knew what was

~ 153 ~

going on. The oldest of the Bryan daughters, age twelve at the time, had made the call to the neighbor lady and Ricky, age 14, also knew. He would never forgive his mother.

Brennan should have done everything possible to cover up the circumstances surrounding Jack's disappearance, including moving the Bryan's out of New London as soon as possible. However, Brennan was so obsessed with his winning athletic program that he could not bear to lose Ricky Bryan. Ricky was already the best athlete to ever play for Perpetual Help. There were also other good athletes in the lower grades who, as a group, looked like they would provide the next big opportunity to win the state basketball championship. Brennan simply decided to take the risk that he could manage any potential scandal in hopes of winning that state championship.

The Bryan family, however, was destroyed. The kids lived with constant chaos and were never in a stable home. The conflicts over Jack's alcohol problem had triggered fighting that was never hidden from them. The almost constant yelling and fighting burdened them. They were forced to pick sides, with Ricky feeling the greatest affinity for his father, and the six youngest favoring their mother. Meredith, the oldest daughter hated them both. The result of this toxic mix would be the alienation of the Bryan children from each other and a lifelong bitterness that would permanently prevent reconciliation.

Ricky was at an age where he was the most likely to act out. He created constant turmoil as he proved uncontrollable and defiant. He began drinking, and Margaret worried he would end up like Jack. There was great concern that Ricky would create so much attention with his rebellious behavior, that the family secret would be exposed. To keep him from being suspended from the basketball team for drinking, Brennan had to personally protect him. School discipline kept things under control during the school year, but once summer vacation arrived there seemed to be no way to predict what Ricky would do. Joe Brennan had a solution.

He owned three motels at Disney Land. His brother oversaw his real estate empire and would do whatever he was asked. He could get rid of Ricky for the summer and look like the good guy who gave him a summer job in a place every kid dreamed of visiting. Ricky was unlikely to object. He wanted desperately to get away from his family anyway, so Brennan packed up all that Ricky would need for a three month stay at Disney Land and off they went in Brennan's Chrysler.

Two days later they arrived in Anaheim, CA and Ricky began his first job. There was a problem though. Ricky understood that he could do as he pleased, and no one would do anything about it for fear that he would expose what really caused his father's disappearance. So, Ricky did a lot of playing and very little work.

When Bill Brennan confronted him, Ricky simply explained why he was there and the circumstances surrounding Big Dad's seeming generosity. Bill refused to believe any of it. That assured that Ricky would never respect him. He seldom listened to him or obeyed any of his orders. Nothing good could come out of this toxic mix of adolescent rebellion and family turmoil. What happened next was almost predictable.

Bill Brennan's son Bill Jr. was helping manage the hotels and owned a motorcycle. Ricky bugged him to try it out. At first Bill Jr. resisted, thinking that Ricky was too wild to be trusted, but Ricky had the same engaging personality as his father that made him a successful coach, and eventually persuaded Bill Jr. to teach him how to drive it, and allow him to take it for a spin.

Bill Jr. was happy to have found a way to occupy Ricky. He was useless as an employee anyway. Bill senior wanted to prevent the spreading of rumors he was sure were false, so he played along with brother Joe and allowed Ricky to hang out and occupy himself with the motorcycle. Ricky would disappear for hours at a time joyriding around Southern California. Bill ignored his concern that Ricky was too young to be off on his own so much, because his other choice was to put up with Ricky's insolence and disrespect. Not having him around was a big relief. As for Ricky, he was having the time of his life. He raced up U. S. Highway 1 getting acquainted with the California coast. Watching the bikini clad women cavorting on the beaches was eye popping mind candy for the young man whose sexual urges were just beginning to emerge.

The fun ended suddenly. It was mid-morning, after traffic had cleared, and the roads were wide open. Ricky was speeding down the street in a commercial area of Anaheim when an eighteen-wheeler blew through a red light. Ricky was too close to stop and his speed prevented any change of direction. In a move that was remarkable for an inexperience driver, Ricky laid the motorcycle down to avoid being decapitated. Miraculously, he slid under the trailer and avoided being crushed under its wheels. He was momentarily stunned however, so for a few minutes he lay by the curb, not completely sure why he was still alive, feeling nothing. When he returned to reality, he suddenly became aware of excruciating pain in his leg. When he looked down he realized that the motorcycle's hot manifold was lying on the calf of his right leg. Before he could lift the bike off himself, the manifold had burned half way through his calf.

Emergency medical treatment stabilized his leg, but a prolonged period of rehab was necessary to enable Ricky to walk again. He would wear a leg brace for the rest of his life. His basketball playing days appeared to be over.

When Ricky returned to New London following his accident, he was re-immersed into the family chaos. Brennan and his mother continued in a relationship that scandalized the children and perpetrated a deception that became ever more difficult to maintain. Ricky no longer received the deference he had been given as the future of the Perpetual Help basketball program. He was also no longer inclined to keep quiet about what was going on behind the closed doors of the Bryan residence. Brennan's hidden life would soon begin to unravel.

Chapter 30

No Longer Just a Symbolic Father Part II

<u>FIRST FRIDAY THIS WEEK:</u> <u>Exposition of the Blessed Sacrament</u> after the first Mass. Ladies of the Guild are supposed to keep these hours of <u>adoration</u> occupied, but too often to be accidental, it has not been done lately; so to make sure that Our Lord has some visitors, I am asking the grade and high school students who are able to come and please do so on that day. <u>It is only a half an hour.</u> By the time you say the rosary, some private prayers, look at your watch a few times, think of how you could be sitting at home, and a few prayers to Christ in the Blessed Sacrament—talking to him about how good or bad things are at home (don't pray for Our Lady of Perpetual Help School that we get good teachers and the right students for next year—leave that to the other guy because he is leaving that for you,) well the half hour will be gone and you can be on your way again.

Sunday Bulletin July 2, 1972

The Bryan story stunned Frank.

He asked Therese "Is that how the scandal began to emerge?"

"Not exactly," she responded, "Brennan's lackeys do not give up easily. We suspect that he has been blackmailing them with information they revealed in the confessional. It's the only reason we can come up with why these otherwise good people, would go to such lengths to protect him. We have testimony to that fact from one parishioner. People persist in defending him and turning every attempt to expose Brennan into an attack on the school. They accuse us of being anti-school and anti-Brennan.

"The school is so important to these people because of the sports programs. They feel proud to be from New London. Perpetual Help's success gives them bragging rights wherever they go. They are afraid if Brennan goes the teams will no longer dominate. He is publishing attacks on us in the Sunday bulletins. Here, take a look."

She continued as she tossed a stack of Sunday bulletins at him.

"We've been saving every bulletin for the last three years. The only thing keeping us going is the support of a couple of the former assistant pastors who have taken a stand against this blatant immorality. The Bishop is resisting to protect the Church and because of Brennan's rock star status as a school administrator, but they persist, as do we, along with our small cohort of principled parishioners."

"I was wondering about Ricky Bryan" remarked Frank, "he had an amazing year and an even more amazing state tournament despite the brace on his leg." "I wondered what had happened to him. He must have worked very hard to be able to play ball again after such a devastating injury."

"He is a very driven young man," Therese conceded. "As you probably know, he was named to the all- state team."

"Yes, I know, it is remarkable," Frank said.

By now Frank was emotionally drained from hearing the story of a man he had formerly held in high regard.

He asked Therese, "Would you mind if we took a break? I need to process this a bit."

Therese agreed to resume after lunch and invited him to stay and eat. Frank was happy to accept given the dearth of good restaurants in New London. Their conversation, over lunch, revolved around Frank's new-found determination to help the New London group get justice for the people whose lives had been ravaged by Brennan. He told Therese he was sure that the article he would soon publish would get the bishop's attention for sure.

Therese expressed her appreciation saying, "We have been at this for such a long time and are feeling abused by the process. All the bishop does is defend the Church. He is accusing us of the same thing as you read about in those anonymous letters. He persists in calling the charges against Brennan rumors, despite all the hard evidence we have. Both priests who are helping us arc talking about leaving the priesthood over this. One of the former assistant pastors already has. We aren't in touch with him, but we understand he has become a flaming Fundamentalist. Arnold and I are both questioning whether we will continue in the Catholic Church. Arnold is a convert who turned Catholic, so I could get married in the Church. Believe me, he is not impressed. Totally disgusted would be a better description."

Wait till I tell you about the affidavit we have from one of the candidates who wants to become a Notre Dame nun. But first, let's talk about the Brandt family."

*****

"The George Brandt family is a typical New London family. They have four girls and a boy. All are popular with their peers, active in school activities, and like most of the kids in town, want to get through school and get out of New London as fast as they can.

Darlene, the second oldest, has an understated beauty, and when she smiles and laughs, you can't help but smile along too. She was homecoming queen her senior year. She is easy going and self-confident. She got Brennan's attention because she was still living at home and working as a waitress. Her mom said she was trying to save money to go to college. She was nineteen years old.

She was committing the unforgivable sin of dating a non-Catholic. They appeared to be in a serious relationship. We are not sure if he was just obsessed with preventing a mixed marriage or if he targeted her because of her good looks, but her love interest was the excuse he used to harass her.

*****

At first it was counseling sessions in his office. He creeped her out by implying that she was having sex with her boyfriend, Roy. She was turned off because of the way he leered at her when making the accusations. She expected to be admonished, but it looked more like he was taking a sick pleasure in a sexual fantasy he had of their imaginary sex in the back seat of Roy's car. Then he would get serious and threaten her with eternal damnation if she would not give up her relationship. She resisted these meetings, so one night he showed up at the Brandt home unannounced. He had timed the visit knowing that Darlene was home.

This did not set well with George who never liked Brennan. He threatened to throw him out of their home if he did not stop harassing his daughter. Roy was the son of Wilmer Johnson, a good friend of George's. He worked for Wilmer for years after his own farm failed. He considered Wilmer's son the perfect man for Darlene. He accused Brennan of being unchristian. He believed the scripture where it said,

"Love one another as I have loved you."

~ 159 ~

He wondered why this did not apply to Protestants.

"Any way" he said, "She is old enough to make her own decisions."

"Mr. Brandt," Brennan replied, "God will hold your daughter over the pit of hell with one hand, while He torments her with the other. As for you, the wrath of God will be poured out upon you without mercy."

With that, he turned and walked away.

"Ooooo, that was excellent!"

Bubby had returned and was ecstatic to see Brennan sow the hate that served evil so well. He continued to impose himself as Brennan drove back to the rectory.

"She's ripe for the taking."

"She's an innocent young woman. I'm trying to protect her from the likes of you."

"Don't be silly. You know you don't really believe in that wrath of God stuff. She's been banging that boyfriend of hers. Innocent, what B.S."

"She hates me. There is no way I'm going to get in her pants."

"You'll find a way."

With the usual whisper of frigid wind, Bubby was gone.

Brennan hated himself for what Bubby put into his mind, but again, he was helpless to resist. He decided that reforming her was hopeless, but a more aggressive approach just might serve a dual purpose. In his sick mind, he thought he would be God's instrument in punishing her, by manipulating her into having sex with him. So, he invited her out to dinner at a restaurant in Dickinson.

Darlene did not want to go with Brennan, but like most of the kids who were educated at Perpetual Help, she feared the consequences of mortal sin, and disrespecting a priest was, in her mind, very possibly a mortal sin. Being unaware of any ulterior motives, she decided to accept the invitation.

Truth be told, Brennan loved situations where women did not rigidly live the faith. Rather than condemn them because they were not obeying his rules, he assumed that there were other rules they would compromise as well.

He was always on the lookout for women who would believe anything when it came to respecting God's representative, the priest. Darlene Brandt never questioned her religious education. She would be an easy target.

He could make her aware of his money and give her a small dose of a potential lifestyle that would certainly attract her. She was about to see a side of Brennan that she never dreamed of, and another New London family saga was about to begin.

They met at the rectory to avoid attention from her father. When Brennan heard the knock on his door, he removed his shirt, unbuckled his belt, and lowered his zipper just enough to keep his pants from falling off. When he opened the door, Darlene recoiled at seeing the half-naked priest, and immediately dropped her eyes to the ground.

"Oh Father, I'm so sorry, please, I'll wait outside. I thought you would be ready."

Brennan assured her that all was okay and insisted she come in and wait in his office. She reluctantly did so but was shocked again when Brennan left the door to his bedroom ajar, and allowed her to see him as he slowly prepared himself for their outing. This unnerved her but raised no suspicions about his agenda. When he was dressed and ready to go, he opened the car door for her like they were going on a date. Darlene found a single red rose sitting on the dash board. Brennan saw the surprised look on Nancy's face.

"You know, priests are human too. We know that women love flowers. I just thought that it would be nice. I know you are nervous about this meeting. Just relax and enjoy your flower."

They said little on the trip to Dickinson. Before entering the restaurant, Brennan opened his trunk saying,

"I keep a little stash for occasions like this."

Darlene thought nothing of it and did not notice that the trunk was overflowing with cash.

The dinner was uneventful until Brennan asked her if she would enjoy an after-dinner cocktail before they talked.

She said, "I'm not old enough, they won't serve me."

He replied with a knowing smirk,

"Don't worry, I'm a priest; they won't even ask for an ID. Priests don't encourage minors to drink."

So, Darlene ordered a cocktail then excused herself to go to the restroom. The drink order came before she returned, and Brennan had the opportunity he had hoped for. He reached into his coat pocket, removed a small vial of pills, and dropped one of them into Darlene's drink. It would take time for the affects to be felt, and while he waited, they could have their conversation about dating non-Catholics.

When the effect of the alcohol and drugs began to take their toll, Brennan asked for the check. As they walked to the car, Darlene remarked that she had never felt so high from one drink before. She apologized again saying,

"I'm sorry Father, I won't be very good company on the way back. I'm feeling very drunk and tired. I hope you don't mind if I sleep."

"No problem," he responded. "Sweet dreams."

As she drifted off she had a vague realization that she was being undressed, but at first dismissed it as the effect of the alcohol. But soon she realized, despite her mind fog, that something very disturbing was happening. She became aware that she was naked, and that someone was lying on top of her. His fingers were attempting to enter her, and she began to reflexively struggle to get him off. The drugs had done their dirty work though and she soon drifted off into oblivion.

When they arrived back home, Darlene was still only semi-conscious, so Brennan threw her over his shoulder and carried her into the house. It was late, so the Brandt family were all sleeping. No one in New London locked their doors so Brennan needed no help to enter the house. As he was going up the steps of the landing, he stumbled and almost fell. The leg he injured in his car accident was weak and made it difficult to carry Darlene. Luckily, none of the Brandt's, save one, awakened as Brennan lay Darlene onto her bed.

On his way out, he stuck his head into Darlene's sister Donnie's bedroom. She was the one who had awakened. When she saw Brennan, she pretended to be asleep. She was so intimidated by him, and priests in general, that she never questioned why he would be in their house. She never dared bring it up to her parents. It unnerved her however, so she told some of her friends. It became a part of the legend surrounding Brennan that had been building in New London. It was often repeated by Donnie's high school friends who were delighted at any story they could use to disparage "Big Dad."

When Darlene woke up the following morning she had only vague memories of the events of the previous evening. She felt depressed but could not understand why. She remembered she had been drinking, but one drink should not make her feel this way. Her depression gave way to anger with herself for not being able to figure out the source of her upset. She wondered what happened that she could not remember. She was sure it was something bad that had to do with Brennan. She promised herself that she would stay as far away from him as possible in the future.

Two months later her resolve was superseded by events that would change her life. She had missed her period, which mildly concerned her, but she had missed it on rare occasions in the past. But now she was beginning to feel nauseous and noticed she had gained some weight.

When she discussed it with her mother, she said, "It sounds like morning sickness. You haven't been sleeping with Roy Johnson, have you?"

Darlene said, "Mom, he has tried a few times, but I want to wait until we are married, plus, if I had sex with him and got pregnant, I'd never hear the end of it. You and dad would kill me and "Big Dad" would have a field day in religion class. No, I love Roy, but I have not slept with him. I don't know what's wrong with me, but I can't be pregnant."

"Well, then you better see the Doctor." Her mom responded.

When the nausea recurred almost every day for the next week, Darlene went to see Dr. Kreskas the town doctor. The minute she walked into his office he said,

"Your pregnant, I would recognize that look anywhere."

Darlene chuckled at the thought and said,

"Well, it must be the second Immaculate Conception, because I'm a virgin."

Dr. Kreskas looked at her skeptically, then proceeded with the exam. No physical problems were diagnosed, but the Doctor's suspicions were confirmed. He was sure she was not a virgin, but he told Darlene to wait for the results of her pregnancy test. His office would call her in a couple of days with the results.

Darlene was incensed when she walked out of Dr. Kreskas' office.

"He doesn't believe I'm a virgin," she said aloud.

How the hell could he say something like that? I don't care about his damn tests. The blood test will surely come back negative.

Then it hit her.

"Oh my god," she said aloud, "Is that what happened that night with Brennan? Did that bastard rape me? Please God, don't tell me I'm carrying his baby, I'll shoot myself."

In the end, when the blood test confirmed the pregnancy, Darlene was not surprised. Events had begun to restore her memory from that night. What was she going to do now? She promised herself that she would never tell Brennan and began reading articles about abortion. She could not envision herself having a priest's child. She was determined to rid herself of it. First, she had to tell her mother.

Her mother, Emilia, was a typical tough, but mild-mannered woman. The love she had for her children was of the ordinary kind. It was like most mothers. It was the kind that would move heaven and earth for them if she had the power. It was the kind that all mothers have inside. She became hysterical when she heard Darlene's suspicions. She was a convert to the Catholic Church and had never liked the condescending attitude that Brennan exhibited toward non-Catholics. Her ancestors were all Lutherans and she had always resented Brennan's condemnation of her daughter for dating a non-Catholic. The unbelievable hypocrisy she was now confronting confirmed all her past regrets for having turned Catholic. She called George and told him to meet her at the rectory. They were about to have a "come to Jesus" meeting with the pastor.

The Brandt's did not bother to knock when they arrived at the rectory. They barged into Brennan's office unannounced. What they saw profoundly changed the conversation they were about to have. Margaret Bryan was standing in the doorway to Brennan's bedroom in a flimsy night shirt. The bedroom door was open, and the Brandt's could see Brennan lying naked in the bed. There had been rumors about Brennan and Margaret Bryan for months but until Darlene's problem surfaced, they, like most of the people they knew, were not inclined to believe them.

George yelled at Margaret to get her cloths on and get out of the house.

"We have business with the Reverend," he exclaimed.

Brennan protested meekly, but George cut him off.

"You can just keep your mouth shut; we will be doing the talking," he said.

Few people dared talk to Brennan that way and he was rendered temporarily speechless. Margaret, who was devastatingly embarrassed, complied with George's demand to remove herself, and left quickly.

"You goddamn hypocritical low life," shouted George. "We came up here hoping we were wrong about what you did to Darlene. There is no longer any doubt about you. It's obvious that all the rumors we have been hearing are true. You raped my daughter you sonofabitch, and now she is pregnant. I'll see you put in prison if it's the last thing I ever do."

Brennan was scared and intimidated by the surprise confrontation and the only thing he could think of was to try to buy his way out of the situation.

"I've got money!" he pleaded, "I'll do whatever it takes to make things right if you keep quiet."

George looked at Emilia and saw that she had mixed feelings. She loved her children dearly, but their marriage had been rocky because George had failed in farming, and the residual debt they were left with, created stresses that neither was able to handle without a great deal of emotion. When they were forced to sell out, the money they received was not enough to pay off their debt. And they had unpaid taxes. The IRS had been hounding them for years leaving them only with the bare minimum to live on. It had not been easy. Brennan's obvious bribe caused them to retreat for a moment and reconsider their actions.

There was a prolonged period of silence before George spoke again.

"I have a past due tax bill that has been killing us financially, what are you willing to do to help?"

"I'll pay it off," Brennan replied.

"It's a significant amount of money," George responded.

"Don't worry, I guarantee you I have more than enough to pay it off," declared Brennan.

"We've been living hand to mouth for a long time, and there are few decent jobs for a failed farmer. You must know lots of people you could persuade to hire me," George suggested.

"Let me think about that for a while, said Brennan. I will see what I can do. Come back here after Mass on Sunday and we will talk more. In the meantime, I expect you to keep your mouth shut about what you saw here today. We will get this resolved."

By the time the Brandt's returned on Sunday, Brennan had a plan that he felt would resolve all their joint problems. The most pressing issue to him was Darlene's pregnancy. He thought it would be easy to convince the community that Roy Johnson was the father of Darlene's baby.

He needed to protect himself at all costs. He had narrowly escaped responsibility the last time he fathered a child. But that was before anyone had been spreading rumors about him, and it was such an outrageous situation that it was virtually certain that, if word had gotten out, it would have been dismissed out of hand. No one would have believed that a priest was capable of such a thing.

Things were different this time. Persistent rumors about his escapades had been around for several years now. A few in the community were beginning to believe them. The high school kids were spreading them nonstop. His surrogates were having a tough time suppressing them. At the last three meetings with his advisors, Floyd Sieger, and Paul Grower, Sieger had reported confrontations in the bar with people who were spreading rumors. One had resulted in a fist fight. Sieger and Grower were getting a bit concerned because these confrontations were beginning to affect their business. Sieger remarked that he was getting a little old to be an enforcer. The three of them had had a little chuckle over the last remark, but their concern that it was getting more difficult to protect Brennan was well founded.

It was critical that Brennan make sure that the Brandt scandal never saw the light of day. But, if it did, the Brandt's would be the most adamant in denying it. First, he needed to get the Johnson's and Brandt's to agree to a shotgun wedding. To get the Brandt's on board would be a simple matter of putting together financial arrangements that would solve their financial problems. He had three motels in the Dallas Fort Worth area and was having problems with his manager there. It would be a simple matter to replace him with George Brandt. It did not seem likely that George would decline if he made the job a part of a package in which he would pay off Brandt's debts at the bank and the IRS and give him a substantial salary as motel manager. It would be a take it or leave it proposition; all or none.

George and Emilia quickly agreed to the financial terms, but they were still concerned about their daughter. A quick marriage for Darlene was a nice thought, but getting the Johnson's to agree would not be easy. They liked Darlene, and Roy was obviously in love with her, but he was very hurt by what seemed like a betrayal by Darlene. Though he trusted her word that she had been raped, even he had a tough time believing that a Catholic priest was capable of such a thing. He wondered why she did not just call the cops. It would take many long conversations to convince him that it was likely that she had been drugged. Eventually he realized that the only way he was going to continue their relationship was to marry her. Once he was convinced that Darlene was a completely innocent party he agreed, and a date was set.

The Johnson's were more agreeable than their son had been. They loved the Brandt family and were willing to do everything possible to help. They were confident that Roy and Darlene were right for each other and were more than happy to help Darlene make a home for her baby.

As hoped, the community bought the entire charade. Having to get married was not very unusual even in these puritanical times. People were compassionate towards virtually everyone who did not live up to the strict standards. They inherently understood the human condition and made allowances for it.

Things did not play out entirely as Brennan had hoped. The wedding would be in the Lutheran Church. He was not invited to the celebration. He had hoped to perform the ceremony. Small town weddings were always public affairs and everybody's business. Being excluded hurt even the callous Brennan. Though he had, so far, taken little account of whose child Roy Johnson would be father to, he inexplicably thought it was his proper role to marry the couple. He was forced to reflect for the first time on how wrong this whole affair really was. He wondered why it was so easy for him to father a child, then walk away with almost no remorse.

"You are so pathetic."

This time the voice sounded like it had come over a loud speaker. It startled him and he almost lost control of his car as he was speeding down the main street of New London.

"God almighty, I could have had an accident."

"Do you not realize that if you had married that couple you would have compromised every principle you stand for? You get sentimental, and suddenly you lose control over everyone who has been cowering. Catholics should be punished for marrying protestants. This is a principle you have hammered home from the pulpit time after time. Get control of yourself. If you don't stay consistent, people will think you are weak and the rumors will become more persistent."

This is the price I pay for listening to you.

"You get plenty of return on your investment. Quit complaining."

Brennan could not afford to brood for long. He had important business to attend to. He and the Brandt's had to keep up appearances of being on good terms. It was important to keep them happy as they transitioned from New London to their new position in Dallas. He arranged to fly them to Dallas to see the facilities and arrange for housing. The Brandt's had never flown before. The new business arrangement got off to an exciting start.

Chapter 31

Revenge

I WILL GLADLY FINANCE....<u>IN FULL</u> FOR <u>ALL</u> OF THE INDIAN STUDENTS IF YOU PEOPLE WILL SEE THAT THE WHITES PAY THEIR SHARE OF WHAT IT COSTS TO OPERATE THE SCHOOL. MY VIEWS ON THE EDUCATION OF INDIANS HERE IS THAT WE ARE SUPPOSED TO BE MISSIONARY, and our school is one of the best ways of doing it. Their education has not cost the parish one cent so do not feel that you are supporting or educating Indians at a cost <u>to you</u>. It cost to educate them all right, but you are not paying the bill.

Sunday Bulletin July 9, 1972

"Hello, Sean, how are you? This is Joe."

It had been awhile since the brothers had talked. Sean Brennan was Joe's younger brother who had been working for the JW Marriot hotel chain and was in the midst of a successful career. He was the fortunate male child in the Brennan household. He was three years younger and had not come under the same pressures as the oldest, Joe, after his dad died. His childhood was more normal than Joe's - if the word normal can be used for a life of extreme poverty, living with a mother who had become unstable as the stresses of raising a family in a remote rural area with no money, no assets and little hope, proved nigh impossible. There were the normal pressures to enter the priesthood, but those waned when Joe went to the seminary.

Sean was allowed more autonomy in making career decisions from that point on. Instead of the pressures of a job at an early age, Sean became more the handy man around the house. He learned mechanics from his grandfather and was able to keep things in repair around the Brennan home and was very diligent in keeping things tidied up. Because he learned to make his own decisions at an early age, Sean developed a self confidence that put him in good stead as he entered the world of work. Thus, he rose quickly up the corporate ladder at JW Marriot.

Joe and Sean had sworn an oath to be there for one another – not to judge, to accept each other unconditionally. Growing up, they had cooked up get rich schemes together. But Joe had become like a permanent case of flu to him and was always a couple personal disasters away from catching it again. He had tried from time to time to distance himself for Joe's own good, but that proved to be impossible. Every time he had hit a bump in the road Joe had found a way to bail him out. His connections with important people in the Catholic Church had put him in the position to get the job at Marriot and elevate him through the ranks while he was proving himself. He was on a nice run and gave Joe all the credit. It happened that he had been offered a promotion to VP of Operations the previous day.

After hearing about his brother's good fortune, Joe said,

"This is quite a coincidence. I just liquidated the stock portfolio I've been bragging about the past few years. I want to go in another direction. Will you help me buy a string of motels?"

Sean, a bit shocked by the news, assumed that his new position would not allow the time for him to help.

"Geez Joe," Sean replied, "I was just about to write you about my new promotion. Boy, this is an inconvenient time for me. I am going to have to commit all my time to this new position; let me think about it and I will get back to you. But first tell me what you have in mind."

Joe explained his plan to copy a strategy that Joe Kennedy was implementing with his stock profits. He had been tipped off by Monsignor Ben Havok. Havok was in the Vatican a few weeks prior and had run into Kennedy while Kennedy was waiting for an audience with the pope. He was a personal friend of the pope and was there with his grandkids. Kennedy mentioned how much he appreciated the help he was getting from several of the Churches real estate specialists and said he was liquidating his oil stocks to ramp up a real estate portfolio. Havok was doing real estate deals in Los Angeles as well, so he scheduled a meeting with Kennedy to pick his brain on how he was making his buying decisions. It was after that meeting that Havok called Brennan to pass on the information.

"Wow," Sean said, I need to sleep on this. I'll call you tomorrow morning."

As he thought about it overnight, he realized that there may be opportunity he had not recognized at first. He was very happy at JW Marriot, but was having to spend increasingly long hours on the job as he moved up the corporate ladder. Growing up on the prairie and the wide-open spaces of SW North Dakota caused an ill-defined discontent within Sean. He had not realized how constrained he had felt in the rigid work environment of a large corporation. An opportunity to run his own business created an excitement he did not expect. Running his own operation would give him control of his time and the flexibility to enjoy life on his own terms. He decided to inquire further with Joe to understand the full scope of the project. He arranged a meeting with him at Marriot's facility at Disney Land, and was ready with a proposal of his own when the time arrived.

Before the meeting started, Sean laid a quickly prepared business plan on the table.

"Joe, the real estate market is absolutely booming in California, I would like to do more than just help you identify a few suitable properties. We could make a fortune in the hotel business if we approached things properly. We can start small and grow as big as we want. You've apparently got the money, and I have some expertise. We can do very well together. I've already sketched out a proposed business plan."

Joe was surprised by Sean's enthusiasm, and was excited by how aggressively he picked up on the idea. He had never let on about the true extent of his wealth, so Sean was going to be happy to hear that the opportunity was bigger than he imagined. Sean laid out his plan for a national effort to place motels in strategic locations throughout the country. They would start here in Disney Land. He had already found three properties that were on the market. The only question in his mind was, was the money to buy them available.

Joe smiled at the question. He assured Sean that they had the funding and suggested that the sooner they could get started, the quicker they could cash in. The next morning Sean called his boss at JW Marriot and gave his notice. The Brennan brothers were in the motel business. All went well as the acquisition phase proceeded. Within two years the portfolio included motels and hotels in Texas, and Colorado in addition to three motels at Disney Land.

*****

Sean proved to be a masterful managing partner. Joe, seldom called, but they saw each other often. Joe liked to bring girls from Perpetual Help

School to Disney Land as a reward for their commitment to a vocation to the convent. His wife Bridget, occasionally saw him enter the room with the girls. She wanted Sean to confront him about it, but he always assured her that Joe had a strongly held devotion to the Blessed Virgin and was simply meeting the girls to say a daily rosary.

*****

The call from Joe dismayed Sean. He was calling to inform him that they would be getting a new manager for their Dallas properties. Typically, all business decisions of this type were left to Sean. This was the first time that Joe had ever tried to mandate anything.

"What are you talking about?" Sean asked, "We have an excellent management team in Dallas."

"Sean, I have a family here in New London in distress. I've promised I'd help them and cannot back out. I'm sorry, but it is my money that is financing this operation and I am going to insist that we make this change. My credibility as pastor of Perpetual Help is at stake and I cannot risk losing my peoples respect."

Sean was adamantly opposed to allowing an unknown quantity to run three of his motels, but the reminder that Joe was supplying all the financing, forced him to reluctantly agree. He was agitated enough though, to constantly hassle Joe about his reasons for making such a decision. Joe never truthfully disclosed his rationale. He told Sean that the family was down and out due to the loss of their farm. He was just being compassionate in helping the best way he knew how. Sean knew Joe well enough to be suspicious of his explanation. But the man with the money usually got his way. He dearly hoped that the future of farming in New London would forever be profitable. He could not deal with too many more failed farmers as motel managers.

*****

From the beginning the Brandt family was ambivalent about the move to Dallas. Their family had always been in farming. Their ancestors had been a part of the German migration to the Odessa area of the Ukraine. They emigrated to the United States in the early 1900's and settled in North Dakota where the family operated a small farm that George ultimately inherited. Rural folks always ridiculed city life. They believed city people to be soft and lacking in the self-reliant qualities most admired by those who lived

~ 172 ~

off the land and on whose surplus city people depended. The term "city slicker" was often part of the bar talk in rural America when discussing those who fled the farm. Now the Brandt's would be city slickers too.

George and Emilia had long conversations before making the final decision to take Brennan up on his offer. They could not get over their anger at what had happened to their daughter. They felt a decision to take over the motels in Dallas was a compromise of the moral principles they had always assumed were shared by their pastor. They had always been good people, well regarded in the community, and now, because of their desperate financial circumstances they found themselves diminished in their own eyes. They felt an urge to get revenge, and they hated the feeling, but the fact that the injustice to their family had been done by a priest who was held in such high regard in the community, as well as by the Bishop, besieged them. They were embittered, and their consciences were confused. Right and wrong ceased to be black and white.

Revenge would be sweet and everlastingly profitable. The Brandt's had Brennan "by the balls" as was the common expression amongst the boys downtown when someone was up against a difficult problem. They would be unconstrained when handling motel money. Significant numbers of transactions were in cash. They did all the record keeping, so no one would really know how many rooms were occupied in a given night. Wasn't it Brennan's version of justice that was in play? Skimming cash was easily justified. Brennan might never know, but even if he found out, he would be desperate to keep his secrets. Father Joseph Brennan had met his match, and the ersatz life he had so carefully crafted was beginning to unravel.

When Sean discovered the Brandt's phony bookkeeping, and reported it to Joe, he just shrugged his shoulders and dismissed it as the actions of a family under great stress with needs with which they were unable to cope. He counseled giving them some time to resolve their financial matters and said that he would talk to them. However, he refused to take any further action. Because it was a new discovery and Sean thought Joe knew the Brandt's better than he did, he let him handle the situation.

As time went on, and the fraud continued, the official books began showing a loss. These had always been profitable entities and Sean found the situation to be increasingly unacceptable. This led to frequent confrontations. Sean no longer gave Joe the benefit of the doubt. He viewed the Brandt's as nothing more than common criminals and could not understand why Joe refused to prosecute them. As COO, much of Sean's income was affected by the profitability of each of the motels. The Brandt's were regularly taking money out of his pocket.

Sean remarked to his wife, "I didn't leave the security of the corporate world just to be defrauded by some hick farmer from North Dakota."

The relationship between Joe and Sean deteriorated till it became irreparable. Sean demanded that his interest in the enterprise be bought out. But, Sean was never satisfied with the settlement. While their separation was being negotiated, Sean had a heart attack. His family blamed the decline in Sean's health on the conflict with Joe. He never fully recovered and died before the separation could be completed. His family felt that they were cheated and sued to recover their losses. That law suit was fought vigorously by Joe whose money made it easy to pay the lawyers indefinitely. In the end, Sean's family received only a fraction of what they thought they were owed. Bridget's faith in the Catholic Church was destroyed. She could never again reconcile her experience with Joe, a revered priest, and a Church that allowed a person like him to serve.

The Brandt's did not stay in Dallas for long. They never could adjust to city life, and the yearning to return to their roots assured that they would eventually return to North Dakota. With their debts paid and the IRS off their backs, they were able to embezzle enough money to live comfortably the rest of their lives. Five years from the day they arrived in Dallas, they returned to their home in New London.

No one ever discovered the true story of their odyssey in Texas. Darlene's secret was less fortunate. Rumors about the real father of her first-born son soon leaked into the student body of Perpetual Help School. The kids delighted in the environment that gave them ammunition to use against their antagonist. The story was repeated so often that it became difficult to tell truth from fiction. It would eventually become instrumental in the demise of Brennan's control of Our Lady of Perpetual Help Parish and its people. No one ever heard if the rumor ever reached the ears of Brennan's child, Reid. All mention of Brennan, and any connection he had with the Brandt family, was avoided. When anyone dared suggest that there was a special relationship between them, they were informed plainly, that the subject was off limits, that whatever they had heard was all a lie, and that if they wanted to continue to be friends they were never to bring it up again.

Chapter 32

She's Legal Now

I AM NOT HAPPY WITH THE WAY OUR YOUNG HIGH SCHOOL BOYS AND GIRLS have kept the First Fridays, Perpetual Help Feast Day, Holy Communion on Sundays, Church support when I see the same ones have money for other things. THE PARENTS OBVIOUSLY DO NOT PUT MUCH PRESSURE ON THEM. The attitude of these many young people forces one to question what appreciation there is for the quality here in New London. I hear strong rumors that one of our big Catholic high schools might not open a year from now—ARE YOU YOUNG PEOPLE SO INDIFFERENT THAT YOU WILL LET IT HAPPEN HERE SOME DAY?

Sunday Bulletin July 16, 1972

There was a long pause as Therese finished the story of the Brandt Family. Frank was so angry at what he was hearing that his own faith was coming into question.

He thought to himself, *if this can take place without repercussion in the Catholic Church, how can it have any legitimacy in matters of faith? Have I been lied to all my life? Is the Church a sham? This story is bigger than anything I can write in a small-town newspaper. Someone needs to write a book.*

He asked Therese, "Have you thought about writing a book about this?"

"No," Therese answered, we have been interviewing many people in building a case against Brennan. I've pledged to some of them that I would never reveal what they told me. I'm afraid that a book would be a betrayal of confidence. I'll leave the book writing to someone else.

Have you had enough for today, or would you like me to continue?"

"How much more is there" asked Frank?

"Well, as Brennan himself said in one of our meetings with the Bishop, looking me directly in the eye; "there is a lot more. You think you are so smart, but you don't know the half of it.""

"So yes, there is more. We interviewed five women in the parish all who claim that they were preyed upon when they sought marriage counseling from Brennan. They were struggling in their marriages, very unhappy, and vulnerable. Every one of them slept with him. When thinking back, they found it hard to believe that they let it happen. None of them found him at all attractive but said that he had a way of creating sympathy for the plight of a celibate priest that made it seem okay. They all report the same thing. He convinced them that he could hear their confessions, and all would be well. He claimed that God gave his priests special graces so that, when they sinned, their service was their penance. The natural law that dictated sexual relationships applied to priests, but God understood that the urges were too strong for most priests to resist. He quoted scriptures that seemed to support his assertions. All the women bought into this. However, this is a small town. It didn't take long for their husbands to find out. Rumors got out into the wider community as well, but Brennan's minions stifled them. One incident stands out, and since it is already out in public view I am free to tell you about it. "

"Cliff Wentz was married to Ginny, one of the women I was talking about. Cliff was an alcoholic and spent a lot of time at the local pub. Once he got drunk, he was liable to say just about anything, and one night he was telling everyone who would listen, that his wife was sleeping with "Big Dad." Floyd Sieger was in the bar, and took exception to Cliff's drunken rant, and warned him to stop telling lies about Brennan. When Cliff told him to shove it, Sieger beat the daylights out of him. Some of the other guys in the bar had to pull him off for fear he would hurt him badly. Sieger is one of Brennan's enforcers. He keeps the wraps on all the rumors about Brennan. In any event, all five of the women are now divorced. Their families are in shambles.

Then we have the tragedy of Karen Helms. She was a good friend of my sister, Kaylee.

*****

"She's been cleaning your house for three years. She knows too much. She is beginning to be suspicious of much of the activity around here. You need to protect yourself."

It was 4 AM and Joe was being tormented by Bubby as he awakened on a pitch-dark Saturday morning in January. He clearly understood the implications of the message he was getting. Karen was of age now. He could not be accused of a crime, and she had seen things that if discovered by the wider community, would cause him significant grief. He had wanted to have sex with her ever since she began coming to the rectory every Saturday morning in her freshman year. He had masturbated at times to stop himself from attacking her. He did not want to be guilty of statutory rape. But now she was of age. If she feared exposing him, and felt too guilty to admit what had happened, there would be little threat of her telling about others. But more important than even the prodigious number of women whom he had subtly propositioned in her presence was how careless he had been about the cash he was embezzling from the parish. She saw substantial amounts of it lying around his office which she knew came from the Sunday offertory, but if she was listening at all attentively, she could have easily overheard conversations indicating that it was not all ending up in the parish bank account. His life was in such a frenzy all the time that he was often unable to make regular transfers to his Minneapolis broker. His faithful currier, Jack Bryan was no longer doing his dirty work.

He sometimes wanted to kick himself for getting into Margaret Bryan's pants. There had been so much turmoil when the relationship was discovered, that it would have been less of a hassle if he had just pursued satisfaction elsewhere, far from home. Karen was present more than once when he was in the bedroom with Margaret.

*****

Karen Helms was a boarding student from Plentywood Montana. She assumed her parents were making significant financial sacrifices to send her to Perpetual Help. Her brother Gary attracted Brennan's attention when he was on one of his frequent recruiting trips He always asked the locals about the best ballplayers in their towns. Everyone automatically trusted a priest and people were seldom aware of who he was, so they were more than happy to brag about the community's best athletes.

He was most interested in the eighth graders. The sooner he could get them to Perpetual Help, under the guidance of superior coaching, the better able they would be to help him achieve the state championship he was obsessed with. When he happened to stop in Plentywood, Montana to fill gas, he engaged the attendant in conversation who told him that the best athlete who had ever grown up there was an eighth grader at Plentywood Jr. High by the name of Gary Helms. Brennan made a mental note to call on his parents and decided to attend one of his games on his next trip through town.

Despite the significant distance Plentywood was from New London, Brennan was back in Plentywood by the next weekend. His efforts were rewarded. He saw a six foot-two-inch athlete who was only thirteen years old and had the ball handling skills of a point guard. His skills were remarkable for an athlete in small town Montana. He vowed to get him to Perpetual Help.

The effort proved to be more difficult than expected. Gary's parents owned one of the local taverns and were not Church going types. When a man wearing a roman collar walked into their bar one morning they were automatically suspicious that he was another new priest in town coming to lecture them about responsibilities they had to help their customers avoid, what they always called, "the occasion of sin." Priests were always trying to offload responsibility for the bad habits of their flock on the bar owners in town.

This encounter was different though. Brennan began by complimenting them on the skills their young son showed on the basketball court.

"Your son is the best eighth grade athlete I have ever seen."

He very bluntly made it clear that he would do anything to get them to send him to Perpetual Help.

"It would be a shame if his talent was wasted because he lacked good coaching."

The Helm's response was not what he hoped for. They looked at him incredulously and said,

"Who the hell are you to come barging in here and suggesting we send our kid off to school four hours away from home. It'll be a cold day in hell before we do something like that. Why would he be better off in New London than playing ball in his home town where everybody knows him and who frankly, already treat him like a hero?"

"Our Lady of Perpetual Help School is positioned to play in the state tournament every year, and your son will get exposure to college recruiters. That will be much less likely if he stays in Plentywood. He will also get an outstanding education and be prepared to succeed academically as well as athletically in college."

He also appealed to their egos by suggesting that Gary looked like he could be even better in football and that there would be no better place to display his skills than in a place that had given Don Earnhardt his start in coaching.

"You are no doubt aware," he said, "that Earnhardt is now the very successful head coach of the North Dakota State Bison who got his start in coaching at Perpetual Help."

They knew nothing about Earnhardt, but Brennan continued,

"We are committed to maintaining the best coaching staff in the state of North Dakota. Our current head coach in both football and basketball is someone I am sure you have heard of. Jack Bryan may be the best high school coach to ever come out of Montana. He is currently at Perpetual Help and is doing an outstanding job developing our programs. Your son will thrive under his guidance."

"We can't afford to send our kids to a private school!"

"I will take both of your kids and you won't get a bill. I've got resources to handle tough situations like yours, and your daughter can do some housework for me in lieu of tuition."

"I don't get why you are all on fire about my kids, "said Mrs. Helms, "Why are your athletic programs so important that you have to pay for an athlete's education under the table? You can't run a school without revenue that's for sure, and isn't recruiting illegal? You make an attractive offer, but we want our kids at home."

"Mrs. Helms" Brennan replied, "We are a Catholic institution. I may talk a lot about sports, but the bottom line is, we are doing God's work. We are preparing the next generation to live honorable and holy lives for His greater honor and glory. Efforts to stop us from recruiting are anti-Catholic and morally wrong. I will make my offer even better. If Gary does not get an athletic scholarship to play ball in college, I will pay for his college education, and your daughters too."

The Helms impressed by the zeal of a man whom they had never met, and who had appeared out of nowhere proposing to take their children from them at a time when they were enjoying them the most. But the prospect of free education all the way through college was very difficult to pass up. They refused to make an immediate decision but told Brennan they would talk it over and let him know.

When school started in the fall the Helm's children were enrolled at Our Lady of Perpetual Help.

Although Karen Helms was an afterthought in the negotiations to recruit her brother, Brennan secretly thought of her as his coup de grace. For nine months of the year for the next four years she would be cleaning his office every Saturday. She was an adorable, bright, and cheerful young girl. Her shape already had the beginnings of womanhood. She was still a child, who seldom displayed her delicate side and kept her natural smile under lock and key. Her eyes, which peaked through bangs of chestnut brown hair, were the color of a blazing emerald green. Her smile was warm with a hint of shyness.

It won't be easy keeping the boys away from her, he thought.

Whenever he had time to talk with her he would caution her that boys would desire her with impure hearts. His copy of "A Portrait of the Artist as a Young Man" was a handy reference when he was at a loss for new ways to instill the kind of fear in her that would motivate her to keep them at bay. He would play mind games with her by periodically quoting from "A Portrait" while purporting to give her spiritual counseling.

Karen never questioned Brennan's "teachings" and became a reliable helper and something of a confidant. She filled a key role. He was always in need of information about the kids' social activities that would enable him to keep control. Knowing what questions to ask when disciplining a student always kept them off guard and was an easy way to intimidate an adolescent. Knowing who was dating whom, how often they were together, who was bringing alcohol into the dorm, who was bootlegging alcohol to minors, where the parties were held every weekend, and more, is how he maintained discipline. Karen became a reliable snitch and he occasionally rewarded her with one of the rolls of cash that often laid around his office.

He resisted his almost constant felt need for sex with her. The demon "Bubby" helped. Every time he looked at her with carnal desire, Bubby would manifest as severe headache pain and Brennan would hear a faint but audible,

"Stop it you fool"

Both were aware of her value as a tool, but more important, she was underage. He was never held to account for manipulating dozens of young women into sexual relations with him, but he was always aware of the possibility that the system he had built to protect himself was not perfect. The last thing he needed was a charge of statutory rape.

*****

Things were different now though. Karen was of age and she was privy to some of his efforts to get her contemporaries into bed with him. "Bubby" was now on his case every day, urging him to sleep with her, and reminding him that his empire could come crumbling down if she came forward as a witness when someone he had abused brought charges against him. Once she had slept with him "Bubby" assured him that she would be too vulnerable to go public and support charges made by others. As with every one of his conquests, Brennan agonized over the temptation, but he could never resist "Bubby" for long. Karen would be his next victim.

When she arrived for her regular Saturday visit, she found the door open just enough that it appeared to be latched, but when she knocked, it swung open enough for her to hear him yell to come in. As she stepped into the house he called out to her from his bedroom,

"I want to show you something."

When she walked into the bedroom she found him lying naked on his bed smiling broadly. She turned on her heels and fled the room, but he threatened her.

"It's time for you to pay for that college education I promised your parents."

He ordered her back into the room. While her instincts told her to run and never come back, she realized that if she alienated Brennan her dream of a college education would evaporate. Her parent's business had declined significantly. The farm economy that sustained Plentywood was in a prolonged depression and her father's tavern had suffered along with the other businesses in town. He would never be able to afford to pay for her college education. Her brother had been fortunate. He was as good an athlete as forecast and was in college on an athletic scholarship. She was not so lucky. There were no girls' sports at Perpetual Help.

Despite the panic that overwhelmed her, she knew that others had survived a similar ordeal.

How bad could it be, she thought. *Is it really any different than all the guys who pressured me for sex?*

This time she had no choice. She could think of only one thing that might get him to back off.

"Father," she said, "what you are asking me to do is wrong. You know better than anyone that we would be committing a mortal sin."

His sly smile was followed by his stock answer,

"Don't forget, Karen, I am a priest, I can forgive your sins. God has ordained me and empowered me to forgive sins. In confession I don't say God pardons you, I say, I absolve you. You can have your college paid for and absolution for your sin. I have that power."

He then got up, grabbed her by the hand, and led her into the bedroom. When she felt his erect penis she began to tremble. He then slowly began to unbutton her blouse and remove her bra. He pushed her on to the bed, removed her panties and lay next to her. He grabbed her hand and forced her to caress him.

All the while she moaned quietly, "no Father, please Father no."

Her moans were muffled as he rolled on top of her and forced himself into her. When it was over she was too shocked to cry. As she lay there in a daze she heard what she had heard so often during confession,

"In nomine Patris et Filii et Spiritus Sancti."

Her sin would be forgiven, but she would never forgive herself.

Karen stayed at the Hunter home on the weekends. Her best friend in New London was Kaylee Hunter and the Hunters had graciously asked her to stay with them. They had eight children of their own, but the older ones were off to college, so there was plenty of room for guests. When she arrived at the Hunter residence on the afternoon of that fateful day Kaylee took one look at her and said,

"Oh my God, what happened to you?" Karen uncharacteristically snapped back at her, "Leave me alone, I'm fine."

"Did he do something to you?"

"Please, Kaylee. I'm fine, I don't want to talk about it."

Like every one of his victims she blamed herself. She carried her shame throughout her life. It affected all her future relationships with men and helped destroy her marriage.

*****

"Karen later confided in Kaylee and told her the full story. When Kaylee told her mother, she adamantly forbid her to repeat such "nonsense.""

"Mom was so conflicted. I told her everything I learned about Brennan, but she always refused to believe it. She didn't want to have to choose between her brothers and me. Plus, she thought all priests were saints. It will be really hard for her when all the charges are proven"

"But you haven't heard the sickest story of all."

Chapter 33

Reward for Religious Vocations

<u>FOOTBALL</u>: High School students are up and down and psychology plays a greater part in coaching than most people think. If you are not up for each game, you are subject to defeat by almost anyone. We lost at New Salem Friday night 26-20. We did not look good in beating Belfield last week. We lacked much that goes to make a good team, but from reading papers and listening to people the players thought they were better than they really were so the New Salem defeat will (I hope) get the team down to facing reality and work now to win the conference. I really think our football team is living in a dream world. I hope it does not take another defeat to bring them out of it. One should be enough.

Sunday Bulletin September 10, 1972

Anne beamed with pride as she walked across the stage to receive her diploma, Father Brennan had just announced that she would be entering the Notre Dame convent in the fall. He also announced, as was his practice, that she would be receiving an all-expense paid trip to Disney Land as reward for dedicating her life to God's service. He would be providing the transportation and be the chaperone. As usual, the applause for her and others with a vocation was extra loud. Anne's parents were showered with congratulations. It was a night filled with pride in their daughter, and thanks for the blessings God had granted them.

Anne Mandarich was the oldest of six children who grew up on a farm near New London. She had always been a very shy girl who wanted to be around people, and connect with them, but just did not know how. Her family was ethnic German where children were to be "seen and not heard."

When she was a young child she used to hide behind her mother whenever she was in the presence of strangers. When she went to school, she held back, wanting to talk to the other kids but not knowing what to say or how to say it. As a result, she found it difficult to get to know them. In class the teacher had to drag every word out of her.

As a teenager she kept to a few good friends and used them to shield herself much the same as she had with her mother when she was young. She let her friends do the talking in social situations and blushed furiously if a boy she was interested in entered the same room as her.

Her shyness would plague her throughout her school years. The girls from town tended to be more outgoing and therefore got most of the attention from both teachers, and more important, the boys. She was pretty enough, but lacked the self-confidence to stand out. She graduated from high school without ever having been asked out on a date.

Without the distractions that most teenage girls struggle with when fully engaged in the affairs of the heart, Anne spent a lot of her free time alone, often hiking the prairie and contemplating a love that came from a higher place; elevated above any love she felt from humankind. She felt called to service by the God she knew mostly from her religion class. She loved the nuns who taught her and who had become her role models. Her favorite class was religion, though she wished they spent more time talking about the love of Jesus than all the rules that were hard for even a committed Catholic like her to obey.

Father Brennan intimidated her as much as the kids who were breaking all the rules, but she saw something more important in him that came out only rarely, and required certain heightened sensitivity to notice. He portrayed a genuine love for the Blessed Virgin and a commitment to service that showed only rarely and for brief periods. Others never seemed to believe this side of him.

Because she had voiced her desire to become a nun during her sophomore year, she was privileged to meet privately with him regularly for spiritual direction. His love of the Virgin Mary was especially clear in these meetings, but she always left with a feeling of foreboding she did not understand. He sometimes let slip a fear of Satan that tormented him. At these times he would appear depressed, and the absolute control he typically projected would disappear. He would become more human, and this is when Anne would feel most attracted to him. However, he would always recover quickly as if he was embarrassed by his temporary vulnerability. Anne often wondered what was really troubling him.

Because she saw this side of him, Anne had a much more positive impression of Brennan. When he spent entire religion classes disciplining students for perceived bad behavior, she tuned him out. She wondered why Brennan spent so much time talking about Satan and temptations and mortal sin. Her reading of the Catechism made her much more positive about the Church. While explanations of things to avoid were a prominent part of it, she saw a much more hopeful message in the seven gifts of the Holy Ghost, the twelve fruits of the Holy Ghost, the eight beatitudes, and the moral virtues of prudence, justice, fortitude, and temperance. So much of what she read pointed to all the reasons that she should avoid condemning or judging Brennan like most of the other students. She developed a respect and trust for him that most found hard to countenance.

She looked forward with great anticipation to spending time with him as they traveled to Disneyland in his brand-new Chrysler. She had never been out of the state of North Dakota. The prospect of seeing a big part of the West excited her.

*****

Las Vegas! I never thought I would get to see Las Vegas, thought Anne as they dropped down from the Spring Mountains into the city.

They had pushed hard to get there on the first day. Brennan wanted Anne to see sights she would never see again once she took her final vows. They arrived at dusk having not stopped to eat since before noon. When they pulled up to the restaurant, Anne wondered if he was lost. The structure before them was palatial. She had never seen anything like it even in pictures. As he got out of the car, Brennan assured her that they were in the right place,

"But," he said, "this place will charge more than I carry in my wallet."

He opened the trunk of the car. Anne was shocked to see grocery bags full of cash. Without comment, he grabbed a roll of the cash and turned toward the entrance to the restaurant saying,

"This ought to do it. You are about to have the dining experience of your life."

This simple farm girl was indeed impressed. Brennan encouraged her to eat whatever she wanted. Since she had never seen a menu like this before, she had no idea what to order.

Brennan said, "Order the rib-eye steak. It's the house specialty. It will be nothing like the steak you've eaten at home. Order it a little rare. It's better that way."

It was difficult for Anne to enjoy her meal despite the fact she had never tasted anything quite so good. She was so in awe of her surroundings and overtaken with excitement, she started to wonder if she should rethink her vocation. Did she really want to deny herself the experience of things she previously had no idea existed? Life was looking much more exciting away from the farm.

Maybe I should reconsider my decision, she thought. The idea passed soon enough, but the wonderment persisted.

Instead of continuing to their hotel upon leaving the restaurant, they took a walk down The Strip. She was awed by the bright lights and the crowds of people scurrying along to get to she knew not where. Every step was a new experience.

"Where are they all going in such a hurry?" she asked.

"Some are hurrying to get to their favorite casino, some are going to a show. I'll take you to one of the shows before we leave. They are just excellent entertainment."

She wondered why Brennan seemed so tolerant of the gambling, a behavior he always condemned as mortal sin. The neon lights and billboards with near naked girls advertising the nightly shows scandalized her but did not seem to faze Brennan. She wondered if Brennan was really the person she thought he was. The bright lights seemed to change him. It concerned her a little. She was naïve but not stupid. Something about this new version of Father Brennan dismayed her. She let go of her fears though, because this might be the one and only travel adventure of her life and she dearly wanted to make the most of it.

When they reached their hotel, Brennan showed Anne to her room.

"It's the Landmark," he said. "Las Vegas' newest"

It was one of the most luxurious in the whole United States. Her room was huge and was not what she had envisioned at all. It reminded her of the hotel where Audrey Hepburn stayed in "Breakfast at Tiffany's." The bed was king-sized with pure white, Egyptian cotton sheets. She had a sprawling leather sofa, and, on the other side of the floor-to-ceiling windows was her own private terrace. And the bathroom! Along with the power shower, there was a bath tub big enough for a football team, and a Jacuzzi. Everything in marble and handcrafted tiles. The millionaire suite.

"What? This can't be for me!"

"Anne, you deserve a room like this. You are giving up a lot because of your vocation. Enjoy it while you can."

Then he bid her good night.

Alone for the first time in a hotel room, she dallied to absorb the newness and excitement. She walked to the window and stared out at all the glories of Las Vegas. As she turned to ready herself for bed, she noticed a man with a severe limp walking across the street and entering a building plastered with signs of scantily clad girls.

She wondered, *is that Father Brennan?*

The unsettling feelings she had earlier returned. She decided to find someone who could tell her more about what really went on in Las Vegas. She found the concierge in the hotel lobby and asked about the place she thought she had seen Brennan enter. They told her that it was a strip club and a brothel. That confused her. She had never heard either of these terms before. When the concierge explained to her what went on there she decided that she must have misidentified the person she thought was Brennan. She went back to her room and went to bed, but she could not sleep. She wanted to believe that the man had not been Father Brennan, but her intuition told her otherwise.

The rest of the trip was uneventful. Anne was much quieter on the final leg of the trip to Disneyland. They arrived in the late evening and again stopped at an expensive restaurant. As before, Brennan opened his trunk and removed a roll of cash. After the experience of the night before, Anne felt less intimidated by Brennan and decided to ask,

"Father where did all that money come from?"

Brennan completely dismissed the question and told her brusquely, "Anne, there are some things you never ask about; that is none of your business."

Anne got a sense of how others felt when he bullied them in religion class. This was the "Big Dad" everyone feared. She thought that being a "good girl" all these years would have sheltered her from Brennan's wrath. She was finding that her initial discomfort with this new Brennan was proving to be prescient. She was beginning to be afraid of him.

Chapter 34

"It's OK I Will Give You Absolution"

He called Father Sipe, Father Bryan, and the sisters that left the school, liars. He said they had no proof to back up their accusations. He also said there were accusations made that he was having affairs with several different women at the same time.

-Transcript of Brennan's talk to Junior and Senior Religion Class –

May 18, 1971

Anne was expecting the knock on the door. They were going home the next day and they had been saying the rosary every evening together just before retiring. When she heard, "it's me," she was already opening the door. The minute she saw him, the ugly feeling she had first experienced when she thought she saw him entering the brothel, returned as it had whenever she knew she would be alone with him. She loved the Virgin Mary and prayed the rosary religiously but praying with Brennan had become an unpleasant experience.

Devotion to the Blessed Virgin was his most prominent spiritual admonition. He conducted weekly services in honor of Our Lady of Perpetual Help and encouraged his people in the Sunday bulletins and sermons to attend regularly. When he got frustrated at often low attendance, he would admonish them in the bulletin as well. Sometimes he would display an annoying sarcasm castigating them for asking for gifts from God while not honoring Jesus' mother. On her feast days he would schedule special devotions and hours of prayer and assign families to pray during specific hours of the day. He chose the families that modeled devotion to Mary to their children, and who made sure they attended daily Mass and Perpetual Help devotions. He sarcastically feigned to not want to burden the majority who were less committed, and intimated that they were failing in their parental duties. He always scheduled in an hour of prayer for himself as well to make sure that people knew how much he too revered the Blessed Virgin. When he led the rosary, Brennan made sure that his devotion was unmistakable. There would be long pauses in the Hail Mary to show special reverence by not rushing through the prayer. People were impressed by his professed love of the Virgin Mary.

His real aim, though, was quite different. Behind closed doors he used the mother of Jesus to gain access to women and young girls. The invitation to say the rosary before retiring for the evening was his classic ploy. At the end of the rosary, he asked for a period of quiet reflection. While Anne sat on the edge of her bed, eyes closed, meditating on her prayer period, Brennan gently positioned himself next to her, quietly whispering to her how much Mary loved her and placing his hand on her thigh in what seemed at first to project a fatherly touch intended to reinforce and deepen her devotion.

Anne opened her eyes when she felt Brennan's touch. Without warning Brennan's tone began to change from one of spiritual direction to a pitiable pleading for understanding of the sacrifices that he was making as a priest. Anne recoiled as she sensed danger in his tone of voice.

She wondered, *why is he telling me these things?*

Then his hand began to move up her leg and he asked her to think about how difficult it was to live a life of celibacy.

He said to her, "God has made man and women attractive to each other in ways that will assure the permanent propagation of the human species, yet the Church asks its priests to ignore the natural urgings that actually fulfill this purpose. I have worked hard to maintain a school so that you could have the finest of educations and have given you special honors in recognizing your vocation to the convent. Now I am spending my own money to reward you for that decision. Will you show me a little mercy? Give me pleasure. It won't really be wrong. You will just be giving back to the person who has done so much for you, and you will be helping relieve a burden imposed on me by my vows. I know that I have preached over and over that what I am asking of you is a mortal sin. Priests use every means to control the baser natures of their flock. If the Church did not try to constrain sexual activity outside of marriage, there would be no limit to the doctrines they would question. Pleasure so often overwhelms common sense. But sex is a very natural and necessary part of being human, and I am most definitely human. I will not hurt you and you will benefit from the experience. You will experience the very act about which you will someday counsel your students. You will be able to better empathize with their emerging sexual natures. As God's ordained minister I will give you absolution and forgive your sin. I have all power in Heaven and on earth. Those who listen to me, listen to God. As a nun, you will learn the importance of rightly elevating the image of the priest. That which seeks to magnify the image of the priest magnifies the image of the whole Church. I will also make sure that your mother house never wants for financial support. I will make a gift in your name as a token of my appreciation. And remember, just make an act of perfect contrition and you will be forgiven of all sin."

As she heard these words, Anne became disoriented. She could not think clearly. His pleadings were hypocritical, and she realized why she was feeling so uncomfortable around him. Her entire value system was under attack from the very priest who had helped form those values.

She thought, *I can't do this. I've pledged myself to lifelong virginity. My model is the Blessed Virgin. He is the person who counseled me that this would be a grace filled decision.*

"Why are you asking me to do this Father?" she pleaded, "no please, this is wrong. Please don't ask me to do this."

Panic set in as he ignored her pleading. He began ripping at the buttons on her dress then pulled off her panties. She began to scream, but he put his hand over her mouth and she feared he would suffocate her. He was too strong, and the only way to avoid physical injury was to cease fighting. As she became limply resigned to her fate, her mind became so confused and tormented she wondered if it was all a dream. This man could not be acting out this way. He was her confessor after all. Her parents thought he was a saint and God's direct representative. This could not be happening.

Then she remembered the rumors.

"Oh my God," she shouted as he forcibly entered her, "you are Satan himself!"

When it was over, but for her shoes and socks, she lay naked on the bed weeping softly, sickened as she heard the words

"In nomine Patris et Filii et Spiritus sancti."

He was preparing to hear her confession. This re-energized her and she shouted,

"No, get out."

~ 192 ~

She kicked at him as hard as she was able, and screamed, "get out of my room," over and over until Brennan, fearing the commotion would cause someone to call for help, left the room.

As soon as he was gone Anne picked up the phone to call her parents. Her mother answered and was shocked by the story that Anne blurted into the phone. She refused to believe it. It was more than she could absorb given her love for the priesthood.

This was completely out of character for the man who she considered to be a Godly man. She had heard the rumors about him but dismissed them out of hand. To hear this from her daughter distressed her, and she shouted at Anne to stop.

"What is wrong with you Anne? Why are you lying to me about Father Brennan? He has done so much for you. He is devoted to the Blessed Virgin. He has put Perpetual Help on the map. We are the envy of the diocese. What has come over you?"

Anne retorted, "Mother listen to me. He did these things to me. I have never lied to you. I will not drive home with this animal. You have to come and get me."

"Anne," her mother snapped, "we cannot possibly drive to California at this time of the year. The fields need tilling and your father is working 16-hour days."

Anne insisted that her mom call her dad to the phone. She told him the same story and pleaded with him to come get her. She got a different response from him. His fatherly instincts triggered fears he had harbored for a long time. Many of his friends believed the rumors about Brennan's abuse. He trusted their judgments in virtually every interaction they had with each other except for their opinions about Brennan. Hearing this from his daughter sent up a red flag.

Maybe the guys had been right all along, he thought.

"Anne," he said, "I will arrange for you to fly home. I believe you. I've always believed that the rumors about him were farfetched, but I will not trust him over my own daughter. Give me his room number. I will order him to stay away from you. You tell me if he tries anything. I will call the police if necessary. I will call you back and tell you how you will be getting home."

The plane ride home was the first ever for Anne. The thrill was wrecked by the trauma of her experience with Brennan. She spent many sleepless nights blaming herself and wondering if she really had a vocation to the convent. She thought that people should know who Brennan really was, but her faithfulness to the Church and fear of public shame prevented her from telling anyone about her experience.

As time passed she became increasingly conflicted. She even began to question her faith. But in the end, she decided that she needed to stick to her decision to enter the convent. She hoped that immersing herself in the religious life would enable her to sort out her conflicts.

*****

Frank leaned back in his chair, gulped down his third cup of coffee and sighed,

"Wow, this is mind blowing. I started out to write a story about a priest whom I believed to be a superstar; an accomplished leader and administrator, and you are telling a tale of the most immoral and likely criminal behavior I have ever heard. I'm not sure that I can even write the story now. I will need documentation. Without the cooperation of the Bishop I'm afraid that facts will be difficult to substantiate. It would make for a great novel though. I assume you aren't finished yet."

"You may have to come back tomorrow," joked Therese, "but let me go on."

Anne's story would stay in the family until Father Tim Bryan contacted her a year after she entered the convent. Father Bryan was the assistant pastor at Perpetual Help her senior year in high school. After the incident with Brennan, her father had approached Father Bryan to get counseling regarding his daughter's rape by Brennan. He asked that the seal of confession apply to the conversation and Bryan had granted his request. Now, however, Bryan was leading an effort to have Brennan removed as pastor of Our Lady of Perpetual Help and was asking that he be defrocked. He went to Mr. Mandarich and got permission to use the information he received in the, now year old, counseling session.

After getting permission from her father he asked her for an affidavit he could present to the Bishop. Anne at first refused to get involved. She had informed her Mother Superior about her experience when she entered the convent. She was told to let it go for the good of the Church, and to offer it up for those who needed the strength to deal with their own difficult circumstances. Anne agreed, but she never felt certain she had done the right thing. It caused her to re-consider her vocation. After asking for guidance from the Blessed Virgin, she decided to submit the affidavit. When she was informed Bishop Whacker was considering the removal of Brennan, she reluctantly left the convent.

As shocking as Anne Mandarich's story was, it was only the beginning. During her stay in the convent, she discovered that five other Perpetual Help graduates had the same experience. All of them stayed in the convent and eventually took final vows. They would go on to long careers teaching in Notre Dame schools. Three of the five claimed that they were drugged when they had intercourse with him, and that they were barely aware of it at the time. All had the same experience when they told their parents. They refused to believe a priest could do such a thing and said that they must have been hallucinating. When they related their experiences to the Mother Superior, she gave them the same advice. Remain silent for the greater good of the Church.

Had the problem with Brennan been confined to a few candidates to the convent, it is likely no outsider would have ever discovered the truth. Anne's affidavit would have never seen the light of day. But, in addition to the easy, unsophisticated, immature, and naïve targets amongst graduating seniors, he was so sex obsessed that he could not avoid higher risk targets. When candidates left the convent to resume a secular life, he called on them, took them out to dinner, and tried to talk them out of leaving the convent. After dinner he would invite them to his motel room to say the rosary. Some of them fell for the ploy and became victims. Some were on to him and refused. Still his perpetrations were kept concealed. Until, that is, he scored with members of his teaching staff.

He had an uncanny ability to identify the young nuns who were still unsure of their decision to stay in the convent. These tended to be the best looking of the group. When he found one that seemed vulnerable he targeted her.

Chapter 35

Rebellion at the Mother House

There is a rumor that he was having affairs with several different women at the same time. Also, a rumor said that he was making a play for three upper class girls that year, and that he carried on at least one affair with a past graduate. He then stated, "Who are the lucky ones?"

-Transcript of Brennan's talk to Junior and Senior Religion Class –

May 18, 1971

We can no longer sit back and allow this man to disgrace The School Sisters of Notre Dame, thought Mother Superior.

Sister Margaret Ann had been chosen Mother Superior only three weeks prior, amongst a virtual rebellion of the young nuns. Notre Dame nuns had anchored the teaching staff at Our Lady of Perpetual Help School for over fifty years. Many of the existing members of the community were graduates of the school. The relationship had always been harmonious with both sides benefitting.

However, beginning in 1965 the rumors about Father Joseph Brennan began to reach the Mother House. At first, they were dismissed as the typical rumor mongering that occurs in every small town. Father Brennan's integrity had never been questioned, and he was noted for being an outstanding administrator and a very successful superintendent. It was not unusual for successful pastors to generate resentment in their communities. They often had to step on a few toes to maintain a high-quality institution.

Some students did not measure up to standards, and their parents were sometimes upset when their children were disciplined or expelled. Others in the community objected to the frequent harangues from the pulpit about money. Rumors about the pastor could sometimes impact opinions about the institutions they ran and would be used to influence a change in direction. As a result, the nuns tended to ignore them.

There was also the need to protect the Church. The nuns, more than most in the clerical class, understood that men were especially human when it came to sexual matters. They were especially aware of the admonition that circulated among the priests themselves about making sure if they were going to stray they should do so at least 500 miles from home. So, when they heard of a priest who succumbed to his male imperfections, they tended to be very forgiving. It was more important to protect the image of the priest and the Church.

When Sister Margaret Ann was first confronted by one of her postulants with a claim of sexual assault by Brennan, she was not naïve; she knew that this sometimes happened, but she never expected to have to deal with the kind of charges that were being levelled at Brennan.

She grew up in a small town in Central Minnesota that was virtually 100% Catholic. Her parents ran a hardware store and depended on the prosperity of the local farmers for their survival. Both parents were raised in strict Catholic families and were dedicated supporters of the pastor. He was a well-liked and generous man who loved to play whist over a couple of beers and was a frequent guest in their home. No one ever had a bad word to say about him. Growing up, Sister Margaret Ann thought most priests were just like him.

She was dumbfounded as she listened to the story of Sharon Miller, one of the members of the community who had attended Our Lady of Perpetual Help school. Sharon told of the reward trip she had received from Brennan, who she instinctively called "Big Dad", the summer before entering the convent. She claimed he seduced her with alcohol and stories of woe and rigors of the celibate life. He claimed she would be doing God's work by relieving him of the stress he encountered by abstaining from sex. She recounted that he claimed the power to grant forgiveness by an immediate confession and that having the experience of intercourse would hold her in good stead as she worked with girls who were confronting their first demands for sex. She said she consented because she believed that, being his representative on earth, he spoke with authority from God himself. She was only vaguely aware at the time of the hypocrisy inherent in what he was asking. Plus, she was drunk for the first time.

She never considered revealing her secret before because she was embarrassed by her behavior and desperately wanted to avoid exposure. She had only recently become fully aware of the significance of what had happened to her and felt a need to discuss it. The nightmares she was having were a motivating factor as well. She assumed they were the normal result of having done something that violated her conscience. But she did not understand the full psychological impact of what he did to her.

Finally, she said, "and there are at least five others."

When she finished telling her story there was a prolonged period of silence. The new Mother Superior had expected many challenges in leading a community of nuns, but she was unprepared for a situation like this. Then Sharon dropped a second bomb.

"I'm pretty sure two of the sisters currently serving in New London are having affairs with him at the present time."

Horrified, Sister Margaret Ann dismissed Sharon with a wave of her hand, saying,

"Please leave. We'll talk again later."

Before Sharon was out the door Sister Margaret Ann was on the phone to her bishop in Winona.

"Bishop Watters?" This is Sister Margaret Ann at Good Counsel."

After a few pleasantries she continued,

"We have a severe problem at our school in New London, ND that I feel unqualified to handle. I need your help."

After hearing her story, the Bishop admonished her saying,

"Sister Margaret Ann, you must keep this to yourself until I can think it through and consult with the Vatican. I will also call Bishop Whacker in Bismarck to see what he knows about this. If this gets out, the Church could be severely damaged. It is critical that the Church be protected. At the same time, we must see that this evil doing stops at once."

Bishop Watters' conversation with Bishop Whacker confused him.

He asserted, "Everything you have been told is a lie. Father Brennan is not only a good and holy man, but he is my most outstanding school administrator. He has done more to advance the mission of the Church than any of my pastors. Sister Margaret Ann has a lot to learn as a new Mother

Superior, and she should be more skeptical of rumors regardless of their source."

Bishop Watters had no reason to mistrust Whacker, so the conversation ended on that note. He notified Sister Margaret Ann and asked her to inform her sisters that Bishop Whacker had thoroughly investigated these matters and found them to be false. He had no further advice for her.

In the meantime, all hell was breaking loose in the convent at Our Lady of Perpetual Help Parish. The two nuns who had been sleeping with Brennan were guilt ridden. They tried to break off their relationship, and he did not take it well. He berated them angrily and threatened to inform the Mother Superior that he had caught them sleeping with high school boys. He demanded that they continue their relationship lest he ruin their reputations.

If Brennan thought that his response was going to end the problem, he seriously underestimated the nuns. He had been successful for 20 years in stifling the rumors about his predations. His allies in the parish had successfully limited the rumors, but this time those threatening to speak out were nuns. They could not be easily dismissed as Brennan haters. When the word came down from Good Counsel Hill that nothing was going to be done about Brennan because Bishop Whacker was accusing the nuns of lying, to a person, the nuns said they would refuse to return the next school year. They demanded a meeting with Sister Margaret Ann to air the truth and demand the removal of Brennan as a condition of their return to Perpetual Help.

Mother Superior was dismayed that an entire group of nuns were willing to violate their vow of obedience in a cause where she was told there was no offense. But she had no choice but to address the problem. She hopped on the train and traveled to New London for the conference the nuns were demanding. The meeting resulted in a total reversal of Sister Margaret Ann's attitude about conditions at Perpetual Help. There was near unanimity about the concerns that were expressed, and she was forced to act.

The next phone call she made to Bishop Whacker was a bitter exchange with Whacker continuing to defend Brennan and Margaret Ann taking exception to the inference that her nuns must be lying. She informed Whacker that unless he did something about Brennan, the School Sisters of Notre Dame would be ending their relationship with Our Lady of Perpetual Help Parish.

Chapter 36

Wearying of the Battle

Father Brennan also said that Sister Mary Kevin signed a two page affidavit that said he enticed her twice. But, he said, the facts were that she had been griping to him about the system and he told her that if she didn't like it, why in the hell doesn't she quit. She said she still wanted to get her Masters, and he told her that she could borrow money, and if nothing else worked, she could borrow the money from him.

-Transcript of Brennan's talk to Junior and Senior Religion Class –

May 18, 1971

"So, amid all the clear success at Perpetual Help there is a rebellion among the nuns," sighed Frank.

"Yes," answered Therese. "We are hoping it will force the Bishops hand and finally enable us to rid ourselves of the "Big Dad.""

"But you indicated earlier that Brennan declared that there was much more. What else do you know?"

"We have the testimony from the five families whose marriages were broken up because the wives fell for Brennan's line. These are the people to whom I've pledged confidentiality. We suspect he violated several high school girls, but these are only rumors. I doubt if they can be verified. I recommend that you talk to more of the kids. They may be able to lead you to the victims. I suspect also that Brennan was referring to activities away from home. He spends considerable time away from New London. Who knows what goes on when he is on his trips."

"Given the fact that Brennan is still running Perpetual Help, I assume the Bishop has not been all that receptive to your attempts to get him removed. Tell me how that has played out."

Therese's response was punctuated with a hardy guffaw.

"This process has become a complete joke. The Bishop has resisted us every step of the way. At first, we were mystified at his unwillingness to help us. It seems almost uncatholic, if that's a word. Why would a Bishop ignore a problem of this magnitude and risk the bad publicity that could result? We got our answer a couple of weeks after our first meeting with Whacker. The clergy tightly controls information about their members, but apparently someone is trying to help us covertly. Word leaked out that Bishop Whacker is a homosexual and that Brennan is threatening to expose him if he tries to remove him from Perpetual Help. Brennan walked into his office unannounced one day and caught him in the act with one of his assistants. It's kind of a hysterical visual to say the least, but if true, it explains everything. At any rate the process has been painful."

"Good lord!" Frank responded.

Therese continued with a litany of meetings and obfuscations and delays. She showed Frank some of the letters the group had received from the Bishop that documented his long effort to keep the critics at bay.

First, he tried to intimidate the group by requiring testimony under oath. Someone had told him that this would cause them to back off since none of them had personally experienced any of the immoral behavior. When the members of the group held their next meeting they unanimously agreed that the advice had come from Brennan himself. It was obvious that Whacker wanted to keep information as close to the vest as possible and was unlikely to allow word of the controversy to get out into the broader clergy group. He could not risk exposure of his homosexuality. When they expressed how absurd the whole idea of testimony under oath was, he tried to shut down any further investigation. They were prepared to bring some of the victims along to future meetings, but Whacker would have nothing to do with it.

Next, they asked to get Brennan evaluated by a psychologist. They declared that no priest in his right mind could conduct himself in such an outrageous manner. He had to be mentally ill. Whacker seized the idea and offered to have Brennan evaluated. He suspected that he could get a positive endorsement of his excellent mental health if the therapist was a practicing Catholic. Despite a very unsatisfactory few meetings with Brennan and the abrupt ending of the sessions, Dr. Walter Drake was a Catholic and agreed to spin the report in any way Bishop Whacker wanted. He hoped this would end the affair.

He was right about the first part. A positive report in hand, Brennan bragged in the Sunday Bulletin,

"After having doctors put me through tests, etc., they wrote to the Bishop and told him that they could find nothing wrong with me mentally and that I needed no treatment. Either Mayo Clinic is behind the local experts or far ahead of them, but it is not with them. Thus, I have another document to display in the due process of educational life."

He was wrong however about the persistence of the "rebel" group. They refused to quit and the scandal at the Notre Dame Convent reinvigorated their effort.

The rebellion of the young nuns was what triggered the threat to remove them from Perpetual Help. They felt empowered by their success in getting Margaret Ann to address the abuses. Seven of them refused to return to New London after Christmas vacation in 1971. This left a vacuum in the teaching staff that caused great consternation among the parents. It also fed the narrative that the so called "rebels" were trying to destroy the school and triggered the threatening letters that Frank had read earlier.

"One can imagine the smirk on Brennan's face when his minions agreed to write the letters," Therese said with a chuckle.

The nuns had been the bedrock underlying the success of Perpetual Help School. The prospect of operating without them pushed Brennan over the edge. He began seriously considering resigning. It was his money that was supporting the music and sports departments. Personally, funding significant numbers of lay teachers was not a part of his bargain with the devil. He was becoming weary of the battle. Then the Bishop received the affidavit from Anne Mandarich. He ordered Brennan to come to the Chancery at once.

*****

"Good Council Hill is already in revolt and now I get this," Whacker shouted as he handed the affidavit to Brennan.

There was a long pause as Brennan read it, then he looked up and said,

"So, what, what's the big deal? Am I the first of your priests to have strayed? What about the skeletons in your own closet? I've built an educational institution that is highly regarded by educators all over the state. Most of them are jealous, in fact. You should hear how they talk every time we beat them in sports. I've contributed my own money to support programs and recruit the best coaches in the state. So, I have a strong sexual appetite. Am I so different than other priests? I'm just more persuasive, and therefore get more opportunities. Look at John Kennedy. He was out there banging every good-looking woman who dared smile at him. No one seemed to care, and he was president of the United States. I'm just a small-town pastor who works for peanuts and happens to run the best school in the diocese."

There was a long silence while Whacker mulled what he had just heard. He feared that his homosexuality would be exposed. His weakness was now being used to justify multiple sinful acts, and he did not feel he had the moral authority to act. He knew that he was going to have to take a stand because this case was about to be blown wide open and would get out into the press if action was not taken.

So, he said to Brennan, "Joe, if I thought for a minute that my other priests were acting out in their communities like you are, I would resign as Bishop. My priests are mostly good men trying their best to serve their communities as God's representatives. Most them have stayed loyal to their vows and are worthy of their people's respect and admiration. You have let your ability go to your head."

"Somehow you seem to have amassed a fortune, and you are using it to build an empire and justify your immorality. I have great concerns about where all that money came from. I fear that you have not been honest with me about financial matters. I've ignored it only because your school is so important to the work of the Church, and of course, because of that unfortunate incident that you witnessed in my office the day you so rudely barged in unannounced."

"I have no doubt that you will follow through on your threat to expose me if I try to discipline you. So, here is what I propose. Please give it serious thought. I will give you a year to wrap up your affairs at Perpetual Help. During that time, you prepare your people for your resignation. You can claim fatigue after twenty years of demanding work. Use your diabetes as rationale for resigning as well. I know that you have been living in constant pain since your accident. Surely you can communicate that to make your people understand why you must leave. Joe, the bottom line is, my hands are tied. If the nuns escalate their grievances up to the Vatican, or this affair gets blown up in the press, we will have an unmitigated disaster on our hands."

"You must leave Perpetual Help. Give serious thought to leaving the priesthood. Your lifestyle is not conducive to serving in the clergy. The psychologists suspect you might be a sex addict. If true, you will need long term therapy. I'm guessing you are not going to cooperate, so if you refuse, I will strongly consider defrocking you."

Brennan protested mildly before saying that he would consider resigning but warned Whacker not to get his hopes up. As he walked out the door, he looked over his shoulder and said,

"Don't push me too hard or I will let the word out about you. The whole diocese will go down in flames with me."

Chapter 37

What to Do?

He said that Coach Thomas signed an affidavit that Father Brennan caused his divorce. He had the priest that married Coach Thomas investigate and he found that Father Brennan had nothing to do with it. He (Father Brennan) also said that Coach Thomas called Dan North, next years music teacher, and told him what an immoral man Father Brennan was, and told him he should look for another job.

-Transcript of Brennan's talk to Junior and Senior Religion Class –

May 18, 1971

"Therese, I appreciate the time you've spent with me. I'm not sure what I am going to do with this story. I would like to follow up with the various assistant pastors who have served here during the Brennan reign. I will seek a meeting with Bishop Whacker as well. He is right about one thing. If I publish this story, the church will get hurt. I have to evaluate the right of the people to know versus the potential damage to the church. I am very disturbed by how the image of the priest, and the way people grant automatic respect and authority to men who often do not deserve either, has worked to enable grossly abusive behavior. I also wonder how much of this I would find if I broadened my mission."

Frank left the Koch residence with a heavy heart. When he got to his car he sat for over an hour before he drove away. He reflected about the implication of the events he planned to publicize. The Catholic Church was a powerful institution. Given what he had just heard, it was clear to him that they would go to great lengths to protect it. They might even try to destroy him. More likely, they would confront the victims and try to destroy their credibility. Some of them were, in a sick sort of way, preprogrammed to allow Brennan to take advantage of them. Many have parents who will fight to prevent their children from doing harm to Brennan or the Church.

He wondered if it was even justifiable to go public with a story that would inevitably dig up old hurts and cause families to suffer needlessly. He decided that it was too early to decide. He would call on the assistant pastors to see what he could learn from them, and then confront the Bishop.

He was curious about what he could learn if he offered not to publish the story in exchange for a frank discussion with Whacker. Maybe he could persuade him that these situations could be prevented in the future if they were made public now. Maybe they could have a conversation about how the Bishop himself felt about being put on a pedestal that was impossible to live up to. He doubted all of this, but there was only one way to satisfy himself and that was to follow through to the bitter end.

He would start with Father Kenny Kahl who appeared to be the first to report Brennan's predations to the Bishop. Our Lady of Perpetual Help was his first assignment after his ordination.

*****

They called him Father Kenny because he never put on airs like most other priests. He always thought the image of the priest was over glorified and the humanity that he projected never fit the gilded image of priest as venerable, incorruptible, saintly, or Godlike. He was devout in his faith and set a good example to his flock. He was the opposite of Joe Brennan as clerics go. He was happy go lucky and sought the friendship of his people. He was a rock in the troubled times of his parish, and principled in his teaching and in guiding his charges in the demands of the Church. His concern for everyone was genuine, and he always took the trouble to ask how you and your family were whenever you met. He was raised in a strict German family and felt strongly about his view of right and wrong. He was a tough disciplinarian if you crossed him, but quick to forgive and eager to restore comity to any relationship. He did not take himself too seriously, but he was rigidly compliant about the vows he took as a priest.

He was furious when he discovered that the man who had been chosen to be his mentor was nothing more than a serial abuser of women. The abused were all good Catholics who went to confession regularly. They chose Father Kahl as their confessor to avoid contact with Brennan. Virtually every one of them blamed themselves for what had happened. They assumed it was their sin and they must confess it. When he first heard their stories, Kenny was overcome with doubt. This was not the image of the priest he had grown up

~ 206 ~

with, and it certainly was not the type of person he aspired to be. At first, he wondered about the veracity of what he was hearing. Soon however, the magnitude of the information led him to approach Bishop Whacker to see if he would address the problem. His initial conversation was hindered because of the source of the information. He could not be specific for fear of violating the seal of confession. Whacker told him that if there were no specifics he could not act. Further, he warned Kenny that publicizing information of this kind would be very unwise. It would unleash forces that would rapidly get out of control. The Church itself would become the primary victim. He told Kenny that unless the evidence was overwhelming, and reliable witnesses came forward with testimony directed to him personally, he could do nothing.

Father Kenny left the Bishop's office completely unsatisfied. He went back to New London determined to get permission from the victims to discuss their situation with the Bishop. He always tried to avoid identifying those whose confession he was hearing, because he did not want what he heard to influence his regular relationship with them. He found more than two dozen victims. Most refused to meet with him, but he was able to talk with several, and their stories were depressing and disturbing. Judy was a 30-year-old mother of three who lived with an abusive husband. Helen was married to a local businessman who worked hard and seldom came home before ten at night. He often had alcohol on his breath and was sometimes stumbling drunk. They had eight children. Veronica was a high school senior. She had been disciplined several times during her high school years for partying and she had a steady boyfriend that lived in another community. Brennan was pressing her to break off the relationship and had persuaded the Postmaster to stop delivering the love letters he was sending her. All of them blamed themselves.

Father Kenny compiled this information and went back to the Bishop. The reaction he got was not what he expected. Whacker angrily dismissed him after scolding him and communicating how much he regretted that he had not been more forceful about the importance of protecting the Church. Kenny was given the impression that in fact, sexual sin among the clergy was not all that rare, and was to be expected given the fallen nature of man.

His parting words were, "we are all human and the celibate life is often too difficult for the weakest among us. Do not judge your fellow priests; you may be the next to fail. And, finally, never approach me about this again."

Father Kenny Kahl took his vow of obedience seriously. He never approached the Bishop about such matters again. He did discuss them with his contemporaries though. With few exceptions, most supported the Bishop.

Frank was impressed by Father Kenny. He saw him as the epitome of what a Catholic priest should be. They had a mutual interest in sports and their time together was both productive and fun. However, as he left their meeting, he could not help but be less than sympathetic with Kahl's rigid compliance with his vow of obedience. Not exposing the kind of activity engaged in by Joe Brennan felt as sinful as the scandalous behavior itself. He felt he had made a new friend but left more disturbed about the situation than ever.

*****

It was less than a hundred miles between Raleigh, where he had met with Kahl and Amidon where he would meet with Father John O'Grady, so Frank had scheduled both meetings on the same day. The North Dakota highways were straight and narrow and had very little traffic. He once measured the time between meeting other cars when it dawned on him that he had not met a single car for a long time. He timed the next interval. It was twenty minutes, so he was not too concerned about driving a little above the speed limit. There was little chance that there would be any law enforcement with so little traffic. It would not take very long to go the 100 miles.

Father O'Grady was congenial and friendly. He graciously welcomed Frank as he arrived in Amidon. He was under the impression that Frank was writing a complimentary article about Our Lady of Perpetual Help School and was eager to sing its praises.

Everybody loved Father O'Grady, and his famously Irish sense of humor. But despite that, he seemed to lack confidence in himself. He had a nervous laugh that arose whenever he was confronted with anything uncomfortable. When he discovered the real reason for Frank's visit, the nervous laugh manifest as a device he used to cover disappointingly evasive behavior.

While he acknowledged that all was not well with the pastor of Our Lady of Perpetual Help, he was not willing to discuss any of the things that he knew. O'Grady was a good man, but a true believer. Like the Bishop, he was as inclined to defend the Church more than anything else. He encouraged Frank to write a complimentary article and to stay away from scandal. He thought nothing good could come from exposing Brennan.

As he left Amidon, Nash felt uncharacteristically depressed. He was a traditional Catholic himself, and his belief system was being challenged by an attitude among the clergy that did not represent what he had always assumed to be the basic message of Jesus,

"Love one another as I have loved you."

How did any of these priests truly manifest God's love by hiding activities that were destroying lives; especially young lives? He would be meeting with Father Gus Williams in Dickinson the next day. He hoped he would be able to leave that meeting a little more hopeful.

*****

Nash's hope that the Williams interview would be more encouraging was dashed just a few minutes into the meeting. Father Williams was a very large, balding, jovial guy. He was incapable of hurting an insect. His sense of humor enabled him to keep students engaged. Religion classes were much more fun when he was the instructor. They saw him as a push over compared to Brennan, so his classes were sometimes a bit chaotic.

He was angry with the Bishop and disenchanted with the Church for hiding Brennan's activities. He characterized them as borderline criminal. The meeting started with Nash laying out what he knew about Brennan.

Before he could finish, Williams interrupted him saying,

"This isn't even the worst of it. My immediate predecessor was the dorm prefect for four years. He had special boyfriends and he sexually abused them. When a few of the football players rose up and tried to stop him, they were summarily dismissed from school. When I confronted Brennan, he didn't even try to hide what happened.

He said, "I was helpless to do anything about it. He knew that I had skeletons in my closet and threatened to expose me from the pulpit if I interfered with him. He said it was just sex. There is no sin confessed as often by the mothers and fathers of these boys. What did it hurt? He was just a human being with a weakness that was common among men, and other priests as well. There was no real harm done. These boys were just getting early sex education. It might even help them eventually. I frankly couldn't argue with him."

Father Williams face was bright red with anger. He continued by telling Frank about his next meeting with the Bishop which was a repeat of what Frank had heard from Kahl. He added that these events were seriously affecting his faith, and that it was likely that he would be leaving the priesthood, and probably the Church as well. He said he was confident that God had not created a Church that enabled power hungry abusive priests to destroy families and he was going to find a Church that taught God as love. He felt that was the only way to change people's lives for the better and the world too for that matter.

Chapter 38

The Church Must Be Protected

Father Brennan also said an old rumor had been revived that he had an affair with Brenda Baumgartner and he heard that she had signed an affidavit. He said he called her and she just laughed. One of the trustees was listening in and after they hung up he agreed to sign an affidavit about the conversation. Then the trustee went down to the boy's dorm and called Father Bryan a "god-damn hypocrite.

-Transcript of Brennan's talk to Junior and Senior Religion Class –

May 18, 1971

As he walked up the steps of the chancery in Bismarck, Frank took note of the majesty and splendor in which Bishop Whacker lived.

I wonder what happened to the poverty of spirit that Jesus preached, he thought.

Was it not almost impossible for someone to live amongst such opulence and remain poor in spirit? He supposed that some could, but he was highly doubtful that Whacker was one of them.

As he walked into the front door of the Chancery he could not help marveling at the gorgeous architecture. It was built with large blocks of white Concord granite and featured a massive freestanding Corinthian portico in front of a magnificent dome. Inside in the large foyer stood a replica of the Pieta, a work of Renaissance sculpture by Michelangelo, that is housed in St. Peter's Basilica.

How do they finance these places, he wondered? *The maintenance costs alone must be backbreaking. Maybe they used Brennan's investment genius to support the budget.*

As he stood admiring his surroundings a receptionist approached him to ask if she could help. He mentioned his appointment with the Bishop and was escorted into the waiting area outside his office. The Bishop had a busy schedule on this particular day and would have preferred not meeting with someone from the press. He had intentionally scheduled meetings close to each other, and true to form, they ran together. One of his staff people was waiting to see him so he was ushered in ahead of Frank. The wait irritated Frank. He feared it would be followed by a request to state his business quickly so that Whacker could get on with more important business. After a thirty-minute wait he was greeted by the Bishop.

"This will have to be quick; I have a noon luncheon that I cannot be late for."

Frank reacted by blurting out a bit angrily,

"You might want to rethink your schedule. I am about to publish an expose on Father Joe Brennan that will shake the Church at its very foundation."

Whacker was taken by surprise and said nothing for what seemed like an eternity. Finally, he said,

"I assume you have examined your conscience over this. Printing scandal about the Catholic Church is a serious issue. You will be judged without sympathy for any unproven allegations made by any of Brennan's enemies. I advise you to proceed with care."

"Your Excellency, I set out to write a complimentary article about a man who I considered a genius and one of the best leaders I had ever met. I thought what he had accomplished at Our Lady of Perpetual Help was worthy of spreading to a wider, even nationwide, audience. I interviewed him hoping to tell our readers how a man from a small town, with a simple background as a Catholic priest, had accomplishments that would be a model to anyone who sought excellence in all that they do. My interview with him was not what I had expected. I was disturbed by references he made to wealth that seemed extremely excessive for a man of such simple background. He also referred to interactions with certain young people that seemed unusual for a priest. I decide to ask around the community if others knew anything about such things. What I found out is one of the most disturbing experiences of my life. I'm told that assistant pastors, and members of his parish, have asked you to look into certain allegations, and that you have resisted. What can you tell me about these matters?"

"Mr. Nash, these are not issues that I can discuss outside of the presence of a select group of advisors and my superiors in the Church. I suggest that these are issues you must trust that we will handle in the best interests of the Church and the flock that we serve."

Frank was beginning to realize that being respectful and deferential was not going to work with this man.

"Sir," he responded, dropping the Excellency, a term of respect he was suddenly doubtful he deserved,

"You don't seem to understand. I am unsure whether the Church deserves any deference. We are dealing with a man who is, arguably, a criminal and who has fathered children and manipulated their families to hide his paternity. He has divided and destroyed families. He has accumulated wealth beyond anything that a normal investor with limited funds, working in a small parish, in a small town, in a remote part of North Dakota, could honestly achieve. He has traveled with trunk loads of cash and is suspected of dealing drugs. He has abused his position by taking advantage of candidates for the convent and somehow convincing them to sleep with him in hotels, that he owns, under the guise of rewarding them for their decision to become nuns."

Bishop Whacker, there is much, much more and you are telling me that this is an internal matter and people should trust you. I am sorry sir, but that is simply wrong. If you are going to refuse to answer my questions, then you are right, this will be a short meeting, but trust me this is not the end of the story. I will not stop until the entire world knows what happened in New London. I will find evidence of this man's crimes and see that he is arrested and prosecuted. We will let the public decide what is best for your Church."

Bishop Whacker was stunned and could only respond with a request for Frank to remove himself from his presence at once.

As he walked out the door, Whacker yelled after him, "I am not devoid of resources that could totally discredit anything you write and destroy both you and your newspaper."

Frank was so upset he found it difficult to resist giving the arrogant prelate the finger, but he contented himself by muttering a "fuck you" and slamming the door behind him. *Ok*, he said to himself, *I guess we go ahead and publish.*

*****

"Doris, get Joe Brennan on the phone at once," Whacker yelled into the intercom to his administrative assistant, "then call The Congregation of Bishops at the Vatican and set up a telephone meeting with Cardinal Lovelace ASAP."

The Bishop never expected the situation in New London to escalate to this level. For centuries bishops had been masters of their own flocks. There had been many complaints in the past from parishioners about misconduct on the part of their pastors. In every case he had been able keep the lid on scandal. He depended on the conscience of every Catholic to understand that they would be in direct opposition to the will of God if they pursued charges against a priest. Under the pain of mortal sin, they were to trust the internal processes the Church prescribed for these types of things. He had a stock answer whenever confronted by these issues. It was St. Jean Marie Baptiste Vianney's statement about priests that credits them with everything considered holy.

"If there was no such thing as the Sacrament of Holy Orders, we would not have Our Lord.... After God, the priest is everything."

Virtually anyone who had entered his office with complaints against a priest could be thwarted by this defense. When it seemed not to make the desired impression, he would insinuate that attacking a priest was a mortal sin. This usually ended the discussion, and Whacker would deal with his priest in his own way.

Whacker never resorted to requesting help from the Vatican. He was proud of this. Pope Pius XII had even singled him out for praise at a recent Synod. So, this was a stressful development indeed.

Chapter 39

Manning the Ramparts

Father Brennan said that if the troublemakers in Amidon and the small handful in New London would quit like the Bishop told them they would keep out of things that were none of their business. Father Brennan said that Father Sipe called in the Amidon people to tell them these lies.

-Transcript of Brennan's talk to Junior And Senior Religion Class –

May 18, 1971

When Brennan walked out of his Monday morning religion class he was agitated by the lack of feedback he had gotten about his Sunday sermon. This class of seniors were the most rebellious he had worked with in his 19 years at Our Lady of Perpetual Help. The previous Saturday night he had seen Carl Hunter and Sheila Kronk together again as he drove up main street at midnight. He was angry over the defiance the two showed despite being suspended from school three times for going steady. It angered him even more that they had waved at him like he was their best friend or something. He was surprised that Sheila still had an interest in Hunter after their sexual encounter. He was, in fact jealous; something he had not felt before. He made a mental note to find a way to retaliate against Hunter.

Not a single student could summarize his Sunday sermon. He had preached about his concern that students were acting out in defiance of school rules and had admonished parents to be more forceful in controlling their children. He accused them of being complicit in the mortal sins their children were committing at parties, and in the back seats of cars late at night, when they should be home in bed.

Students were losing their fear of him. He wondered if it was time for him to let someone else run Perpetual Help School. He had spent the previous 18 months preparing his supporters to operate without him. Most of his building projects were complete. He had successfully persuaded the sports enthusiasts to form a booster club which was now generating enough revenue to offset what he had been funding from his own resources. He had hired a band instructor and funded the band program himself until a band booster club was able to take up the slack. His popularity was at an all-time high because of the state championship in basketball and the continued excellence on the football field. He had lost outstanding coaches and been able to replace them with even better ones. If he walked out now though, he was sure that the school would struggle to survive.

In addition, his brother had died suddenly, and he had no backup to run his growing hotel empire. It would be the right time for him to cut a deal with the Bishop and allow himself a graceful exit from the pressure the rebels were bringing to bear.

When he got to the rectory he was met by Margaret Bryan. She had decided to surprise him with a prepared lunch as an excuse to spend some time with him. His love making the night before had been a bit frenetic and she hoped that they could talk through whatever seemed to be bothering him. But first, she told Brennan that the Bishop had called and left an urgent message and that he needed to call him back right away.

"You're Excellency."

Brennan always began with the formal greeting of Whacker. The Bishop took his position very seriously and his large ego always needed to be considered when dealing with him.

"What can I do for you today?"

Whacker recounted his meeting with Frank Nash and told Brennan that he was so concerned about the negative publicity that he was going to consult with the Vatican about the matter.

He asked Brennan to consider resigning at once if it was the only thing that could prevent public disclosure. Then he ordered him to keep his schedule flexible because he was going to meet with Father Bryan and the Perpetual Help parishioners who were harassing him. "You must be at that meeting," he demanded.

*****

Frank Nash was drained from his activities in New London and his confrontation with Whacker. When the phone rang, the day after he returned home, he had been taking a rare nap and his brain was a little foggy when he first heard Whacker's greeting. He was not ready for another confrontation, so he was happy when he heard Whacker say,

"Mr. Nash, I beg of you to hold off on the article you are planning to publish. I am going to meet with a group of Perpetual Help people and am consulting with the Vatican over what my options might be. I will call you as soon as I decide what to do."

Unable to confidently evaluate what he had just heard, Frank asked if he could call back in a few minutes to give him some time to get his composure. When he hung up, a sense of excitement overtook him, and he shouted, "halleluiah."

He called Therese Koch before getting back to the Bishop.

"Therese, thank goodness you are home. I just got a call from Bishop Whacker. I went to visit him yesterday and left the meeting about as angry as I've ever been. I told him I was going to publish my article about the New London scandal and he dismissed me out of hand. But, I just got a phone call from him asking me to delay publication and that he was requesting a meeting with the New London people and that he had been in touch with the Vatican about Brennan. Have you heard anything yet?"

Therese had heard nothing, but was elated that the Bishop was ready to deal seriously with the Brennan problem. Since she was the leader of the so-called rebels, she assured Frank that she would make sure to invite all the relevant people, and thanked Frank for the heads up. She then called Father Bryan to make sure that he would keep his calendar clear for the meeting with the Bishop.

He surprised her when he showed a lack of enthusiasm for such a meeting.

"What is your concern," she asked.

"I know Bishop Whacker, and he has something up his sleeve. We had better be sure we know exactly who will be attending the meeting. He is obviously very afraid of Nash's article, but he will not go down without a fight. His mission is to protect the Church, and he sees protecting his priests as part of that mission. He will try his damnedest to keep Brennan in place. We must be well prepared if we hope to achieve anything."

When Therese received the call from the Bishop's office, Bryan's concerns were confirmed. He asked her to bring any of the Perpetual Help dissidents who wanted to attend, and that Father Bryan and Frank Nash would be there, but when she asked for a list of the other attendees she was stonewalled.

"Bishop Whacker asks that you give him the benefit of the doubt and trust that he will do the right thing," the assistant said.

Therese vigorously objected, but she was told that the meeting was going to be held according to the wishes of Bishop Whacker or it would not be held at all. Therese reluctantly backed down and agreed to attend. When she next talked with Frank and Father Bryan they both recommended that she make certain that her group came ready to support every one of their accusations. They feared that Whacker would use the meeting to intimidate them into backing down.

When Therese walked into the meeting at the appointed time, the Bishop was at the head of his conference table. Next to him were Father Joe Brennan, Floyd Sieger, Cleo Sieger, Paul Grower, and the Papal Nuncio to the United States, Cardinal Lovelace.

Therese respectfully greeted them as she remarked to herself,

Good lord, I cannot believe this.

Accompanying Therese were Dan Thomas, Ricky Bryan, Brenda Baumgartner, Norman Black, and five of the women in New London who had lost their families because of their dalliance with Brennan. The Whacker contingency looked at each other sensing that they were in for a far different meeting than they expected.

"Bishop Whacker, it appears that you called this meeting for the express purpose of intimidating us into backing off from the charges we are making against Father Brennan. Why else would you keep the identity of participants secret? Now I walk into a meeting and who do I see sitting at the table with you but two of my own flesh and blood. We see each other almost every day. They are my mother's brothers. So far, we have been able to respectfully disagree about Father Brennan, and now you put us in a position where conflict could permanently divide us. Your Excellency, what you are trying to do is unchristian. Father Brennan is a sex obsessed abuser and we are here today to prove it."

With that she reached into her purse and pulled out a letter from Anne Mandarich, tossed it onto the table and said,

"Here, we can start with this."

Anne was leaving the convent. The psychological trauma she endured had ruined her commitment to serve God in a special way. She was now struggling with her faith and was even doubting the existence of God. Sister Margaret Ann would not let her pursue action against Brennan so long as she was a postulate. She felt that the entire incident had been so unjust that God would not allow it. She had called Therese from Mankato and informed her that she would be writing an affidavit telling about her experience. Therese asked for a copy.

Whacker was now staring apprehensively at Anne's story. There was no hope to keep it confidential. Cardinal Lovelace asked to read it.

When finished he looked at Therese and her contingent and said, "This is indeed disturbing, but we simply cannot expose something like this to the public. It would fundamentally damage the Church."

Along with the others, Ricky Bryan had been sitting silently holding back the wrath that was engulfing him, but when he heard Lovelace imply that Brennan's actions should still be secret, he exploded.

"You people are fucking nuts. This puke destroyed my father and alienated my brothers and sisters from each other. He has held my mother hostage as his mistress for eight years. He sees her whenever he goes to Billings. He is the evilest bastard I have ever known."

"Cardinal Lovelace, do you realize that this man and my mother conspired to put my dad in a mental institution, so they could live their life of sin together without any interference?"

Ricky's outburst enraged Floyd Sieger who got up from the table and lunged at Ricky. He had to be restrained by Cleo.

Cleo yelled at him, "what in the devil is wrong with you? This isn't the Golden West Bar for crying out loud. Get hold of yourself!"

Silence engulfed the room. The outburst shocked everyone. Therese was the first to speak.

"Bishop Whacker, do you see the extent of the problem? The rest of his victims feel just as strongly. You must remove him from Our Lady of Perpetual Help. You may think you can shove this under the rug, but you cannot control this man. He will continue to perpetrate his abuse as long as he has the power of the church and the priesthood behind him."

Cardinal Lovelace could see that Whacker no longer had any credibility with the aggrieved group, so he motioned to him to let him take control.

"Mr. Bryan," he said, "I understand that you are angry, but there is a much larger issue before us than the grievances of a small group of people."

Before he could finish Therese interrupted him to assure him that if they had brought all of Brennan's victims to the meeting they would have needed an auditorium to hold them.

"Surely Mrs. Koch that is a gross exaggeration, but none the less, let me emphasize that the wider issues I speak of, take precedence over the actions of any individual member of the clergy. False accusations will be met by excommunication. The evidence must be clear and convincing. We will brook no vague charges, so each one of you here must have compelling evidence to support your allegations. I will personally see to the excommunication of anyone who tries to smear Father Brennan without clear and convincing evidence. Priests are God's instruments. False charges against them are a mortal sin that will not be absolved until retracted, and damages repaired. Each one of you here risks condemnation to hell. The Sieger's and Mr. Grower are prominent members of your parish and the wider New London community. They do not believe these charges. Your burden of proof will be heavy indeed."

Frank Nash could not hold himself back any longer.

He slammed his fist on the table and shouted, "You speak of excommunicating victims but seek to protect the perpetrator. What charges are you talking about? You have ignored the victims and have not asked about their charges against Brennan. How could you have any idea if the charges are credible if you have not heard what they are? It is obvious that you seek first to intimidate the victims with threats of excommunication and eternal damnation. I think you want them to shut up and go home. Your Excellency, understand that if you refuse to hold Father Joseph Brennan to account, I will write the story of your lifetime, and trust me, it will be published internationally in every secular journal I can think of. Maybe you should hear these people out."

Floyd Sieger looked at him with scorn.

He muttered, "You dirty son-of-a-bitch!" Then threatened, "You come to us talking about writing a laudatory piece about Perpetual Help and deceive us into supporting your effort. I'll see that you are fired. I'll be damned if I will let you get rich and famous at our expense."

However, Lovelace could see that threats were not going to stop the New London contingent. For the first time, he looked at them and in a soft voice assured them that they were a valued part of the Catholic community and that he wanted to hear their complaints. What followed was an outpouring of anguish as each of the victims related their stories.

When they were finished, the room was again dead silent. The tension in the room mounted with each passing second.

Finally, Lovelace said, "Father Brennan, what do you have to say for yourself?" Brennan had been sitting throughout the proceedings with a smirk on his face that made it plain that he was finding it all very amusing. As he began to respond to Lovelace, he broke out with a chuckle that seemed surreal. It was an almost demonic spasm of evil that took even his victims by surprise.

"Your Excellency," he chirped, "this isn't the half of it. There is much more. Too much to handle in one meeting."

Then, his demeanor returned to normal.

He addressed the group saying, "You people can't touch me. The Church is bigger than all of us. All authority comes from the Roman Curia and the Pope himself. The role of the clergy is bigger than ministering and instructing. We hear your confessions and forgive your sins, lay the very body of Christ on your tongues in the sacrament of the Holy Eucharist, and assure the salvation of your souls through the last rites, but our role does not stop there. None of these things would be possible if not for the Church itself. Therefore, we have an even greater and higher role, and that is more than anything else, to protect the image of the Church and see to its eternal survival."

Lovelace did not appreciate Brennan jumping in with his arrogant and hubristic tirade.

He looked at Bishop Whacker and asked, "Does he always act like this?

"He has been known to try to appropriate my authority," Whacker said, "but I've never heard an outburst like this one."

Lovelace then looked at Brennan and said, "Bishop Whacker and I will be having a conference with you at the end of this meeting. I am not aware that I gave you authority to speak for the Church. After having heard these people and the charges they bring against you, I am not sure that you are even morally qualified to serve as a pastor. You do not appear to be mentally stable."

"On the other hand," he said as he turned to the victims, "what Father Brennan said about preserving the image of the church is absolutely correct. It is not only paramount, but we must also protect its finances and its property. If a scandal of this proportion becomes public, multiple law suits could be triggered putting our assets at risk.

I must caution you that despite the outrage you feel, you will be condemned and excommunicated if you attack the Church."

"As for you, Mr. Frank Nash, even the threat of publishing your article puts you at risk of excommunication. The diocese does not abide interference from the press. We will handle issues internally. I order you to cease your investigation and halt any activity leading to the publication of your New London story."

With that he asked Whacker if there was any reason to continue the meeting, and was assured that there was none.

He turned to Brennan and said, "The three of us will take a short break to allow the New London contingency a respectful departure. We will then resume. We have much to discuss."

When the meeting resumed, Cardinal Lovelace surprised Brennan by insisting that he would hear his confession before continuing with any further discussion. He reminded Brennan to examine his conscience thoroughly, and reminded him that any unconfessed mortal sin would result in his soul being condemned to everlasting hellfire. He then asked him to go into the adjoining room and take 30 minutes to examine his conscience.

Brennan sat at one of the desks in the room and the smirk that he had exhibited earlier returned. Unsurprisingly his friend, Bubby appeared. He came as fire masked by thick black smoke.

He chuckled at Brennan and said in an evil voice with the familiar slight echo, "Mortal sin? What garbage! You have served your people well. Their school is extraordinary. You have transformed the physical plant; sometimes using your own money. Your people are excited about the success of your athletic teams. Your students will be easy marks for me as I go about competing for souls. I am elated by the anger and upset you have engendered in them."

"The Church be damned. It's time for you to move on and enjoy your wealth. There are hundreds of women looking for men with money. Tend to your estate."

Just as suddenly as he had appeared, Bubby left the room. Ignoring the 30 minutes he was given to examine his conscience, Brennan returned to the conference room where Whacker and Loveless were discussing his fate.

"Your Excellency," he grumbled, "I will not be making any confessions. You will have my resignation on your desk within a week."

Chapter 40

Sudden Resignation and Nash's Frustration

Father Brennan said that this group of people were trying to shut down the school and ruin his good name and that they had failed. He stated that he had more education in psychology and philosophy that Father Sipe and Father Bryan put together and therefore they couldn't say that he was crazy.

-Transcript of Brennan's talk to Junior And Senior Religion Class –

May 18, 1971

The Perpetual Help contingency left the meeting with Bishop Whacker discouraged. They stopped at The Castle Lunch Cafe to discuss their next steps. Father Bryan started the conversation by saying, "I am reluctant to continue pursuing Brennan's ouster. "I am under extreme pressure. The Bishop has warned me that I would be the one being defrocked if I do not desist. I dare not approach him about this matter again."

The rest of the group agreed.

Therese said, "If nothing positive results from this meeting, there is no reason to continue. Several families are pulling their kids out of school and sending them to boarding school elsewhere. We are already sending our kids to public school. Maybe that's the best we can do."

Then she turned to Frank and said, "Frank, it looks like you are our last hope. Have you decided to publish your story?"

Frank looked at the group with resignation and said,

"Most of my article is already written. Today's meeting will certainly provide an exciting ending. Yes, I will present it to my newspaper next week. I haven't even mentioned I was writing anything yet. I've been so unsure whether telling the story is the right thing to do, but after today's meeting, I've made up my mind."

*****

Your Excellency,

I hereby resign as pastor of Our Lady of Perpetual Help Parish and Superintendent of Perpetual Help School. I leave both after 20 years knowing that they have prospered under my leadership.

I have rebuilt the entire physical plant. The offertory contributions have more than tripled, and the school continues to be a first-class educational institution. Our sports programs, as well as virtually all the extracurricular activities, have achieved high honors every year the past fifteen years. The sports program is the envy of every small town in the state.

Others have worked hard to help make Perpetual Help school a success, but there is one element that cannot be replaced. Despite the tremendous generosity of hard working parishioners, the growth of the offertory collections has not been enough to fund the improvements. I have been personally funding a significant percentage of the budget, especially the coaching salaries. We could never have become so dominant in sports without the best coach's money could buy. To continue the excellence, we have become accustomed to, I will need some time to implement certain changes to prepare the community to become self-reliant.

I hereby ask that my resignation be effective at the end of the 1972-73 school year. I will use the remaining time to assure that my successor has the resources to continue my successes. Let me remind you of the Church's mandate regarding Catholic Schools.

Pastors of souls (priests) have the duty of making all possible arrangements so that all the faithful may avail themselves of a Catholic education.

Parents are to send their children to schools which will provide for their Catholic education.

A Catholic school is understood to be one which is under the control of the competent ecclesiastical authority (the bishop).

It is your duty to enforce the mandate. I have worked my entire career to serve this mandate. I will need just a little more time to assure that my successor can do so as well.

As to the charges leveled against me by the rebel group, I have admitted guilt. I assure you today, as I have on several occasions previously, that there is much that they do not know. I do not apologize for my actions. I am leaving them with an institution that is second to none. It is a vastly better place than when I arrived. I am a human being with flaws, but a lot of good came with the bad.

My sexual appetite, exceeds that of most men. I do not understand why. I have spent many hours in prayer asking for healing and forgiveness, but I am not able to control myself. I have visions of Satan talking to me and tempting me and surrounding me with unearthly sights and sounds. I hate him but cannot resist him. Even now my decision to resign is influenced by him. He tells me about all of life that I am missing, tempts me with all that I can have with my great wealth, and urges me to move on.

In hindsight, the priesthood was probably the wrong choice for me, but I firmly believe that everyone who thinks they were victimized by me will survive whatever psychological damage they think I have done. They are not, in fact, guilt free. I have been burdened by the many women who secretly wanted to seduce me. I am simply unable to resist. They got what they really wanted.

In the case of the Bryan family, they are much better off since their mother and I began our relationship. Their father was a drunk and an abuser. They lived on the edge of poverty. I have the financial wherewithal to give them a much better life. I say, without apology, that Margaret is in love with me. It is an exaggeration to say that I love her. She is just a tool for my sexual gratification. I owe her nothing except a little gratitude for taking care of me after my accident. However, she is the one person I feel obligated to treat well, and I am determined to do so. Her children will get their college paid for even though some of them hate me. I would love to reconcile with Ricky, but that seems unlikely.

I tell you all of this because I do not want you to think that I am all bad. I leave with both a heavy heart and a certain amount of excitement about future possibilities. I will be especially relieved not to have to feel guilty about the violation of my vows. My Bubby (That is what I call Satan) has been ridiculing me for years about respecting my vows.

I assure you that the day I walk away from Our Lady of Perpetual Help Parish, it will be positioned to continue the traditions I have built, and that the people will be relieved to be rid of my constant hounding about money, the ten commandments, hell and damnation, devotions to the Blessed Mother, and all the other things that irritate them about me.

In Christ,

Father Joseph Brennan

Pastor of Our Lady of Perpetual Help Parish

*****

Frank was seldom stressed in his Sports reporting job. He did it because he loved sports and it helped him stay connected to young athletes he could sometimes help counsel, especially if they had the ability to play college or professional ball. He was financially secure because of his dad's professional career, so he never concerned himself with job security. He always gave his best to his employer and assumed that he would continue to be employed if he continued to find it fulfilling.

When he set the meeting with his publisher, Richard Donner, to discuss the Brennan story he had no reason to believe it would be any different than earlier meetings. So, he was surprised that, before the usual pleasantries, his boss blurted out,

"You can forget about publishing that story about Father Joe Brennan."

"What in the world?" Frank responded, "How would anyone at the paper know I was writing about Brennan? I haven't told a soul."

They had never discussed religion, so Frank was unaware that Donner was a committed, orthodox Catholic. He had become personal friends with Bishop Whacker over the years as he collaborated with him on publishing articles favorable to the Church. He was one of the first people Whacker called after the meeting with the Perpetual Help contingent. The message was delivered in a tone of voice that belied their friendship. Whacker told him about the meeting and said he was sure that Frank was going to write an expose' and ordered him not to publish it. He used the standard threat of excommunication. The threat triggered an angry reaction in Donner who demanded to know why Whacker was talking to him like that.

He said, "I have no knowledge of any pending expose' being written by Nash. Settle down for crying out loud."

Then he realized who he was talking to and reverently apologized.

Whacker went on to explain why he was upset, and adamantly insisted that the article not be published. Donner assured him that he would meet with Nash and inform him that no such article would ever see the light of day, and forbid him to publish it anywhere else under threat of dismissal from his job.

Richard Donner grew up in a strict German family on a small farm near Dickinson. He was the oldest of 18 children. His dad forced him to assume adult responsibilities at a very early age. Once the daily chores were assigned he acted as enforcer. He was held responsible for everything that went wrong. And a lot of things went wrong amongst the Donner siblings. Ten of the children were boys and they were doing farm chores by the time they were six years old. Richard's job was to make sure that the work got finished and done right. His dad stayed busy seeding, fertilizing, summer fallowing, and harvesting. He did not have time to mentor ten boys. He expected Richard to take care of his brothers. When things went wrong he would angrily castigate him and sometimes beat him with a leather strap.

He put the fear of God in all his kids and was not much gentler with his wife. He dominated her to the point that she completely forfeited her own personality. Her interaction with her children was confined to reinforcing her husband's orders. Richard hated him but feared him too much to disobey orders. He never voiced any objections, nor did he dare to differ.

He used the same approach in their religious training. The rules were absolute. They never missed Mass on Sundays or Holy Days of Obligation. They knelt on the hard kitchen floor, straight up, every night while saying the rosary. He chastised any hint of criticism of a priest. Dating was forbidden well into high school years and monitored strictly once allowed. The fear of committing mortal sin prevented romantic involvement of the most innocent kind. They all went to Catholic School.

Despite being the first college graduate in Donner family history, Richard remained a prisoner of his Catholic background. When his friend the Bishop ordered him to censor Frank Nash, he never questioned him.

The meeting with Frank was short. As he was walking out the door, Richard remarked that he could not understand why anyone would risk excommunication to dishonor a priest. His last words were, "Priests are human too, and God knows, we need more of them, we better keep the ones we have."

Chapter 41

A Long Goodbye

When someone asked why he doesn't sue people for writing these affidavits, he said these people aren't the ones who should be sued but the priests and nuns who are making them do these things.

-Transcript of Brennan's talk to Junior and Senior Religion Class –

May 18, 1971

Brennan's departure was never announced. He returned to Perpetual Help and began planning for the survival of his legacy. His anger with the "rebels" consumed him, and he resolved to get revenge. He made sure everyone was aware that the survival of the school had been jeopardized by the "rebels." His periodic tirades from the pulpit, extremely cynical and manipulative insinuations in the Sunday Bulletins, and the creation of booster clubs for sports and band that he charged with raising the funds needed to replace his personal subsidy, were used to sow fear amongst the majority who supported him. He used the clubs to emphasize that, without him, money would be tight. For the school to survive they would have to fundraise. If they wanted to blame anybody they had only to look to the "rebels." They had created bad publicity, and it was affecting his ability to attract teachers, coaches, and enough boarding students to keep the school viable.

If there was ever any doubt that an evil influence was in control of Brennan, it was dispensed by the weekly rantings in the bulletin on all matter of issues. He decided to implant so much suspicion within the community, that all blame for whatever happened after his departure would be assigned to the "rebels."

Anger, cynicism, arrogance, and sarcasm were on weekly display. Shortly after submitting his letter of resignation, he published the following in the Sunday Bulletin.

"In case some get their hopes high, the pastor is not leaving the parish and so when he is gone now and then it is because he has other things to do."

He was implying that the school had been so damaged by bad publicity that he was having to spend more time away recruiting new boarding students. This was only partially true. While some of his trips were for legitimate school and parish business, Brennan had to attend to his personal business interests along with a bevy of female consorts who required attention.

The laying of guilt for not restraining the rebels, who were ostensibly trying to destroy the school, filled the pages of the bulletins. He insinuated that when the school closed, it would be because they had been insufficiently faithful to their Catholic principles.

The Catholic Church was in the midst of turmoil at the time, due to changes mandated by Vatican II. There was significant resistance to the changes from the people, but no one resisted more than Father Joe Brennan. One of the first changes that was obvious from the moment one entered a Church, was that the altar had been turned around. Prior to Vatican II the priest conducted Mass in Latin with his back to the people. Brennan refused to adopt this change. Some believed that Brennan resisted change because he was conservative and disagreed with Rome. The reality was, he knew that his congregation was conservative and left it to his successor implement the changes. He hoped to trigger a reaction against the new pastor and nostalgia for the old.

Everything that he did from the day he submitted his resignation till the day he left New London was designed to gain revenge on the rebels. He made it clear that school revenues were at risk. Most people assumed he was genuinely concerned about the school, but without stating it he wanted them to know that it was his money that supported the shortfall from the parish, and when he was gone it would fall on the people to raise the necessary funds.

He employed two strategies to drive home this point. First, he demanded that the sports booster club be created, so they would be able to continue to afford excellent coaches and maintain the dominance that they enjoyed for so many years. He constantly drove home the point, without voicing it, that money was short, and the school was in jeopardy. He implied that without his money, they were in trouble, and it is the rebels who were responsible.

Secondly, he hired a band instructor. Perpetual Help School had never had a band in its entire history. There was demand by some of the parents over the years to start one, but Brennan had no interest in music and he knew that it would be his money that financed it. But once he was on his way out, he relented and hired Dan North, an able alumnus to start the program. He came at a high price which was exactly what Brennan wanted. It gave him an excuse to polish his image while making it more difficult to support all the school programs after he left. He knew that insufficient finances would create a need to prioritize and some programs would have to be ended. The conflict that would result would be perfect evidence of the damage that the rebels did to the school.

The band program would also need a booster club. Brennan would use it as a constant reminder that certain people would work hard to maintain the program, while the rebels took their kids out of the school and ceased all financial support. After he was gone, and without his personal funds, the program would not be sustainable, and the blame game would further elevate his legacy. The prevailing attitude amongst his supporters would be, "Look what he built, and now that he is gone it is falling apart. You rebels destroyed our school."

At every opportunity he would imply in the bulletin that the rebels were harming the efforts of his supporters who were trying to keep the school going.

"SCHOOL CARNIVAL IS COMING. As you know, this is one of the resources used to support the school. IF OUR PEOPLE AND THE STUDENTS DO NOT SUPPORT THE CARNIVAL, THEN THE SCHOOL IS DEFINITELY THE LOSER."

And later, "OUR THANKS TO ALL WHO HELPED IN ANY WAY WITH THE SUCCESS OF THE SCHOOL CARNIVAL. Some are just good supporters of a good cause. Some know it is supporting Christ's work. A FEW WITH NARROW VIEWS take the position that my children are all through at Perpetual Help so why should I help now? Let others do it. But I will bet anything that others helped you when you had children here and the little you paid for tuition and church dues never came close to doing the job. The boarders helped carry this school for a long time."

He would remind people repeatedly that the time was coming when they would have to provide the funds that would be missing once he was gone.

"BAND BOOSTERS HAVE THEIR MEETING NEXT SUNDAY. I SHOULD KNOW FROM THE BAND BOOSTERS HOW MUCH MONEY THEY ARE GOING TO RAISE, AND HOW THIS WEEK. It is contract time and you cannot leave the teachers wondering whether the parish is going to have the money to pay the salary or not. But I must repeat that there is no other source to obtain money for the band department needs than the BOOSTER CLUB. It is either we do, or we don't. BAND BOOSTERS MEETING THIS SUNDAY. The band is planning to go to Moose Jaw in May. I hope they are going to practice hard for that trip, and if they do not, I hope Mr. North cancels it. Before that, they have district music contests and a local performance. YOU BAND BOOSTERS HAVE YOUR HANDS FULL FINANCING THIS GROWING PROJECT."

He seldom passed up the opportunity to remind people that there were some in the parish who were no longer contributing.

"IT WOULD BE APPRECIATED IF PARISHIONERS COULD MAKE A SPECIAL DONATION TO THE CHURCH PARISH SUPPORT FOR EASTER SUNDAY, as many have done nothing for the year so far and our bills are many."

"WOULD WE HAVE A PARISH CHURCH – JUST A PARISH (No school by any means) if these people were our support?" A list of shirkers followed.

"SPORTS BOOSTER CLUB: The Booster Club gave a check recently to the school for $12,000. I expect $30,000 next year, and this is the minimum. We have to cover the expenses from the athletic department and the salaries connected with the coaching. You do not have to worry about raising too much money, for the expenses are greater than you think."

The expenses were greater than people thought because Brennan was paying inordinately high coaching salaries only a select few knew about it. When he leaves the parish, he takes his money with him. So, his message is obvious. If you like what you have, you better keep me as your pastor. Of course, he already knew he was leaving so what he really meant was the "rebels" have ruined what he built.

"FOOTBALL AND WRESTLING BOYS CANNOT BE PRAYING MUCH SO THAT WE COMPLETE THE COACHING AND TEACHING STAFF. The teaching vacancies are math and science, which should not upset the students too much as most of them don't like either subject too well and would rather take courses like folk dancing, how to fish, wine tasting, proper grooming, and many others. So, let none of us worry or pray about it, and let the superintendent worry about it—and he is tempted to fill the vacancies with

~ 233 ~

young people who cannot coach. There are many ways to solve problems. Maybe we should try a new approach so some can appreciate the old approach."

So, he is saying, sarcastically, that he has things under control even if no one is praying. He will save them, and the coaches will be signed.

Without saying it, he was thinking, *but wait until next year when you don't have my money to bail you out.*

Again, in preparation for his unannounced departure he wrote,

"CHURCH SUPPORT: It is amazing how little church support people have given the first half of the year. I am going to present to some of the men of the parish the schools financial books for the past year. (I WILL TELL THEM WHY I HAVE NOT PRESENTED THEM IN THE PAST.) I will also give them the contributions for the first half of the year and see what they want to do with things as they are."

For the first time they are given detailed information about school finances, but only to make the point that there are problems looming when he leaves.

"I AM NOT HAPPY WITH THE WAY OUR YOUNG BOYS AND GIRLS have kept the First Fridays, Perpetual Help Feast Day, Holy communion on Sundays, and Church support, when I have seen the same ones have money for other things. THE PARENTS OBVIOUSLY DO NOT PUT MUCH PRESSURE ON THEM. The attitude of these young people forces one to question what appreciation there is for quality here in New London. I hear strong rumors that one of our big Catholic high schools will not open next year. ARE YOU YOUNG PEOPLE SO INDIFFERENT THAT YOU WILL LET IT HAPPEN HERE SOME DAY?"

After stirring up all this controversy he disappeared from New London for six weeks in July and August. No one knew where he went. Some speculated that he was ill, or that he was having residual impacts from his car accident. Some had a bad feeling that they might be permanently losing him. Summer time was when priests were transferred. However, he was just driving home a point. See what happens when I am gone for a while. How do you think you will survive when I leave permanently? Don't forget who is working to get rid of me.

WHEN YOU SEND YOUR CHILDREN TO SCHOOL THIS FALL WILL YOU BE FOLLOWING VATICAN II'S TEACHING – which is the official teaching of the Church?

I quote: "The Council also reminds Catholic parents of the duty of entrusting their children to Catholic Schools wherever and whenever it is possible, and cooperating with them for the education of their children."

Note well ---------- the word duty is used ----- not choice - not as I like.

whenever possible – not what is convenient.

whenever possible – not what is easiest

supporting these schools – to the best of their ability – not any way we like.

cooperating with them – working for them – not against."

"WHO IS SUPPOSED TO DO THESE THINGS?

CATHOLIC PARENTS"

These words were meant for the "rebels," some of whom pulled their children out of Our Lady of Perpetual Help School and sent them to public school. Other families sent their children to a Catholic School over 100 miles away. These words were coming from a man who hated the second Vatican Council and all it stood for.

The cynicism and sarcasm continued for the remaining months that Father Joe Brennan controlled Our Lady of Perpetual Help parish. On May 13, 1973 the following announcement was published in the Sunday Bulletin.

"I will leave you sometime soon. I will not say goodbye to any of you because there are too many to do so. I have no definite plans for the future except to live where it is hot and dry. I do not have a definite spot for even that. I am in no hurry to find something to do. In the meantime, you can use as my mailing address, 1759 S. West St. Anaheim, CA 92802. If you think you have an emergency – I do not know what it would be – my nephew might be able to find me, but it might take a day or two. You can find him in the Anaheim telephone directory."

"SCHOOL AND PARISH FINANCES: I have paid up all the school bills. Parish income for the rest of June, July, and August should cover all parish expenses. When I leave the parish will owe for the past school year either the sisters or the diocese $45,000. From the deficit of $120,000 last June plus the increase in salaries for nuns, lay people, and other things of a minimum of $45,000 for a total of $165,000, the deficit now stands at $45,000. We cut the deficit $120,000 in the last year. You have enough money coming in to pay on the debt plus interest for the year. So, you will be in the banker's paradise this fall and winter – money everywhere. It has been since before the rebellion that things were that good."

Most Accountants could not have made sense of such a report, but Brennan's supporters were ecstatic about it. To them it was further evidence of the brilliance of the man, and it reinforced the impression that the rebels had severely damaged the school.

He could not resist a final attack on the "rebels." Nor could he find the decency to admit the psychological devastation he was leaving in his wake. Two unacknowledged children, multiple young women assaulted and raped, marriages destroyed, families in turmoil, and the verbally abused. Most would never acknowledge its impact.

And there were those about whom he bragged as he walked out of the last meeting with the Bishop and the rebels; those among the unknown "You don't know the half of it."

Then, one day he was gone. People showed up for daily mass, and there was no priest. They became concerned that he might have taken sick, but their phone calls went unanswered. A few went to the rectory to see if he was okay. He was nowhere to be found. He had not even locked the door. When they entered they saw nothing that seemed out of the ordinary. He had taken nothing but his clothes. They checked the garage where he kept his car. It was empty. Only two people from New London would ever see him again.

Chapter 42

They Just Can't "get over it"

I want to thank the lay faculty. Many of them have been added since the middle of the year when we had a little revolution. However, the revolution did not put the school out of operation, and so we have many lay people here.

-Recording of Brennan's graduation speech – May 19,1971

The Brennan era was finally history, but his legacy would not be what he might have envisioned. The conference championships in football, the state tournament teams in basketball, the overnight success of the band program, and the men who built all of this would gradually be forgotten, but the emotional trauma he inflicted would last a lifetime.

Nevada Black left New London before her child was born. She would have seven more children from a man she never truly loved. Her husband was abusive and domineering and she stayed with him only because he was wealthy. He spent very little time with her and included her in his social life only when he needed a beautiful woman at his side. Over her lifetime she periodically sought therapy to deal with her hatred of him. She told her therapist that every time they had sex, she would see images of Brennan hovering over her, with a demonic look on his face, laughing at her with an evil sounding chuckle. She could not rid herself of the image and thought she was being punished by God with a husband she could never love. Her mental state prevented the proper nurturing of her children, so they looked to their father to see to their needs. He ridiculed Nevada for her ineptitude as a mother, so the children developed no respect for her as they grew older. She withdrew from her entire family over time and in her later years spent most of her time in bed suffering from severe depression.

*****

Darlene Brandt was luckier. She never saw the inside of a Catholic Church again until her parents died, but her father had retaliated against Brennan and had hurt him where he was most vulnerable. He had exacted a toll on Brennan's fortune which seemed like vindication enough for Darlene. She also married her true love and they built a successful farming operation together. She had nothing to hide from her husband, so it was not difficult to talk with him about her anger, anxiety, and occasional periods of depression. He was not overly religious, so her decision to avoid anything to do with religion, never came between them. Her family rallied around her and would roundly condemn anyone who suggested that Brennan was the father of her first-born son. When pressed the person was ordered never to contact anyone in the family again. The child was never told who his real father was. Brennan was too heartless to care.

*****

Sheila Kronk's life was never the same. She was unable to forgive herself. She had been a true believer who attended Mass more often than most of her contemporaries. She never committed a serious sin that would keep her from receiving Holy Communion, and she went to confession weekly. Carl often ribbed her about her frequent confessions because he could never figure out what she needed to confess. After they broke up, he remembered the sermon about hell and wondered if she was beginning to find it difficult to resist an increasing desire to elevate their relationship in a physical sense and decide to break it off because of the horrors of hell that the sermon had communicated so vividly. She feared committing a mortal sin even more than the possibility of getting pregnant.

The reality was that Sheila knew that if she continued her relationship with Carl, she would eventually tell him about her encounter with Brennan. She witnessed occasional outbursts of rage from Carl when he felt he was treated unjustly, and feared that if he ever found out, he would do something drastic. She did not want him to ruin his life. So, she shut him out of her life, and in a state of psychological ferment, had her second sexual encounter when she seduced Carl's best friend, Tommy Kent. Tommy admitted to the encounter years later when he assured Carl that Shelia had not been a virgin.

Shelia's fear intensified when her brother and Carl's sister got married. This meant that there would be times when the families would be together socially. They both went on with their lives and eventually married, but Sheila would never speak to Carl when the families were together.

For a time, she flirted with atheism, but her rebound was eventually more symptomatic of one whose demons controlled her revenge. In her youth she had been a rigidly compliant Catholic. She would live her life as an equally rigid and compliant Jehovah Witness. She alienated her siblings by repeatedly trying to convert them. She judged them for their "godless" lives, and righteously proclaimed her path to be the only path to God. Eventually she became so alienated from them that she was no longer welcome at family functions.

She worked hard throughout her life to suppress the anger that lingered, but she would never consider psychological counseling. She believed that only God could sustain her. Despite this, her anxiety and depression made it difficult to be a good mother. Her children found the rigid religious environment in the home to be so stifling, that they fled soon after graduating from high school, and maintained little contact with her.

Coincidentally, Carl lived five minutes from her for 15 years and never once talked to her during that time. She could never get past her shame.

*****

Karen Helms had been especially vulnerable because she was aware of many of his activities. Brennan was often careless in leaving evidence lying around. She always feared that she could be his next victim, but she became complacent and was not emotionally ready when Brennan suddenly demanded she have sex with him.

She also sought to hide her encounter. She had overheard both victims and other priests discuss the problems. She was terrified of harming the church and had often heard him threaten excommunication. She took it upon herself do no harm. She later told her therapist:

"I felt like it was my responsibility to keep the code of silence; not to keep it just for myself, but for the Church, the priest, my family, friends and anyone who would be scandalized. I had to protect the Church or people would call me names. I can still hear Brennan's voice,

"Don't you dare tell anyone, or you'll be burn in hell."

"I was trembling and scared to death. But I didn't tell anyone because I felt so guilty. I was still in high school. I couldn't quit because my mother and the principal would have questioned me. And I had no other reason to quit. He was put on a pedestal by the Church, and everyone in the community worshiped him. They were delighted by the winning teams, and desperately wanted it to continue. I saw this, and thought I was the problem. I had to piece

~ 239 ~

together my soul. You are not just raped physically and emotionally, but when a priest messes with your faith, the problems multiply. Priests have so much power. They are supposed to represent Christ at Mass. I could never blame him, only myself."

Unfortunately, Karen did not seek help until she had suffered for many years. She was never able to sustain a long-term relationship with a man. She married and divorced four times. In her later years, after an extended period of psychotherapy, she was able to come to grips with what had happened to her. She was comforted when her children and grandchildren displayed her brother's athletic ability. Every one of her children received scholarships to play in college.

*****

Anne Mandarich never sought psychological counseling. As a result, she remained traumatized for the rest of her life. She had frequent nightmares and found it difficult to form intimate relationships with men. When she eventually fell in love and married, she had difficulty with sexual intimacy. Her marriage survived only because her husband was committed to helping her overcome her issues and forgave her whenever she rejected him.

When her daughters were born she had difficulty being the mother she wanted to be. She responded with extreme anger whenever she disapproved of her daughter's behaviors. She feared giving them a complex about men that would not serve them well in their future relationships. She suffered severe depression.

On the day her oldest daughter graduated from high school she gave up on life. Her husband discovered her body hanging from the hay loft in the barn. She had pinned a sign to her blouse that read,

"He stole my soul, now he steals my life. Please forgive him."

Evan Mandarich had dedicated himself to his wife's recovery from the trauma that "Big Dad" had inflicted on his wife. He fought with his own ego in trying to understand something that no husband can fathom. Anne loved him like no other because he worked so hard to understand. She often said,

"Evan, you are surely a gift from God."

But no matter how hard they worked, she always felt unworthy and the pain persisted. When Evan discovered her body, he wailed in despair, threw himself on the floor of the barn, and sobbed uncontrollably. He was able to get control of himself only because he knew his children must not see their mother this way. As he lowered Anne from the rafters, he hugged her limp body, looked up to the heavens and yelled,

"How can you do this to me."

The faith that had formed him into the good man that he was, let him down. The anger that was boiling in his gut would never subside.

*****

Brennan left his mark on others whose stories emerged as time passed. Fred Katz grew up in New London and attended Perpetual Help School for twelve years. His home life was difficult because his father was an alcoholic and his mother was long suffering. She was a rigid, devout Catholic, who would never contemplate divorce. His father sometimes beat her when he was drunk, and Frank took it upon himself to be her protector. When he was thirteen years old he had his first fistfight with his father. He was severely beaten. He got bigger and smarter though, and over time was able to get the upper hand. The first time he stood over his father who was lying on the floor, bleeding from his nose and both ears, he felt a tremendous sense of euphoria. Never again would his mother have to take a beating from his father. He would see to that. But the euphoria soon turned to shame. He had badly beaten the man he was hardwired to love and honor. It was an internal battle he would fight the rest of his life. By the time he was sixteen he began to walk in his father's path. He had his first beer at a graduation party. One beer was not enough. He could not remember getting home that night.

One summer evening Fred was hanging out with his friends and the discussion turned to "Big Dad." One of them mentioned that he had been window peaking at Brennan's house the previous Sunday night and saw him with a naked woman.

He could not tell who it was, and all he could say was, "that fucking sonofabitch."

The gang had a good laugh, but most of them did not believe the story. None of them liked Brennan, but they could not believe a priest was capable of doing something like that.

Fred was one of the skeptical ones, but on his way home, he remembered that his mother had met with Brennan that Sunday night. She had frequent meetings with him to help resolve the problems in her marriage. When he got home he confronted her. She angrily denied being the woman his friend had seen. Fred would never find out the truth, but his suspicions troubled him for the rest of his life.

In January of 2015 the pastor of Our Lady of Perpetual Help Parish offered one of the classrooms in the now closed school as a meeting place for the newly formed Alcoholics Anonymous group. Fred was one of the first to sign up. Twelve people came to the first meeting. Five of them were longtime residents and had gone to Perpetual Help School during the Brennan era.

The first person to share that evening mentioned that she was still struggling with demons from her days at Perpetual Help School. She talked about how she hated "Big Dad" and wished she had never met him. This began a crescendo of woe from the others who had attended the school. Brennan became the topic of conversation in almost every meeting thereafter. Forty-two years after driving off in yet another brand-new Chrysler Imperial, never to be seen again by most who had known him so long, Father Joe Brennan was still casting a pall over the city of New London, ND.

Chapter 43

Justice

Last, but not least, I want to thank the Sisters, good Sisters, the ones who stayed here, not the ones who left, but the ones who stayed, and did a lot of extra work because it was piled on to them by the ones who left.

-Recording of Brennan's graduation speech- May 19,1972

"Mr. Brennan, we would love to help you with your estate plan, but please understand that our specialty is real estate. Our firm does little else."

Joe Brennan was eager to resolve the guilt that had been gnawing at him since he left New London. He had decided to leave his entire estate to charity. He owned so much real estate that he was sure the best people to plan his estate were the ones who knew the most about his primary assets. The Blantendein Firm in Denver had been representing him for over fifteen years, and he trusted them implicitly.

He responded, "Steve, you know that, I don't trust lawyers. Yours is the only firm that I would ever consider. I trust that your diligence in handling my real estate will translate into the estate planning arena. I have no sophisticated plans in mind; just a straightforward charitable trust."

After strongly encouraging Brennan to engage an estate planning specialist, Steve Blantendein relented and agreed to set up a meeting with Brennan. Secretly, he did not an admire Joe Brennan. He was a Catholic and Brennan worked exclusively with Catholic advisers, but Blantendein deplored Brennan's wealth. His ideal priest was one who spent his time in service to the Church not gallivanting all over the country doing real estate deals. He treated Brennan well and was thankful for his business, but he did not respect him. Having already recommended that he seek the advice of a specialist, Blantendein assigned one of his young lawyers to draft the documents needed to execute the estate plan. He was too busy with the higher paying real estate work of the Firm.

Brennan's plan was a testament to the guilt he carried with him. Since leaving New London, his nemesis, the demon Bubby, had dropped out of site. It was as if he decided that his mission was accomplished, and that Brennan's fate was inescapable. So, there was no pushback when he decided to give his entire estate to charity.

The final plan held an impressive array of beneficiaries, including Our Lady of Perpetual Help parish and school.

Our Lady of Perpetual Help School of New London, North Dakota ...$1,802,862

Our Lady of Perpetual Help Church of New London, $500,000

Carmelite Convent, $2,343,721

Missionaries of the Charity of Mother Theresa, $3,605,724

Oblates of Mary Religious Order, $1,802,862

Columbian Fathers at St. Columbians, $1,802,862

St. Elizabeth Church and Missions, $1,802,862

Latin Archdiocese, $1,802,862

Diocese of Gallup, $1,802,862

Missionaries of the Sacred Heart, $901,432

Archdiocese of Denver, $360,573

Total.............................. $18,528,622

He created a trust that gave an income stream for a period of years to various individuals who were either siblings, or associates who had helped him run his hotel business. The charities were to receive the assets only after the income obligations lapsed. There was a willful and obvious omission of either of his children. Neither was there any mention of the women who had been emotionally abused, or the broken families. It was as if he was angry at his victims for corrupting him.

*****

Evan Mandarich never recovered from Anne's suicide. His grief destroyed him, and he began to neglect his farm. A series of bad crops and declining prices in the early 80's combined with bad management caused his farm to decline and lose productivity. He stopped paying on the principal of his operating loans. They grew beyond his ability to repay them. The banks threatened foreclosure. He began to drink heavily. At one of his frequent visits to the Golden West Bar, he overheard Floyd Sieger talking about a planned trip to Denver. Brennan moved there because he owned several hotel properties there and found the climate suitable. Sieger was telling his friends that he had been invited to spend the weekend and attend a couple of Denver Nuggets games. This was the first that Evan had heard about the whereabouts of Brennan. As he drove home that night, anger and despair welled up in him. Despite having drank heavily, he could not sleep that night. He sat up in bed and pulled his handgun from the drawer of the night stand, massaged it gently and tossed it back and forth from one hand to the other. He thought to himself, "Somehow that sonofabitch has to pay." He made a mental note of the day Sieger would be in Denver with Brennan.

Evan had just celebrated the Christmas Holiday with his family. The absence of **Anne** had been especially disturbing because of the overall decline of his state of mind. Now, as he left the farm and turned south on the highway toward Denver, tears welled up in his eyes and he began to sob. The tears were as much in anger as for the loss of **Anne**. He knew now what he must do.

*****

Sieger and Brennan met at Brennan's home in Cherry Creek, one of Denver's most exclusive neighborhoods. Sieger was shocked by the wealth surrounding him as he drove into the neighborhood. He was just becoming fully aware of the true extent of the wealth of the man he had worked so hard to protect.

When he rang the doorbell, Brennan leaped to his feet as fast as his lame leg allowed, opened the door and greeted Sieger warmly. They hugged each other tightly. Sieger was surprised by his feeling of affection. German males simply did not hug each other, but this time it felt right.

The Nuggets game was scheduled for 7 PM that evening, so Brennan treated Floyd to dinner at the Palm, one of Denver's most exclusive restaurants. Sieger gasped when he saw the bill, but Brennan never hesitated. He gave his credit card to the waiter. As if he needed to prove how generous he was, he tipped the waiter 50%. Then they were off to the game at McNichols Arena.

The two arrived just as the player introductions were concluding. As the arena briefly fell silent just before the players broke their huddle before tipoff, a gunshot echoed through the arena. Panic gripped the fans who desperately began to flee. Floyd's ear drum broke, and he was temporarily deafened by the shot that occurred inches from his head. He looked at Brennan and almost passed out. Brennan's forehead had exploded, and his brains splashed on the fans seated in front of him. As he turned to look behind him, a second shot rang out, and he saw Evan Mandarich falling dead in the row behind him. Sieger knew at once what had happened. People in New London had become concerned with Evan's state of mind, but no one could have conceived that it would come to this.

Joe Brennan and Evan Mandarich lay dead. Sieger noticed a forty-five-revolver lying on the floor next to Evan. Eerily, a cold breeze began to blow, and a sniggling laughter echoed throughout the arena. As both slowly subsided, Sieger sat back in his seat and cursed. Bubby had come to take his servant home.

*****

Frank Nash was at the game. After his confrontation with his editor at the Dickinson Press, he resigned. He had a series of successful stints at ever larger newspapers, and ended up at The Rocky Mountain News in Denver. He had become their lead sportswriter a year earlier.

Frank had shopped his story about Brennan to multiple outlets without success. Once Brennan was defrocked and sent packing, he felt vindicated, and the thought of writing a book faded. He was still a committed Catholic and felt that, in all probability, Bishop Whacker had been right. The Church would be hurt, and much of the good that it did would be questioned.

Frank was unaware that Brennan was living in Denver. When the shots rang out at McNichols Arena his newsgathering instincts kicked in and he rushed to the scene. He did not recognize either of the dead bodies. Then he noticed Floyd Sieger still slumped in his seat, face white as a sheet, still unable to process what had just happened. Tissue, blood, bone, and brain matter had been dispersed many feet from the shooting. Fans sitting in front of Brennan and covered with blood had not panicked and ran. They were in shock and could only stand and stare at the dead bodies.

Frank looked at Sieger and exclaimed, "What the hell happened."

Sieger looked at him with vacant eyes and mumbled, "Mandarich shot Father Brennan."

Then he vomited.

Chapter 44

Compensation Foiled

These Sisters were working to help your children; in some cases, the children of parents who at the same time are trying to harm the school, even close it down. But the Sisters didn't say, "You children go because your parents are working against us." They didn't say anything to the children. They are a lot fairer then some of the parents.

-Recording of Brennan's graduation speech - May 19,1971

"Bill, this is Kathy, I just received a call from our attorney. The IRS has invalidated the charitable trust. They want $12,000,000 in estate taxes."

"Oh my God, that can't be, what is their reason?"

"The income allocated to several of his associates violates the provisions governing charitable trusts and they claim all the assets are included in his estate. We need to fight this."

"Have you talked to Blantendein?"

"Yes, he did some research and is admitting that they screwed up."

"What can we do?"

"I think we have to sue Blantendein and his firm."

"But we don't have $12,000,000 to pay the government. We would have to sell everything."

Kathy let out a long sigh and said, "we have no choice but to challenge the decision. But first, we need a new attorney."

Bill and Kathy were long time confidants of Joe Brennan. Kathy had a brief affair with him, but she ended it when she realized he would never end his relationship with Margaret Bryan. She stayed on good terms with him and consented when he asked her to be his trustee. Bill was a member of the council of advisors in the Denver Archdiocese and had been introduced to Brennan when he applied for reinstatement to the priesthood.

Brennan's last will and testament, designed to compensate for his depredations and make things right again, failed. It was as if his guiding spirit, "Bubby," had drafted the document. No money went to Our Lady of Perpetual Help Parish. No money went to Our Lady of Perpetual Help School. No money went to Mother Teresa.

The attorneys that drafted the charitable trust were incompetent. The IRS jumped all over its flaws and invalidated it entirely. The trustees engaged in a ten-year battle to reverse the decision. They lost in the end. During the years of litigation, the trustees had insufficient cash flow to maintain the twelve hotels included in the estate. The IRS confiscated income with liens and levies. The hotels became dilapidated and their value plummeted. In addition, the tax law that was so favorable to real estate investing was repealed, further contributing to the decline in values. The trustees sued the attorneys who had drafted the charitable trust and won a $2,450,000 settlement, but that too went to the government.

None of the charities received a penny. The entire estate went to the government. The tax exceeded the proceeds from the liquidation of the estate, so it remains perpetually open pending payment of the balance due.

Correction, I said no one got anything. One person did get something and that was "Bubby." He got his boy!

Chapter 45

Postscript

EXCERPTS FROM BRENNAN'S FINAL BULLETIN, JUNE 10, 1973:

"This is printed so you have for future reference."

FINANCES OF THE SCHOOL --- DO NOT WORRY – I HAVE STAYED LONG ENOUGH TO SEE THAT THEY ARE IN GOOD SHAPE – my love for you people and for the school would not let me leave before there was proof of this.

These things will make the finances even better for this year.

The rebels should be so glad to get back to Perpetual Help that they will tithe and then some. Maybe they will make large lump sum payments for the nothing of two and one half years.

Anyone who gave less than what they should have in the past will no longer have my presence as an excuse and therefore give generously to make up for so many years of failure.

The fall festival should increase considerably with the help of the rebels and Amidon.

There should be more boarders at the school because the booster club is working to obtain them and also the rebels can no longer go about the country using me as an excuse for working against the school and against boarders.

This rebellion lead by the three priests, four nuns, and a handful of frustrated lay followers, cost us about $17,000 to finish off the school year in extra salaries…. This will go on for a long time as you have a built-in cost of the rebellion of $15,000 per year.

After a lengthy list of financial concerns and successes he concludes:

Now you have the school finance picture. You see now why I have stayed when the rebels tried to chase me out. At the time of the rebellion you did not have:

~ 250 ~

<u>A BAND PROGRAM</u> – It is now two years old… and it is paying its own way.

<u>BAND BOOSTER CLUB</u> – Now you have a group of parents…paying for the salary of the band man.

<u>PERPETUAL HELP BOOSTER CLUB</u> – a large group of people…all vitally interested in all Perpetual Help is doing.

<u>AN OUTSTANDING LAY FACULTY</u> – which we did not have left when the rebellion was devastating things. But in two years we have assembled one which I will match with anyone else. Two of these faculty…would not be here if the rebels had their way.

So, you see why I did not leave when the rebels did everything they knew to destroy my reputation and worked against Perpetual Help. They were right when they knew I loved Perpetual Help. I had worked a lot more for it than any of them ever had. I know what Perpetual Help meant to Christ and his work and I could not help it if they blinded themselves to this fact by jealousy, hatred, and other things. PERPETUAL HELP IS STILL STANDING BECAUSE YOU PEOPLE CAME TO ITS DEFENSE. NOW I CAN LEAVE IT AS A SCHOOL AND PARISH STRONGER THAN EVER. THE DEVIL VERSUS CHRIST IS ALWAYS A BATTLE.

*****

The impact of the Brennan saga continued until most of the principal players died and their children moved away. The last three years of his church bulletins, and other documents survived. They became the foundation for explaining Brennan's impact. One summarizes a talk to the 1971 junior and senior classes, and another is a transcript of his talk to the 1971 graduation class. They are reproduced from written transcripts and tape recordings.

1971 Talk to the Juniors and Seniors

He started off his discussion with the junior and senior classes by stating that he would swear under oath to the truth of any statement he made during the class period. He said that people would go down to Bismarck to talk to the Bishop and would drive through New London and not even stop to get his side of the story. He called Father Bryan and Father Sipe, and the sisters that left the school, liars. He said they had no proof to back up their accusations. He also said that there were accusations made that he was having affairs with several different women at the same time. Also, he said that there were rumors that he was making a play for three upper class girls that year and that he carried on at least one affair with a past graduate. He then stated, "Who are the lucky ones?"

He also said that Father Sipe said he was carrying on an affair with Mrs. Bryan, but that there was no proof of that and that Sister Francesca had signed a two-page affidavit that said he had enticed her twice. He said that the true story was that Sister Francesca had been griping to him about the way the convent and the Mother House were running things and he told her that if she didn't like it why in the hell didn't she quit? She said that she still wanted to get her Master's Degree, so he told her that she could borrow the money and if nothing else would work she could borrow the money from him.

He said that Father Sipe had come to him and told him that he was mentally ill and should leave immediately and that he needed psychiatric help. Father Brennan said that he would leave as soon as he got a signed document from the Bishop releasing him of his duties.

He said that coach Thomas signed an affidavit that accused him of breaking up his marriage, so he had the priest that married coach Thomas investigate and he found that Father Brennan had nothing to do with the divorce. Father Brennan also said that coach Thomas called the new band instructor and told him what an immoral man Brennan was, and suggested he get a job elsewhere and then told him to call Father Caldwell who told him his contract was invalid and that he would not receive any pay. Also, that the school was closing, and no nuns were going to teach next year.

Father Brennan also said that an old rumor was resurrected that he and Brenda Baumgartner had had an affair and he heard that she had signed an affidavit. So, he called her and invited one of the trustees to listen in. When Brennan told her about the old rumor she just laughed. Afterwards the trustee said he would sign an affidavit regarding the telephone conversation. The trustee went down to the dorm and called Father Bryan a god damned hypocrite.

Brennan also said that Father Sipe went to the Bishop and got permission to investigate him. When Father Brennan talked to the Bishop he denied it, and said that he told Father Sipe to go home and mind his own business. Father Brennan then said that the trouble makers in Amidon and the small handful in New London should quit like the Bishop told them. They should keep out of things that are none of their concern. Father Brennan said that Father Sipe called in the Amidon people to tell them all these lies, and also said that he had a specific date and place where one of the Bryan girls had said that her mother and Father Brennan were having an affair. When Father Bryan asked her if she said this she denied it.

Father Brennan said that the Bishop called up Arnold Koch and the other rebels and told them to bring down their affidavits and accusations and that a lawyer was waiting in Bismarck with the Bishop to notarize the affidavit. But none of them showed up. Arnold Koch called him a few days later and told him that they had shown him all those things already and were not believed, so he doubted they would be believed this time.

Fr, Brennan said that this group of people was trying to close down the school and ruin his good name and that they had failed.

Father Brennan stated that he had more education in psychology and philosophy than the two priest who were out to get him put together so therefore they couldn't call him crazy. He said that Father Sipe and Father Bryan were teaching false teachings in their religion classes and that a lot of parents didn't like what their kids were being taught.

Coach Kowalski is not coming back next year, and Father Brennan said it was more than likely due to the fact that Father Sipe and the rest of the trouble makers gave him a bad picture of Our Lady of Perpetual Help.

Father Brennan pointed out the fact that all the nuns who left Perpetual Help were the young ones, and "as you know, the young are the ones with all the answers." He asked who was more interested in Perpetual Help, the man who is out searching for teachers and such things, or the people who are trying to discredit Perpetual Help and close her down.

He ended the class by saying that the devil assailed everyone who preached strongly for the scapular and the Blessed Virgin.

1971 Graduation Talk

I want to thank the lay faculty. Many of them were added since the middle of the year when we had a little revolution. However, the revolution did not put the school out of business, and so we have many lay people here. So, I want to thank them. And I want to thank the Sisters, the good Sisters, the ones who stayed here not the ones who left, but the ones who stayed and did a lot of extra work because it was piled on to them by the ones who left. We can't single out any one of the Sisters for the extra work because all of them got loaded down with extra work.

These Sisters were working to help our children, in some cases, the children of parents who at the same time were working to harm our school, even close it down. But these Sisters didn't say. "you children go, because your parents are working against us." They didn't say anything to your children. They are a lot fairer than some of the parents with what they are doing.

As for next year, well there is all kinds of talk about next year. Some people don't know what they are talking about. One of the group of trouble makers called our music man that we hired and told him not to come to Perpetual Help because they are going to close it down and all kinds of other lies. I say they don't know what they are talking about because at the same time the Notre Dame's new Mother Superior was in New London telling us what teachers we were going to have for next year and telling me not to let the scandal workers win.

Well Perpetual Help will open next fall regardless of what's been said. You hear reports that the school will not be accredited. The rebels are writing letters asking the Board of Education to scrutinize Perpetual Help. A group from Amidon went down and did their best to take our accreditation away from us. They didn't succeed though.

Well, on top of all this the only new thing we are gonna have next year is a new policy. We are gonna have an admissions board who are gonna scan all applicants and decide whether they are going to be admitted.

We have a lot of new wonderful lay people coming to our school who are well qualified, and then we have this new music teacher.... On top of that we have a new football coach coming.... Everyone we talked to highly recommended him.... On top of that we have a new basketball coach and this young man has been coaching for six years.... he has a Master's Degree from South Dakota State. You'll notice how many new Masters Degrees we have picked up.... He is considered one of the best coaches in South Dakota.... This year he went to the state tournament and won it.... And so maybe our enemies will rejoice in the loss of Coach Kawalski, but their joy will be short lived because this man will pick up where Coach Kawalski left off.... So, we have gone and hired the best that we could find.

While I am gone some people at home, the militants, are trying to tear down the school. I ask you, who is more interested in the school, the man working to build it up, or the people trying to shut it down?

*****

Resentments between the Siegers and the Koch's boiled below the surface until the Siegers died. Some of the other band of rebels left family behind and moved out of town, the Koch's included. Some with children in high school sent them to boarding school 125 miles away where this author was privileged to be one of their teachers.

It was not until this book was being written that I became aware of how angry the non-Catholics in New London were, especially the young people at the time. Once word got out about the, comments on Facebook highlighted their agitation. Kids that grew up together, and spent time with each other in the summertime, ignored each other during the school year, fearing condemnation. They especially resented the whippings that the public-school basketball team took at the hands of a Perpetual Help team aided by out of town recruits and overpaid rock star coaches.

Most people and their children who lived in New London are now dispersed throughout the country. Some are angry that this book was written. They still believe that "the less said, the better," and ask why all of this is being dragged up again. The answer is below in excerpts from historical writings about priest abuse throughout the history of the Catholic Church. There is little doubt that the image of the priest as saintly representative of God, who has been raised above the laity, who forgives their sins, transforms bread and wine into the body and blood of Christ and lays the body of Christ into the palm of their hands at every Mass, and baptizes their babies, freeing them from original sin, and cleanses their souls at the hour of death, saving them from eternal damnation, and all of the rest of it, has contributed greatly to the priest abuse problem. Even today these men are seldom disciplined. The environment in which they perform their duties often attracts the most dysfunctional of men. They see the priesthood as a place where they can get access to young boys and girls in an environment where their status protects them against all suspicion. Deviant behavior continues to be ignored if exposing it will damage the Church.

In my seventy plus years of life I have never heard of priest abuse that was as extensive as what occurred in New London. I suspect, however, there are other similarly outrageous, stories. They simply do not get publicized because the culture of silence in the Church is slow to change. If this book contributes to changes in the Church that convince the hierarchy they can no longer avoid true and thorough reform, it will have been of value. This author is still a practicing Catholic and looks forward to the day he no longer must make excuses for the deeds of a small number of degenerates.

Sex Priests and Secret Codes
The Catholic Church's 2,000 Year Paper Trail of Sexual Abuse
By Father Thomas Doyle, A.W.R Sipe, and Patrick Wall

What's Really Behind the Catholic Church's Sexual Abuse Problem?
Why has the Church been plagued by so much pedophilia – predominantly homosexual? And why has a scandal regarding this situation erupted only now?
by Harriet Fraad

Nuns as sexual victims get little notice
By Bill Smith, St. Louis Post-Dispatch

A National Survey of the Sexual Trauma Experiences of Catholic Nuns
John T. Chibnall, Ann Wolf and Paul N. Duckro
Review of Religious Research

Clergy sex abuse of females complicates intricate issue
By Matt Stearns and Judy L. Thomas
The Kansas City Star - July 12, 2002

BishopAccountability.org
The Second Greatest Scandal in the Church
Priests Stealing from the Sunday Collection
By Michael W. Ryan, New Oxford Review